She reached over for the phone and dialed the number from the flyer. It rang twice before a pleasant voice answered, "Hello, this is Gheena with the Ascendiac weight loss study. How can I help you?"

Suddenly, Sharon was nervous, thinking about the possibility of becoming a guinea pig in a research study. In an instant, she considered hanging up, but the haunting memories of a dozen failed diets and a steadily increasing clothing size convinced her otherwise. "Uh, hi. I saw your flyer about a weight loss study and I wanted to, um, know something about it."

TINA —
THANKS FOR THE SUPPORT!

—Dan

Daniel D. Wambold, MD

Ascendiac®

Iatragraph, LLC
Hoboken, NJ
Printed in U.S.A.

Ascendiac®

Iatragraph, LLC
Hoboken, NJ
Printed in U.S.A.

This book is dedicated to my parents, Lynne and Dave.

Special thanks to:

Gregory Grove
Virginia Hanson
Derek Levy
Megan Moore

for their tireless editing assistance and support!

1.

The alarm woke her up, however Sharon kept her eyes shut as she groped for the snooze bar. Consciousness was fuzzy and indistinct, but even so, she was acutely aware of the date. The dry, unpleasant taste in her mouth reminded her that the third glass of wine last night wasn't enough to change the fact that today marked exactly half a year until her 29th birthday. She winced as she convinced herself that it really was March 10th. Ever since she had been a girl, turning thirty and still being single seemed like a life sentence to live alone. At some point, probably as a teenager, she decided that, allowing a year's engagement and additional time before that for dating and other necessities, she'd have to meet her husband-to-be by the time she was twenty-eight and a half. Although adulthood brought with it a realization that such concrete thinking was absurd, the haunting significance of the date would not entirely fade.

Now, come on, Shar, don't get yourself worked up like this again. You're starting to sound like the woman in that movie, Bridget Jones's Diary. *Thirty isn't even old any more. You've got a good job working for Dr. Sonders, and just because some guy hasn't magically appeared at your door doesn't mean anything. Hell, Alison Sonders herself has to be at least five years older than you and she's coping just fine.* Sharon frowned and shook her head. *Of course, she's so thin and pretty that she doesn't have to worry about these things, does she...?*

The minutes ticked by on the snooze timer as she tried to minimize the impact of the morning, but just as she was at the cusp of figuring out her situation, the alarm rang again. She reluctantly slid her legs out from under the down comforter and planted her feet on the cold wood floor while switching on the radio for the morning news. As she walked over to the bathroom she wasn't even aware that she habitually averted her eyes from the dressing mirror so she wouldn't end up criticizing her body before she'd had a chance to shower and dress.

A mild ache pulled at her forehead— another remnant of last night's excesses— so as the shower warmed up, Sharon found the bottle of Motrin on the top shelf of the medicine cabinet and shook two capsules from the container. She filled the glass by the sink and swallowed the pills, then drank more water to finish off the dry mouth attack. As she replaced the glass, the slightly ajar mirror showed her an unsolicited and somewhat unflattering profile of her midsection, made still less appealing by the harsh florescent lighting above the sink. She gasped slightly in surprise, then stated plainly to the mirror's image, "That's it, Sharon Keating, we're getting you in shape. You're not going down without a fight!"

As she showered, she began contemplating how she would accomplish this new goal. *Maybe I'll join a gym because then I'll have to go since I'm spending so much money each month. Then again, I thought that approach would be enough to convince me to use that stair climbing thing I bought that's been neatly folded under the bed for at least a year. Power walking is supposed to be good for you, but March isn't really a good month to plan to be outside every day. I guess I at least need to pick a diet, but which one actually works? Maybe I should send away for one of those fat burning pills the radio keeps advertising. I wonder if Dr. Sonders knows anything about that stuff. Well, whatever I do, this time I will stick to it.*

She continued washing, quickly massaging a handful of herbal shampoo through her shoulder-length brown hair while contemplating her new outlook, but an eerie sense of fate overcame her. After a moment of distracted preoccupation, she shuddered and decided it was most likely the result of having spent so many years of her life dreading the eventuality of this day.

2.

"Yes, what is it?" Dave Aswari didn't like to be disturbed before 9 a.m. and Laura, his secretary, knew that any violation of this policy required a truly pressing issue. Dave personally credited his own swift ascension to Manager of New Drug Development partly to his self-proclaimed near-genius intellect and partly to his compulsive scrutiny of each project's daily progress. No detail was too small for his examination or, frequently, criticism. Whatever the real reason for his success, there was no denying that Excella Pharmaceuticals of Pearl River, New York, was in a position to begin reaping the rewards of his aggressive manage-rial skills. His weaker subordinates buckled under the stress of such supervision, but those who persevered found that each quarter's bonus check grew quickly, as did the attendant stock options. Now, with this new, potential blockbuster drug entering FDA Phase III clinical trials, Dave was in full stride, and even brief interruptions of his morning risked becoming serious flash points.

"Sir, I have Dr. Finnegan here. He says he needs to speak with you, and he says it's urgent." Laura held her breath as she held the phone, even though she really didn't have reason to worry. Jack Finnegan was the lead medical investigator for Ascendiac, the diet pill that Dave projected would propel Excella to the ranks of Merck and Pfizer. Although he struck Dave as being a little out of touch with the business side of selling pharmaceuticals, Jack certainly was a brilliant researcher. Occasionally the two found themselves at odds, usually over issues that Jack termed "Proper Scientific Techniques," which would clash with what Dave considered to be sound business principles. To Jack's chagrin, dollars and rank usually took precedence in the end, though resolution of these conflicts was rarely unilateral. For his part, Jack was careful to pick his battles and his terms for concession.

"I see," Dave answered Laura in a slightly annoyed tone. "Well, OK, send him in, then." As he hung up the phone he moved a few extra papers and folders onto the center of his desk to make it absolutely clear that he was being interrupted by Jack's unscheduled visit. This display, however, was superfluous since Dave possessed the uncanny ability to telegraph exactly the emotions he wanted to convey solely through his body language. Alone, the dark eyebrows over his Mediterranean complexion could speak volumes across a conference room, and, added to his six foot tall frame and dark brown, razor-sharp eyes, he could intimidate or charm with the charisma of a king.

In truth, the effort Dave was currently making to appear busy was much more an unconscious admission that Jack's continued cooperation with the Ascendiac project was vital to the success of Excella. Although he never fully understood why he felt slightly threatened around Jack, the unease stemmed from Dave's fierce sense of independence which clashed with the occasional and unavoidable need to rely on others. He was used to absolute power over projects, but in the realm of the drug industry, Jack held certain crucial cards, especially when it came to a working knowledge of the biology behind the pharmaceuticals in development.

Dave's background was now firmly entrenched in the business aspect of medicine, having graduated fourth in his class from Columbia Business School in 1993, though the route had been indirect. A decade earlier, his undergraduate years at Penn State were split between football games, parties, and achieving a 3.6 grade point average for his combined English and economics majors. He considered it an accomplishment at the time to have taken the absolute minimum number of credits in science courses, though now he often wondered if he should have taken that subject more seriously. As a freshman, he had even leveraged his charm with the dean of students to garner credit towards Penn State's core requirements from a high school advanced placement class in chemistry which he had barely struggled through.

With two degrees and the drive to succeed, Dave moved to Philadelphia after college to take a job with a financial firm called Cavanaugh, Wilson, and Wu. He was brought on as a stock analyst for their medical devices division, enduring a crash course in the minutiae of health care financing. Each company's evaluation showed him a new facet in the business of health care, ranging from predicted market placement to varied patient populations to the gamut of insurance and government-financed reimbursement. Making money in this field required not only a successful product, but a demand for it and someone willing to pay the ever-rising costs. Losses could be swift and blinding, especially when other companies trumped a clinical accomplishment with their own technological advances and innovations. Long term investments had to be restricted to large, multidisciplinary companies which could effectively protect their products through both solid monopolies and relentless scientific progress. As it was, CW&W's focus was largely on turning quick profits, so Dave learned quickly to dart in and out of positions before the luster had disappeared from the newest medical miracle.

During the late 1980's, with black Monday still weighing heavily on investors' minds, profits were hard-earned by the few analysts lucky enough to stay out of the red ink. The SEC was keeping a particularly close eye on transactions because, especially in difficult times, insider trading and illegal deal-making flourished. Many good people ruined their reputations and their livelihoods by succumbing to the allure of fast money, only to find that they had been ferreted out by the SEC's rapidly expanding application of computer algorithms to identify suspect trades. Although he watched as two colleagues were convicted of securities fraud, Dave himself had never betrayed his belief that business was built on a set of rules that applied to everyone. That's not to say that he didn't feel it was his duty to make every effort to use the rules to his advantage, but he still saw a clear line between manipulating the law and breaking it.

Dave prospered during those years despite a stagnant market. His efforts were rewarded with promotions and bonuses, though he always considered true success to lie further up in the chain of command. So, in 1990, with just over $80,000 in cash and liquid assets, he applied to business school. His unblemished record and glowing references secured him a spot at Columbia's Business School for the 1991 academic year, but despite his rationalization that it was better to study in New York than Philadelphia, he tacitly resented the fact that Wharton had turned him down. To prepare for the transition back to academia, he resigned from CW&W three months before the school's September start date to enjoy some of the fruits of his labors by traveling around Europe. For part of the time he rented a 36' sailboat complete with a two-man Spanish crew. He learned to sail (and he polished his Spanish) while exploring the pockets of culture in the port towns along the coast of Spain and Portugal. A picture of the boat and crew still hung proudly on the wall behind his desk as a constant reminder of the simple beauty and danger embodied in the strength of the ocean.

Jack entered the office and strode purposefully up to Dave's desk, carefully ignoring the attempt Dave was making to appear too busy to be bothered. In comparison, Jack's 5' 7", 155 pound stature failed to carry the conviction of Dave's imposing presence. His fair Irish complexion and light auburn hair fit the stereotype of a hard-working scientist much better than the tall, dark, and handsome look possessed by his superior. Nevertheless, there was a sharp, analytical edge behind Jack's bespectacled face which was always evaluating not only the next stage of a conversation, but the one following that, too. It was akin to the deep insight that chess masters possess which allows them to see the consequences of moves that have not yet been made, but which could be rendered harmless if the right position was taken at that exact moment. Jack decided to let Dave finish his paper charade before beginning, so he stood at the desk quietly until Dave looked up and acknowledged him.

"Jack, good to see you. Have a seat. What's on your mind?" Although the greeting sounded cordial, Dave's eyes told a different story.

"Well, I figured you might already know the answer to that question. I got a copy of the Phase III protocol for Ascendiac this morning and it seems that the changes we discussed last month hadn't been implemented."

Dave cleared his throat briefly, knowing full well what Jack was referring to. "Yes, I'm aware of the parameters of the trial, but you need to understand that the FDA has approved our protocol as it is. If they don't think there's a need for us to collect data outside of the study timeline, then I'm satisfied that we're doing our job here."

"Well, did you specifically *ask* them if they thought that a two week crossover trial was a good idea or did you just decide that, if they didn't complain, it must be the right thing?"

Dave's eyebrows lowered a bit, preparing for combat. "Now come on, Jack, you know how these things work. As soon as you start suggesting to them that there might be something to worry about, they'll triple the requirements for approval. Besides, I've had someone from regulatory looking into the precedent for drug withdrawal studies and they're almost uniformly unnecessary after Phase II."

"Yeah, I know that. I'm also aware that our Phase II data are completely clean, but I really need you to understand that dose range studies don't accurately address the potential changes that receptor-modifying drugs like Ascendiac can cause. Just knowing that a few doses doesn't lead to withdrawal symptoms really won't uncover potential problems that can occur with longer-term use. I'm just not sure I see the reason to pass up the opportunity to collect some more information about the drug."

Dave shrugged dismissively. "It's just as I said during the final multidisciplinary meeting when you brought up the same issue. First of all, it's an expense that can't be justified because the FDA isn't asking us to look at patients several weeks after they've completed their trial. Trying to acquire those data points would just complicate the study as more people dropped out for the usual reasons. I mean, it's hard enough to keep tabs on a few hundred people over the course of two weeks, much less a month or more. How many are expected to be lost to follow-up each week of a study? Something like three to five percent, right? That adds up to a lot of unknowns after an additional month, with each question mark waving a little red flag to Andy Rheinberg and his whole FDA review board. Second, since it's not customary to acquire that information, the fact that we'd take an approved protocol and try to modify it to make it *more* stringent would cause Andy to crawl up our ass with a microscope. Most importantly, Jack, what do you really think we'll find? That they get fat again? I mean, we're marketing an appetite reducer, not a miracle drug. As soon as they're off this stuff, how many are going to stick to some low-calorie diet and exercise routine? Now, I know you've told me that this drug is different— that it's not a stimulant like Fen-Phen— but you don't really think it's going to change peoples' life-long overeating habits, do you?" His expression made it clear that this was strictly a rhetorical question.

Jack paused for a moment, trying to choose the most effective tack from the multitude of objections Dave raised. He savored the opportunity to single one out, eventually deciding to focus on the issues relating to Dave's attempt to understand the physiology of the drug. Treading carefully to avoid insulting him, he nodded thoughtfully and raised his hand. "When you put patients on blood pressure drugs like ACE inhibitors, their pressure definitely drops. When you stop those drugs, the blood pressure climbs back up. That's how some drugs work. However – and I suppose I haven't really made this part clear before, so bear with me for a minute– when you put people on other blood pressure drugs like beta blockers, their pressure also drops, but if you then stop the drug, the pressure increases *beyond* what it started at. It takes a few *more* days for it to normalize again, and during that withdrawal time, patients are at an increased risk for all sorts of problems like heart attacks and strokes."

Throwing up his hands, Dave countered, "But that's the same point you made the other day! I and the FDA have accepted the fact that there could be a rebound – that is the word you used, right?– a rebound increase in the appetite. Even if it happens, and I think we both have to agree that we really don't have any reason to believe it will, it's probably going to look just like a dieter stopping their diet. There's always a period when they overdo it, then they settle back to their normal eating level. Honestly, I still can't comprehend why you're so concerned about this."

Jack already had him wandering down a primrose path towards the trap. In as non-condescending a tone as he could manage, he responded, "You're right insofar as a little overeating probably won't hurt the patients, but what if they continue for several days? I don't think we want to get a drug approved that results in patients *gaining* weight after they stop using it. Just like with the beta blockers, sometimes a little increase is harmless, but other times, it can cause real and very embarrassing problems. I doubt a brief stint of gluttony could lead to serious health concerns, but I just think we're swimming in uncharted waters here, and we could stand to be a little more cautious until we understand the drug better."

Dave realized that he was clearly out of his league arguing about the potential medical aspects of the drug. He decided it might be prudent to throw Jack a bone on this one without actually conceding to changing the approved protocol. He raised his eyebrows invitingly. "Look, what sort of a compromise do you think we could make on this? Is there something I can arrange internally for you so that you can get this information without making it part of the study? I could offer you a few people so you can have them phone your study patients a couple weeks after they're done just to check in on them. You know, spin it as sort of a courtesy thing. 'Our company cares.... How are you doing?'"

"I considered that approach, but I think we need to make it a little less suspicious. No one believes that companies actually *care* about them; That's more of an advertising angle. I had a different concept, but it will cost us a small amount of money." The last phrase caught Dave's attention and he frowned incredulously but held his tongue. "How about a week after they're done with the study we send a $10 coupon for one of our products, like a bottle of multivitamins, along with a market survey that's part of the mailing. We could include a detailed section on diet aids and finish with a section on the patient's current physical status. Anyone who didn't respond could get a follow-up call about the survey. That might help keep things low-key."

Dave ran the numbers in his head briefly before deciding that a $10 coupon would cost next to nothing given their huge markup on vitamins. He decided it seemed like a pretty innocuous idea which might even prove useful if the data showed the weight that patients lost stayed off for more than a week. Without wanting to sound as though he'd given in, he sighed. "Well, I guess it could be worse. You could have asked for a $20 coupon! All right. I don't think I could easily justify the expense to our shareholders, but then again, we just might find that your little miracle pill actually works better than you expect, which would give us a nice marketing angle. Send me a memo.... No, actually, *don't* send me a memo. I think we should keep this discussion between us for now so that there's nothing for the FDA to bite on if they decide to subject us to one of their audits. We can just give the list of study subjects to the marketing people and I'll have their director suggest they organize your survey. OK?" His eyes plainly said that the discussion was over.

"Yeah, that's great. I mean, I'd have liked to have done this the right way, as part of the Phase III study, but despite what you think of me, I also really want this drug to fly. This thing's been my baby for almost two years now, and it will certainly mean great things for Excella and for us personally if it gets a green light. Thanks for your time, Dave. I know you're busy at this hour." He motioned towards the artificially cluttered desk. "Let's just hope this drug does for people what it did for the monkeys." Jack stood and walked to the door.

Dave, slipping back into his charismatic leader role, joked, "Hey, lots of people make *one* blockbuster drug. The *real elite* come up with two!" As the door shut behind Jack, Dave's smile disappeared nearly instantly. *That agreement's fine, Jack, as long as everyone does well when they come off of your drug. I don't know how far I can trust you, though, if you start worrying about some imagined problem with the follow-up patients. I suppose I'll need some sort of contingency plan if you threaten the success of this project with your little survey stunt.*

Dave's mind began to wander through the list of possible responses to that eventuality.

3.

Alison Sonders looked over her schedule for the day, shaking her head while she wondered how she was going to manage to see eleven patients. A few of them were thirty minute follow-up visits, but the majority were full one-hour sessions which, even in the best case, would each require an extra fifteen minutes worth of paperwork. She checked her watch to find she had almost ten free minutes before her first appointment, so she took another sip of her morning coffee and leaned back in her leather chair, allowing a small portion of her blonde hair to fall in front of her face. She closed here eyes briefly and vaguely wondered how this girl from a quiet town in New Jersey had managed to graduate from Dartmouth medical school and build one of the busiest psychiatry practices in Manhattan. While random thoughts fought for attention in her still caffeine-deprived mind, a seemingly disconnected memory from her childhood caught her by surprise.

It was late November, and she was at her eighth birthday party, sitting at her parents' kitchen table with her four girlfriends. She could see their faces so clearly that the party might as well have been this morning. Betsy Staub, with her curly red hair and freckles was to her left, then Liz Whitestone, the girl whose mother was divorced. Liz always struck Alison as being just a little too outgoing most of the time, except on the days before she was going to visit her father for the weekend. Those days, she was uncharacteristically quiet, almost sullen. The fact that she lived just a block away made her an appealing friend, though, so her moods were generally forgiven. Across from her was Jenny Thompson who moved out of town six months later, and finally Tammy Hereford, Alison's best friend that year. Tammy and Alison took dance lessons together after school and they spent countless hours each week talking about how they were going to grow up to be ballerinas who would dance in big, exciting cities around the world.

For gifts, the other girls had given Alison toys which were thoughtful but uninspired. Tammy's present was the last one Alison opened, and she smiled at her friend when she realized the box didn't feel like it contained another doll. The smooth wrapping paper slid under her fingers as she ran her hand along the side of the box, the excitement building every moment as the decorative covering reluctantly yielded to her effort. The box contained within was white with an unmistakable red 'B' on the top, the trademark for the Brandtley Fashions store in New York, twenty-two miles away. Although Alison had never been to the store, their newspaper ads, always featuring attractive models wearing the latest Paris and New York styles, had caught her eye a year earlier. She had decided that any girl lucky enough to wear such beautiful clothes must feel just like a princess.

Her eyes grew wide and she turned to Tammy with a look that asked, "*Is this for real?*" Tammy smiled broadly and nodded.

"Oh my gosh!" Alison squeaked as her now-trembling hands worked to open the box. Inside lay a soft, baby blue sweater with fuzzy cuffs and sequins sewn on in snowflake patterns. "It's *beautiful!*" She pulled the gift from the box and held it up to her shoulders. The sleeves were cut just a little short to show off the owner's wrists, and the waist was tapered in gently to give a feminine shape without being overly revealing.

Beth Sonders, Alison's mother, who had been watching quietly from the doorway, walked into the room to get a better look at the gift. "Wow, Tammy," she said, "it's really beautiful. Did you pick it out yourself?"

"Yes, Mrs. Sonders. My daddy works in Manhattan and he took me to the store. He asked the man there where the young *ladies* clothes were." Tammy savored the word 'ladies,' because she knew that, at eight, all girls became young ladies, and ladies never bought girls' clothes. Tammy had explained this to her father during the car ride to the store, making it clear that, in five and a half weeks, when *she* turned eight, the same rules would apply to her. "We looked at every rack and finally I found this sweater. My dad said it was really pretty, too."

Alison was still completely consumed with this treasure and she was stroking the soft fabric as she held it against her shirt. "It's so soft! I love it, Tam!"

"Why don't you try it on, sweetheart?" Alison's mother suggested, motioning towards her bedroom on the second floor. Alison ran off and returned a few moments later, feeling like she could walk on air. The sweater fit perfectly, and as she walked into the kitchen she imitated the deliberate, accentuated strides of a runway model, complete with a pirouette before retreating to the doorway again. Even her father, who had entered the room, was surprised at how mature his daughter suddenly appeared.

"Hey, is that my little girl?" he quipped, only half-kidding, but mostly wondering to himself how time had managed to pass so quickly.

"*Dad,* I told you! I'm a *lady* now!" She smiled broadly at him as she shook her finger in his direction.

"Oops! I forgot. Well, how would a *lady* like a present from me and your mom? It's not a Brandtley present, but I hope you'll at least *make believe* you like it, too." He produced a small box the size of a paperback book which was wrapped in pink and gold paper. There was a large bow in the center which covered almost the entire top of the box. "Happy birthday, Alison." He kissed her forehead as he gave her the box.

Alison tore the paper off to find a plain blue box inside. There were no tell-tale markings decorating this one, so she opened it. Inside was a white envelope, also bereft of print or designs. The thrill of Tammy's gift overshadowed the suspense of this embedded present, but when she finally reached the contents of the envelope, she found three tickets clipped together in the middle. The words "Nutcracker Suite" were printed prominently across the top, with the show date of December 18th stamped below. The performance was to be at the Metropolitan Opera House at Lincoln Center in New York City, one of Ballet's most prestigious venues. Certain this was too good to be true, Alison read and re-read the ticket, her voice bubbling with uncontrollable excitement.

"Oh, Daddy, *thank you!* This is the best present I've ever gotten! I can't believe we're going to see real ballerinas! I heard they practice for eight hours every day to be good enough to perform there and they are so beautiful and graceful that they look like they're angels floating across the stage!"

"Well, sweetheart, that may be true, but you know that you are *my* angel, and that's why your mom and I wanted to take you to see this show. Happy birthday, Alison."

"I love you," she said as she buried her face in his midriff and gave him a hug. After a moment, she looked up, feeling guilty for lavishing all her affection on her father. "I love you, too, Mom," she said as she proceeded to hug her as well, though she was truly daddy's little woman at heart. "Hey... Can I wear the sweater Tammy gave me to the ballet? Then it would be like Tammy was there with me, too!"

Her mother smiled. "Sure, Al, that would be just fine."

The distant sound of the office's outer door closing snapped Alison back to the present. She blinked briefly as her medical mind began to process the memory, dissecting the feelings and relationships within. Years of complete devotion to psychiatry made this an inexorable and routine exercise in virtually every segment of her life. Talking with friends or family, or even introspecting into her own psyche would prod her professional skills into action. While such mental investigations were only occasionally counterproductive, sometimes she felt like her internal clinical monologue would interfere with her firsthand emotional responses. Although there was a lingering sense that this unexpected recollection of her eighth birthday might have a deeper meaning for her, Alison pushed further consideration of it to the background in favor of focusing on her morning work.

She opened the top chart on the stack, reminding herself that her first patient was a new referral named Charlotte Jonitaur who had been treated for depression for five weeks by a primary care physician, known in medical circles as the PCP. Apparently, the progress was less than expected on the first-line medication which the PCP had chosen, so Charlotte was referred to her for further evaluation and treatment. Alison rose, pushing the last bits of the birthday memory out of her mind, opened her door and nodded to Pearlene, the office receptionist, indicating that she would see her first patient now.

4.

The morning traffic was relatively light today as Sharon piloted her Ford Explorer through the downtown streets to the parking garage. Dr. Sonders' office provided parking as one of the perks for working for her, and as the office manager, Sharon was convinced it was well worth the investment. Before the days when the parking tab was picked up by the office, staff generally chose a lot about three blocks further away because it was the cheapest in the area. The service there was abysmal, though, and at least once a week there would be some delay in getting cars parked. After several frustrating mornings watching patients pile up in the waiting room because she was without staff, Dr. Sonders announced that she'd make the parking arrangements herself for anyone interested. Not only did it amount to a $300 per month bonus for her employees, but it made her a favorite employer in the University Medical Center while reducing *her* stress by having her people in place, on time.

Sharon stopped her truck in the entrance to the garage and gave her key to the attendant. As with most of the garages in the city, the managing companies found they could pack more vehicles into a given space if they were parked by employees rather than customers. The downside, other than allowing others access to your vehicle, was primarily the inconvenience of having to phone ahead for your car so that it was ready when you arrived at the garage. Otherwise, there was often a ten minute wait as it was extricated from several densely arranged rows.

Leaning over to open the glove compartment, Sharon froze in place. It was habit for her to grab a cookie from her stash before leaving the truck to make the trek to the office. To herself, she said, "Wow. Now this is the sort of behavior I have to stop. I just ate breakfast, so there's no reason for me to be hungry." The verbalization helped her a little, but her stomach continued to nag. *Damn it, this is always harder than I think. It's been all of 45 minutes since I ate and I'm already thinking about snacks. I guess I need a diet that allows snacking because I don't know how I'm going to make it until lunch this way. Well, I suppose I'll just have to find a way to do it.*

She started the journey to the office at a brisk pace, having figured that any chance to get in a little exercise would be a good thing. To get her mind off the cookie, she tried to organize a mental litany of the day's responsibilities. Since taking the job as Dr. Sonder's office manager a year ago, Sharon had learned more than she anticipated about medicine. It wasn't her first medically oriented job because she'd started at the University Medical Center nearly eight years ago in the accounting department. However, when her friends had heard she was going to move to a doctor's office, they assured her that working for a psychiatrist would be very different than working for a "regular" doctor. After all, they joked, how hard could it be to schedule crazy people for weekly visits, then get them to pay their bills on time?

Sharon was happy to find that her friends were wrong. Alison Sonders, MD, had a dynamic practice focused on treating adolescents and young adults with severe psychiatric problems. The majority of her patients were referred to her from other psychiatrists who felt that their mental illnesses were too complicated for their own practice, and she knew Alison was proud of her reputation as an avant-garde clinician with a particular skill for crafting multi-drug therapies to help treat particularly resistant conditions.

This reputation did not come without a price, however, and Sharon recognized that Alison spent practically all of what should be her free time either performing her own research, reading other clinician's reports in the journals, or traveling to conferences. Staying on the cutting edge required an extreme commitment to the job, and Alison had made numerous personal sacrifices to this end. It also meant a busy office, a demanding schedule, and seemingly endless reams of paperwork in order to keep the practice running. The benefit was that, with such an onerous workload, Alison gave Sharon wide berth with regard to office financial matters. She was happy as long as the business end ran smoothly, and she rarely asked questions or made demands other than that all issues be kept strictly aboveboard and fair. Rather than worry about squeezing the last few dollars from insurance companies by employing questionable diagnostic and therapeutic codes, Alison preferred that simplicity reign when possible, minimizing the risk that her practice would be accused of falsifying claims.

Medical billing is a bizarre and complex maze which must be navigated carefully in order for physicians to receive proper payment for services rendered. Most insurance companies model their payments and processes after the single largest insurer in the United States: Medicare.

For a while, this arrangement actually reduced the amount of work involved in receiving compensation because there was one standard upon which most companies were based. However, in the 1980's in an attempt to stem a growing tide of Medicare billing fraud, the government decided to change its requirements in several key ways, most of which seem relatively benign on the surface. The thrust of the changes were aimed at ensuring that all claims were correctly coded, meaning that the bill reflected the diagnosis and treatments correctly, and that all diagnoses and procedures were justified by the medical condition.

Each year, Medicare's parent organization, CMS (The Centers for Medicare and Medicaid Services), publishes a list of recognized diagnoses and treatments and the associated code numbers, along with a fee schedule which determines how much the government will pay a physician for treatment of that particular medical problem. The average payment is just a fraction of what the physician normally charges, and federal law prohibits the physician from collecting the difference in cost from the patient. In order to receive even this reduced fee, the physician must submit the proper paperwork (or electronic forms) to Medicare, and they will receive payment in about six weeks.

Generally, the billing codes and associated diagnoses do not change from year to year, but even small modifications must be noted and adhered to, otherwise a claim is considered fraudulent, even if the mistake was accidental or in favor of Medicare. If CMS suspects fraud, they can request an investigation which is handled by the FBI. Agents can show up at a physician's house or office and demand some or all of their office documents for subpoena. If prosecuted, the physician may be subject to penalties including jail time as well as civil fines. This is where the law becomes interesting.

Initially designed to protect the government from unscrupulous companies who may inflate costs reported in government contracts, a law exists which allows the government to recoup the difference in value of a fraudulent claim, plus up to $5,000 as a penalty. If a defense contractor bilked the government for, say, $300,000, they'd have to repay that money, plus the penalty. However, in the case of medical billing, the differences in value are generally quite low. For example, the difference in coding a follow-up visit for a patient as a level two or three may be determined by whether a physician listened to the patient's lungs during the visit, with the resulting monetary reward of an additional $15. In this case, if the visit were coded incorrectly, the physician would pay $15, plus the $5,000 fine. This is just the beginning. Since most physicians submit many claims per week (at least one per patient seen), investigators would need to review thousands of charts to determine whether there was a pattern to the fraudulent billing.

To decrease their workload, the government allows what they call chart sampling, in which a few charts are examined and an average rate of error is determined. That rate is then multiplied by the number of patients seen, and the government can collect an estimated over-billing amount, plus $5,000 *for each expected error.* In short order, the fine can become astronomical. Of course, most doctors wouldn't risk their licenses and the huge fines for an extra $15 here and there, but with several thousand diagnosis codes to choose from, mistakes can happen.

It became evident to most physicians that such billing matters were now dangerously complex, requiring full-time attention to be paid to the ever-changing maze of Medicare regulations. Most physicians hired business managers to handle the billing aspects of the practice, relying on these people to keep up with the intricacies of the codes. Sharon had taken an interest in this aspect of medical finances while she was working in the University Medical Center's accounting department. Even when it required personal funding, she attended at least one national meeting annually to keep up with current Medicare, and therefore private insurance, guidelines.

Fortunately for the medical office staff, computers are especially good at dealing with concrete rules, and several programs are available to help simplify and automate the billing process. A standardized diagnosis list used by the physician can be electronically matched to the latest billing codes, helping to minimize the risk of errors as well as speed the claim submission process. Sharon had been testing a trial of one of the latest versions by entering all of Alison's previous month's receipts. Today, she hoped she'd finish so she could decide whether the new system was worth the $3,000 annual contract fee.

I'll run the whole month this morning, then check it against what we submitted by hand. Ooh, I hope there weren't any mistakes last month! I wonder what we'd do if there were. I guess we could just tell the insurance companies about it, or maybe just resubmit those bills.... But then again, maybe that would just prompt them to run a complete audit of our practice. I'm sure we're as clean as we can be, but an audit would really be an inconvenience for Dr. Sonders and it would make me look pretty bad, too. Wow, I guess this is as much a test of me as it is of the computer. Maybe I should have just made up some bills instead. But then again, it wouldn't really be an accurate assessment of the machine if I did that. I suppose I just have to pray I got everything right last month.

As she waited for the elevator to arrive, she realized that this was yet another time she should be sneaking a little exercise into her life. After all, how hard was it, really, to climb four flights of stairs? Bolstered by her new resolve to get into shape, she turned towards the door to the stairs when a white flyer taped to the wall caught her attention.

"Research volunteers needed for weight loss study." Needless to say, the boldfaced title piqued her curiosity. "Healthy men and women between the ages of 18 and 40 needed for evaluation of a promising new diet medication. Not like Fen-Phen! Free medical screening for eligibility. Successful completion of 14 day protocol pays $400.00. Study organized in conjunction with the University Medical Center's endocrinology division and a well-known pharmaceutical company. Call Gheena, x4-4652, for details." The flyer had a stamp on it indicating that the study had been approved by the University's ethics review board and that it was posted on March 2nd.

This poster's been here for more than a week and I never even noticed it! Well, maybe now that I've really committed to this, I'll notice even more new stuff…. Like what the stairs look like. She wrote down the extension on a scrap of paper and headed up to the office. The stairs were more work than she expected, and she was completely out of breath by the end of the fourth flight, but the small sense of accomplishment made it marginally less painful. *You've got a long way to go, honey,* she thought as she staggered through the access door into the hallway.

5.

Jack Finnegan's morning meeting with Dave regarding the Ascendiac trial had proceeded more smoothly than he anticipated, causing Jack to second-guess his own strategy. *Was this follow-up phone plan so weak that even Dave didn't think it would uncover anything? Maybe I should have pushed more for a person-to-person interview? Then again, what am I really worried about finding? If he knew something I didn't— and that's pretty unlikely anyway— then he would at least have worked a little harder to make sure we didn't end up holding the evidence.* Both men knew that, in the world of pharmaceuticals, having just enough documentation was the goal. Anything extra could come back to haunt you. Jack drummed his fingers on the edge of his desk as he contemplated the issues anew. His eyes wandered around the office.

As with many modern pharmaceutical companies, lead researchers' offices were generally finely appointed rooms directly attached to the primary lab area. There was enough space around the central, dark wood desk for a meeting of four or five, allowing most of the important daily intellectual business to be carried out without straying far from the science. The walls were painted a neutral cream color with slightly contrasting molding along the floor but this failed to camouflage the most glaring break from traditional office décor: The floors were the same bare tile as the lab instead of a more traditional plush carpeting, simply because traffic in and out of the lab area would rapidly deposit chemicals, solvents, and cleaning solutions into a rug, destroying it in short order. Even labs in which the most complicated work was no more intricate than high school biology required a constant supply of household bleach, the most common disinfectant. It never took more than a week for someone to end up creating ugly, yellowish footprints across any stainable surface.

To help compensate for this lack of warmth, office walls were richly decorated. As an office was built, an artist was commissioned to create an original piece for display, complete with a bold, attractive frame. According to the note included with it, Jack's was an abstract, futuristic-appearing airbrush allegedly depicting the artist's concept of a ribosome "reading" the genetic sequence from a piece of mRNA and creating the protein that this gene encoded. Jack was intimately familiar with the paradigm of the DNA-encoded gene which is transcribed by the cell into an mRNA coded message, which, in turn, is translated into a functional protein. Despite having had three years to study the vague lines and sweeping curves of this image, Jack never really figured out which strokes represented which parts of the alleged subject. The actual, biological process of protein synthesis, however, never failed to fascinate him.

College is where Jack learned most of the biology he knew, including the whole chain of command which makes up living organisms, and he loved to lecture occasionally on the subject. His favorite talk, written for a college freshman biology course, summed up the topic: "Proteins are the workhorses of cells which, in turn, are the building blocks of all organisms. While it is true that DNA and the genes it encodes are at the heart of every species, the genes themselves are merely sets of instructions describing how to create different proteins. The proteins, though, actually do the work. For example, one protein might be a miniature factory which creates molecules such as sugars or fats. Another might receive or transmit various signals within or between cells. Some proteins take part in burning fuel molecules to generate energy-containing units which can then power other proteins. In short, virtually every function carried out in a cell requires specific proteins to do so. An analogy can be made to a collection of blueprints for a tool factory. While the blueprints (that is, the DNA) tell the workers *how* to make the tools, they are merely inert plans. A worker, properly equipped, can create a drill or wrench or other tool from the blueprints, but it's the tool (or protein) that will eventually be responsible for doing something. As an aside, the analogy is also accurate in suggesting that, without preexisting tools, all blueprints are useless since new tools cannot be created without using tools, yielding a sort of 'chicken and egg' problem."

Even now, as a physician and researcher, Jack spent countless hours during slow parts of the day contemplating the implications of this codependence.

Next to this art hung several pictures of Jack's seven year old daughter, Lisa. The most recent was taken just six weeks earlier, during a visit to his wife Sandra's parents in Virginia. The sun caught her eyes perfectly, showing their bright, blue color against her light skin. Her hair, a little darker in reality than the almost golden blonde that the picture showed, was tossed back over her shoulders as she sat on the back of a dark brown mare. Sandra's parents had always kept horses, mostly for entertainment, although in the earlier days, they often entered local riding contests. Sandra took top honors at a county competition during her senior year of high school, but she had long before decided to pursue college rather than sports, so she retired, happily, a champion. Now, as though it were handed down to her from her mother, Lisa was discovering the grace and joy of sitting atop a muscular beauty, basking in the view over her father's head as he snapped a picture. Without any training she was merely a passenger as the horse was led around the yard, but her pleasure was undiluted by this fact.

The entire wall opposite the desk consisted of windows which looked out into the lab. There were cloth blinds which could be closed to impart privacy to the office, but Jack generally left them open as a reminder that his office was open to his staff whenever they needed him. The wall behind the desk contained several types of filing cabinets, all made of the same dark wood as the desk itself. In a way, these were relics of the mid 1990's, when the majority of information was still stored on paper in one form or another. Jack used to keep no fewer than 25 major text books at arm's reach, and the stack of "essential" scientific journals grew annually as he rose through the ranks as a research physician. For him, the change occurred as he was promoted to project manager about three years earlier and was given his current lab space, two research assistants, and the office. One of the assistants, Stephen Shin, a young Ph.D. from Princeton, offered to help him relocate. Jack knew Stephen from some work he had published on computer modeling of receptor interactions, and he was thrilled to have such an eager and bright person working for him. He gladly accepted the offer, and the two headed to the adjacent building to begin carrying Jack's personal effects across to their new home.

During one of the seemingly endless trips between the offices, Stephen carefully asked about the stacks of journals. "Jack, I know the pictures in the print journals are better quality than the scans you can see online, but I was wondering why you go to the trouble to save these things when it's so easy to find stuff now on the Internet."

Jack was no technophobe and he was very happy with the way the corporate network had provided fast, unfettered access to the Web. "Uh, well, I don't know. I guess it's really just habit. I've always found it difficult to throw away journals because I always think, 'What if I need this some day?' In truth, with Medline and the electronic texts that Excella has on line, it's probably been years since I've opened one of these after I read it." He stood in place for a moment, staring at the piles of magazines, some as much as 12 years old, before emptying the armload he was carrying into a large trash barrel. "We might as well just dump all of these, and I guess I can leave most of the texts here, too. Stephen, you're already making my life more efficient."

"Well, I hope I'll have half that success in the lab!" Stephen quipped. It was prophetic, for in the intervening three years, he made several important contributions while working for Excella.

Jack's focus habitually returned to his computer's monitors, and after a deep breath, he stopped drumming his fingers and clicked on the e-mail icon on the computer desktop. He ignored the notice that he had 3 new messages waiting for him, instead addressing a new message to Stephen: "SS- Ascendiac has finally entered phase III and I'd like to review our current database of knowledge so we are fully prepared for any potential issues. I'm free most of the day, so stop by when you have time. I'll ask Tina to join us, too. -JF"

Tina Haanlut was a chemist who had been with Excella for eighteen years, specializing in creating the sequence of reactions required to synthesize target molecules. She had an almost instinctive understanding of chemistry as well as a knack for designing synthesis sequences which could be scaled up to industrial size production lots with minimal effort. Although this sort of chemical engineering was often thought of as merely mechanical, with little room for creativity and imagination, the truth was much more telling. Without a way to produce a given chemical, there was no way to make the product the company needed to sell. Making a reaction even marginally more efficient could mean shaving millions off production costs, and Tina had undoubtedly saved the company untold amounts during her long, little-celebrated career.

A meeting with these two, Jack felt, would help him relax just a little now that his pet, Ascendiac, was finally on center stage, performing its first solo, under the harsh glare of scientific spotlights and the FDA's judges.

6.

"Good morning, Pearlene," Sharon puffed as she walked through the office door.

"Lordy, woman, what's got into you? You look like you just run a mile! You OK?" Pearlene's brow was furrowed with sincere concern.

"Yeah, well, I just walked up the stairs is all," Sharon replied. "More than I thought, but I need the exercise." She sat in one of the waiting room seats for a moment.

"Exercise is fine, so long as the elevator's broke. Otherwise, all the workout I need is pressing that number 4 button." Pearlene smiled, making a pointing gesture with her right hand. "See, I'm in training right now!"

Sharon chuckled. "Maybe that's how I should start, huh? Work my way up to the stairs. Anyhow, is Dr. Sonders busy this morning?"

"You know it. She's booked solid again. I tried to tell her, 'Dr. Sonders, you need to take it easy, take some time off for lunch or something.' She just smiles and says that once the patients stop calling, she'll cut back a little."

"That's her, all right. Well, if any of the patients cancel today, please tell me. I'd like her to see the new billing system we're trying out. I should be done entering last months claims in a little while, and she needs to decide if it will make her job any easier. I already know it will simplify mine."

"I'll do that."

"Thanks, Pearlene. I'll be in back if she needs me." Sharon got off the seat and walked to the back office and break room. Although Alison had a beautifully appointed office in which she saw her patients, it was strictly for show. The majority of the paperwork was performed in the back room which was equipped with two computers, a table, several filing cabinets, and a microwave, allowing it to double as a break room. Sharon spent most of her time there, dealing with the endless correspondence between patients, insurance companies, and other physicians. Even Alison preferred to dictate her charts there because she felt she needed to get out of the other office from time to time.

Sharon grabbed her coffee mug from the cabinet and poured herself a cup. Inside the college-dorm-sized refrigerator, she found the container of French vanilla flavored coffee creamer and opened the cap. Before pouring it, though, she peeked at the nutritional label to find that it had far more calories than she had expected. *Wow, I forgot how many things are going to have to change now. No wonder switching from sugar to the blue stuff doesn't make much difference.* She replaced the container and decided to try getting by without it. *Hmmm. No donuts, either. Sitting at this desk all day isn't going to be easy. Must be why all those dieters keep carrots and celery with them all the time. Well, I can pick that stuff up at lunch. How did I get into this mess in the first place?* She starting typing in the last of the billing slips while thinking about her weight, trying to determine just when it was that she started overeating. *It must have been around ninth grade because I remember having trouble with my bathing suit that summer....*

"Mom, how can I go to Jennifer's pool party tomorrow? Look at this thing." She was standing in front of the mirror in her bedroom, wearing a two-piece bathing suit that she'd picked out last year. "It makes me look too fat."

Her mother, who had been folding laundry in the master bedroom, walked in. She knew her daughter had gained a few pounds over the past several months, but ninth grade was often a difficult time for girls and she was reluctant to confront Sharon about her worsening eating habits for fear that they would fight even more than they had been. She tried to cook healthier foods but Sharon often ate dinner at friends houses, and even when she was home, she snacked heavily after school while talking on the phone. This was the obvious consequence. "Well, it doesn't seem to fit as well as it had.... We can go to the mall if you want." Sharon had all but given up shopping with her mother, but she figured it was worth offering anyway.

"Well, I need to do *something*," she snapped. Then softer, with a touch of guilt in her voice, "I mean, I need to start a diet, but that won't fix things for tomorrow." She sat on her bed and hung her head down. "I don't know why I'm always hungry these days. When I come home I pick up a bag of chips and I just keep eating them, even when I think I've had enough. Sometimes, I don't even realize I've started. They're just there, in my hands."

Her mother felt totally helpless at that point, unable to decide what to say. She sat next to Sharon and put her arm around her gently. Pointing out that weight swings were a way of life for many women didn't seem like a solution, but it was the best she could do. "You know, Shar, a lot of girls your age do gain some weight. It's a hormonal thing, sort of like retaining water each month, but on a longer term. I certainly put up with that for years. Eventually, you manage to find a combination of dieting and exercise that helps, but you never really escape. I know that when I get sad, there's nothing like a box of Oreos to cheer me up, so that's why I never buy them, because one day I'll be sad about something and suddenly the whole box will be gone."

"But I'm not sad about stuff every day and I'm still hungry."

"Being sad is only part of it, I think. Another part is that your body learns that eating makes you feel better, so even when you're not sad, it wants to eat so that you feel even better than you do. I don't know that anyone will ever understand why it is, but believe me you aren't the first person to feel this way."

"Will you help me lose this weight again?" She looked up hopefully.

Now her mother was starting to feel better. At least her daughter still respected her enough to ask her help when she really needed it. "Of course, Shar. We'll work on this together, I promise. Now, what do you say we get you a new bathing suit so you can have fun at Jennifer's tomorrow?"

"Thanks, Mom."

"You're welcome, sweetheart. Some day, when you have kids of your own, you'll understand how much it means to you to help them out when they need it. Now lets get to the store before your dad comes home and gets involved in this *womanly* matter, OK?" She winked as she said this.

"Yeah, that's a good idea. I'll get dressed real quick."

Sharon shook her head as she finished entering another insurance claim into the computer system. *I guess Mom was right after all. I know I lost weight that summer, but somewhere along the line, I just gained it back. It was probably that winter because I know the cold weather and short days keep me inside rather than exercising. It's got to be more than that, though, because then the summers should be better but they're not. Part of the problem is when I feel fat in the summer, I don't want to wear shorts. Then it's always too hot outside in jeans, so I end up not wanting to exercise when it's warm, either. Of course, if exercise were the only problem, I could just join a gym, which I seem to do every other year. If I could just eat less and not feel hungry all the time.... Yeah, that's a brilliant conclusion, Sherlock. I might as well look for the zero calorie donut.*

She reached over for the phone and dialed the number from the flyer. It rang twice before a pleasant voice answered, "Hello, this is Gheena with the Ascendiac weight loss study. How can I help you?"

Suddenly, Sharon was nervous, thinking about the possibility of becoming a guinea pig in a research study. In an instant, she considered hanging up, but the haunting memories of a dozen failed diets and a steadily increasing clothing size convinced her otherwise. "Uh, hi. I saw your flyer about a weight loss study and I wanted to, um, know something about it."

"Certainly," came the cheery response. "A lot of people are a little nervous about these things because of the side effects people had with Fen-Phen. The drug we're studying is very different, though, and so far we haven't seen any of the problems that have occurred with other types of diet aids. First, let me say that this study is specifically for people who are basically healthy except for being overweight. Your eligibility will be determined by a doctor after a brief history and physical exam. The medication we're testing is called Ascendiac, and it helps decrease your appetite. If you fit the study requirements, you will be given the study medication for a seven day period, either before or after a seven day course of placebo. You will not know which medication you will be given first. You must see one of our study personnel every weekday, during which time we'll ask a few simple questions and we'll check your weight. If you complete the two week trial, you will receive four hundred dollars, and hopefully you will have lost some weight, too!"

"Well, what sort of diet do I have to follow?"

"Anything you like, or no diet at all. We're studying the effects of this medication on people to see if it can reduce their appetites so that they eat less of the same foods they normally eat."

"Is it... you know... dangerous?" Sharon decided to confront her fear directly.

"The medication has been tested in animals and in people with no signs of serious harmful side effects. However, the reason we're conducting this study is to find out more about how the medication works as well as how it may affect people who use it. It has been safe so far, but this is not a guarantee that you will not encounter unexpected side effects." Gheena paused for half a beat, then added, "You know, I have to read these answers from a special response card, so that's why they sound so dry. I've been working for this hospital's new drug study group for four years now and they do a really good job to make sure the drugs they're testing are safe. I see from your phone number here that you're over in the next building. If you want, you can stop by this afternoon and talk to one of the study doctors to see if you are eligible. It won't cost you anything but a little time, and you won't have to join if you don't want to."

Her personable style and candor made Sharon feel much more comfortable about the study. "You know, I'll do it. What time should I come by? Oh, wait, I'm working today until five."

"Five, huh? That's usually after we stop seeing new candidates. Is there any way you could make four-thirty?"

"I'd have to ask my boss. Actually, she's usually very supportive and flexible. Can you put me down for four-thirty, and I'll call you back if I can't make it?"

"Sure, darling. Now, what's your name?"

"Sharon Keating."

"OK, Sharon, we're in the Green building, third floor, room 306. Dr. Ulster is seeing candidates today. We look forward to meeting you!"

"Thanks, Gheena."

7.

The phone rang twice with the characteristic "outside line" tones before Dave reached over to answer it. He wasn't doing anything specific at that moment, but he always figured that, if he answered more quickly, the caller might suspect he was not busy at the time. It was one of the innumerable idiosyncrasies he had developed during his career, but if asked, he would have sworn it made a difference.

Before he could speak, the voice on the line said, "Hello, Dave. It's me."

Dave's eyes widened slightly as he immediately recognized the caller's voice. "Yeah, uh...." He cleared his throat nervously. "How... I mean, where are you calling me from?"

"Relax, Dave, I'm using a pay phone. Remember, I know more about these things than you do."

"Yeah... right... OK. What do you want?"

"Well, I just need to know how things are going with your little experiment so far."

This question made Dave a little angry. "You *know* we're only a week into this thing. It takes time to collect the data, so you need to sit tight for now. Remember, the whole idea was to put a little distance between entry and exit, right? I'll let you know if anything looks bad, but for now, there's no news. The rest of the company is quiet, so I don't expect any big swings in the short term."

"Uh-huh. And how's your buddy holding up?"

"He's fine. I expected a little more pressure from him, but we had a meeting earlier and he's satisfied with the way things are going. He actually agreed to an off-the-books surveillance study to make sure there are no surprises."

"And if there are?"

"That will depend. Whatever happens, though, I'll have the inside line on it and we'll walk away if we need to."

"OK, but remember that my partners don't like to be kept in the dark for too long. They get nervous, and when they do, they can get persuasive."

"Look," said Dave, "this is a business deal. There are no guarantees, but I think it's a pretty good bet that we're all making here. Remember,

I've got a lot riding on this thing, too. I'll contact you if anything happens, good or bad."

The line went dead and Dave hung up the phone. "Goddamn cloak and dagger nonsense," he said out loud to his empty office as he opened the top drawer of his desk and pulled out a white #10 envelope with the word "Lightfoot" written on the front. He took the paper out of the envelope as he clicked the mouse to wake up his computer. *Alright, Frank, let's see what you did for me.* The paper had a list of typed instructions, starting with "Open a new terminal window. Type 'rlogin –h 16.245.22.7' then log in with LIGHTFOOT username and password." Dave wasn't much of a computer expert, but he managed to make sense of the first line. He keyed in the name, then typed in the password Frank had told him when he gave him the instructions.

The computer responded "Kerberos authentication complete. Interactive session initiated without access logging. THIS MODE FOR DEBUGGING OR MAINTENANCE PURPOSES ONLY. UNAUTHORIZED USE MAY VOID DATA." This cryptic message meant little to Dave as it was, but he understood the deeper meaning behind the warning.

Phase III clinical trials traditionally take months to complete and analyze because they are designed to include multiple study sites in geographically distant regions. The purpose for this is twofold: First, by establishing study locations in, say, several major cities, patient recruitment can be accomplished much more quickly by accessing a larger population at one time. Second, the impact that geographical differences may make on study patients is diluted by including many different regions. As a simple example, if a study of the antibiotic doxycycline were performed only in northern cities during the winter, the study may well have missed the fact that the drug dramatically increases the rate of sun burning.

Once study sties are chosen, each must conform to very strict protocols for patient selection, medication administration, and data acquisition. Unless these steps are followed with religious fervor, the information collected is useless from a scientific standpoint. There is no logical way to evaluate the effects of a medication if patients are treated differently but their results are combined. Again, as a basic example, consider studies evaluating the effectiveness of a new medication to treat arthritis pain. If one study center arbitrarily chose to give the medication to their patients at the time they showed up for a daily pain assessment, the drug may seem less effective than another center which chose to give a bottle of the pills to the patient, who would then take them in the morning, as they got out of bed. Arthritis pain tends to be worst in the morning, so, assuming the pain medication actually *was* effective, then patients who took it early, when their pain was worst, would experience more improvement when compared to patients who took the medication after they already worked through the most painful part of the day.

As part of the effort to minimize these sorts of discrepancies during studies, most companies print forms which are to be completed at each site for each patient during each visit. Properly timed and dated forms can help uncover systematic inconsistencies, but extracting and organizing the data often took weeks of manual labor at the company, assuming they were mailed promptly by the sites. Excella sought to circumvent these pitfalls, so about 18 months prior to the beginning of Ascendiac's phase III trial, they hired a network programmer named Frank Phong to create a user-friendly, secure, electronic system to replace these paper records completely.

Frank's plan was for each study site to receive several computers with dedicated Internet access. As patients were evaluated, data would be entered directly into the system, which would automatically tag the entries with time and date. To take the data acquisition process to an even higher level, Frank also created a way for patients to enter some of their own information, especially with regard to perceived beneficial and unwanted effects of treatment. This reduced the work the researchers needed to do as well as allowed otherwise embarrassing information to be provided by the study patient without direct human confrontation.

Had this sort of system been in use by other companies, a drug like Viagra might have come to market much quicker. As it was, Viagra was initially being studied for its effectiveness at reducing angina in patients who suffered from chest pain. The sexual effect was discovered serendipitously when a significant number of patients began refusing to return the unused portions of their study medications despite their reports that the drug did little to reduce the frequency of their chest pain. When the study researchers pressed the patients, a few bashfully admitted that they noticed a significant improvement in their sexual function. If they been given a more anonymous channel through which to report these findings, patients may have been more candid and this new effect would undoubtedly have been uncovered much earlier.

One final requirement for a sound scientific study is that the patients and the researchers must be kept blinded to the treatment groups. That is, neither one can know whether the pill being given is a placebo or the study drug. Since all human beings respond to suggestion to some degree, this potential source of bias must be minimized, and the only truly effective way to do this is to keep the study groupings secret until all the data are collected. Pills are dispensed by computer in numbered containers, and each patient receives pills only from that container. Once the study is completed, a table matching the container numbers to the true contents can be released. Often, the studies will provide *both* types of pills to every patient in a crossover fashion. That is, half the group will receive the real drug for the first part of the study, then they get the placebo for the second part, while the other group receives pills in the opposite order. This way, each patient can be used to generate actual test data for the drug.

The FDA demands evidence that these rules are followed properly, so the new electronic data collection program had to be designed to monitor any breach of these requirements. Frank chose to have the central server record in a special log file any activity that resulted in reading or writing of information. In theory, the log should only show information written to the server as the sites acquired patient data. Then, once the study period had been completed, data recording would cease and retrieval could begin.

Fortunately for Dave, Frank was a much better computer programmer than a scientific researcher. About six weeks into the project, Dave approached him to discuss the progress he was making. "Hi, Frank, I'm Dave. So, it seems that your program is going to be put to the test with my drug when it enters phase III trials next year."

Frank, a mild-mannered 26 year old, was a little intimidated by this introduction. "Well, if you say so. I don't know a lot about that."

"Oh, it's true. We're really quite excited that you've got this great system for us, though. I mean, it should make these trials much safer for our patients, right?"

"Safer? I don't follow," Frank replied, a little confused. To him, the program was simply a secure database, and the medical implications were all but lost.

Dave smiled, knowing that he wasn't going to meet much resistance here. "Well, you know that we're going to use this to compile data from patients who are trying out new drugs made by our company. So now, since the information is going to be online immediately, I can keep an eye out for any dangerous side effects. We can respond much faster than when we have to rely on the mail, you know."

"Yeah," Frank said slowly. "But I thought the information was supposed to stay secret. That's what I was told to do, at least."

"Oh, absolutely. Secret is very important, and so is recording any attempts to look at the information before the study is over. But that really only applies to the researchers, you see. When things were done on paper, we had to keep them secret from everyone since there was no reliable way to limit access to just a few people. The bias that would get introduced if the study people got the data too early would destroy the whole project. I'm not part of the study, though, and as the project manager, I *can* see the information because I'm independent. That make sense?"

"I suppose. Do you want me to put in a back door for you?"

"Well, I think it would be a good idea, don't you?"

Frank thought for a moment. "If I do this, though, the log is going to look a little strange, don't you think. I've already set it up so that any early read access will generate an automatic e-mail warning. It's a good way to keep hackers out." He smiled vaguely, thinking about the endless wars between hackers and programmers.

Dave was pleased. "Yeah, I think you may be right. I don't want you wasting your time trying to program around that sort of warning system if you don't have to. Just make a way for me to access the database and just don't put it in the log, OK? Oh, and I've seen some of the tests you've put together. You're doing a great job, let me tell you." He'd often found that a little praise went a long way.

"Oh, hey, thanks. That's really nice of you to say. I'll put that together and, uh, I guess I'll just send you the instructions on how to use it."

"Better yet, just stop by my office when you're done. I'm in the Channing building, fourth floor. Last name's Aswari."

Frank showed up the next day with the white envelope labeled "Lightfoot," a code name he was quite proud of. Dave quietly placed it in his desk drawer where it sat idly until today. Now that he was linked to the central server, he proceeded to the section Frank had titled "Data Retrieval." The computer asked him to enter a range of dates and study sites, with the default being "all data." A table appeared on the computer listing names, starting weights, interim weights, and other information collected. Frustrated by the limitations of the screen, Dave clicked on print and retrieved the pages from his laser printer. He was initially impressed by the number of patients who had enrolled already, just over a week into the study.

As he perused the information, several things were immediately apparent. First, patients weren't reporting any serious side effects. In fact, it seemed to Dave that the ones receiving the drug were complaining about minor symptoms even less often than those getting the placebo. He figured that was a good sign. As far as the weight loss progress, it seemed that there was a definite trend downward in the treated patients which didn't exist in the placebo ones.

I'm no statistician, but this definitely seems to be a good start. Looks like we're on the right path, boys. As that thought echoed through his mind, another one, much more disturbing, crept in to compete with it. *What happened that turned you into this?* He couldn't see how pale his face had suddenly become.

8.

"Ah, there you are," Jack announced to the computer screen. He had been combing through the FDA submission documents in search of the specifics on the phase III trials and he just found the one electronically marked as "final version." It was an Adobe PDF document, so when it opened on his computer, it looked just like the standard submission form with Excella's information neatly typed into the requisite fields. He scrolled through the first few pages which contained mostly background information, looking for the Approved Study Location list. Due to the need for complete conformity to protocols, studies are carried out only in approved centers, and only after a considerable amount of time has been spent teaching the research staff all the nuances of the study design. Contingency plans must be made in the event that a primary investigator at a given site cannot complete the study so that there are no gaps in coverage. The loss of study data is not only costly financially, but can have a profound impact on the volunteer patients as well.

People who sign up to participate in clinical trials must be informed of all known and potential risks and benefits related to the investigation. The agreement between investigator and volunteer is that the study will provide a new form of treatment which is believed to be at least as safe and effective as current therapies. Usually, the treatment is provided at no cost to the patient, and as a further incentive, many studies will actually pay cash for completion of the protocol. Also included are periodic medical examinations during which study data are collected, but which can also include discussion and treatment of other health issues. In turn, the patients know that their support can help advance medical science, improving not only their own health care, but the treatments available to everyone else, too. The primary risks are, of course, that the new drug will not be as effective as standard treatment, or that there will be unexpected side effects from the new treatment.

Most study patients, therefore, have a significant amount of anxiety as they begin to participate, but their desire to help the greater cause (as well as their own, when a financial incentive exists) can offset this. When studies are terminated and the data invalidated due to investigator miscues, though, many patients feel that the risks they took were for naught. The pharmaceutical companies, along with the research facilities, are immediately vilified and branded as dangerously incompetent, even when the decision to scrub a flawed study is the scientifically correct approach. Thus, the early study sites are always chosen carefully and are frequently major teaching hospitals which have a significant amount of experience organizing and executing new drug trials. Once the initial stages of the trial are underway, smaller institutions as well as independent drug trial facilities may then enter the fray, often under the auspices of an investigator temporarily transferred from one of the primary study sites.

Jack was pleased to see that there were only two sites listed in the primary stage: the University Medical Center downtown and Stanford Medical School. As he read over the highly technical description of the study design he realized that virtually all of the recommendations he had made during the drafting process had been included verbatim. Despite his initial concerns that the company would try to cut corners to improve the chances for success, the undeniable fact was that the study was very even-handed in its approach. The absence of aggressive post-study follow-up seemed much more reasonable given the built-in checks and balances he had helped to devise. *Maybe this surreptitious phone call thing is a better plan after all. If we find anything, we'll have a chance to do some damage control rather than finding out only after the data are unblinded.*

"Jack? You busy?" The voice came from the doorway, and despite his cold, Stephen's slightly jovial voice was easily recognizable.

"Hey, Stephen, come on in. I was just perusing the phase III application here. I hadn't seen the final form yet."

"You mean you haven't been following the Public Relations releases on the 'Net?" His stuffy nose still kept him from pronouncing "v" sounds properly, so it sounded more like he said "habent."

"Uh, I guess not. Cold still got you, eh?"

"Yeah, it figures that I need to gain a few pounds, but instead I help design a weight loss drug rather than a cure for the cold." Stephen chucked.

"Well, make that your afternoon project, then. Seen Tina today?"

"Not unless I was in Sweden this morning. She's at a conference, remember?"

Jack rolled his eyes briefly. "Of course. I completely forgot about that. I sent an e-mail and even left her a voicemail earlier but I'm so used to skipping the announcement that I didn't bother to listen."

"Anyway, just so you know, just about every move the company makes gets announced on the PR Newswire. The day the FDA accepted our filing, a short report popped up announcing it. All done to manipulate the stock prices, right?"

Jack nodded and shrugged. "Always the last to know. So we've got some live patients out there taking our pill right now. They must have done a great job training these sites because I haven't heard a peep."

"Really? That's great. We've already got 26 patients enrolled and underway, so that's a great sign."

"26? How do you know that?"

"Come on, Jack, didn't they show you the online data system?" Stephen moved over to Jack's keyboard and started typing.

"I thought that system was just for post-study analysis. Isn't that part of the security?"

"It certainly is, but information such as number enrolled really doesn't need to be blinded. In fact, it *can't* be blinded because our power analysis demanded exactly 300 patients to make a valid study. We've got to know exactly how many have started and finished, right?" He tapped on the screen and Jack saw a table showing the names of the two study locations along with a list of how many patients were in each, the number of males versus females, and the average age of patients in each group. "The guy who wrote this... I think his name was Frank... put this feature in. It won't show you anything that would compromise the validity of the study. In a sense, it's an investigator access portal designed to give just enough information so that we know how far we've gotten. Here, I'll leave it up so you can follow the progress. It updates every hour or so."

"Great. I should hang out with you more often!" The two laughed, then Jack continued. "Now, the real reason I wanted to talk to you was to go over the specifics of our drug one more time. I'm one of the first line guys here when it comes to fielding calls from the research sites, so I want to make absolutely sure we've got all the information we know within easy reach."

"OK," Stephen started, "as you know, most of the early data came from predictive computer structuring. Let me just bring up the modeling program on your machine here and I can show you." He typed for a few moments before the computer opened a new window with a large, blob-like shape in it. When he clicked on the shape, it began to rotate, and as the computer automatically shaded and highlighted regions, the picture suddenly looked like a real, tangible 3-D surface. "So, this is the computer predicted structure of the serotonin delta receptor. Obviously, the neurotransmitter serotonin has been studied for some time, but this delta form of the receptor was a new finding to come out of the human genome project."

"That much, I remember. The alpha, beta, and gamma receptors are widespread, but this one seems to be much more localized in the brain."

"Right. In fact, once the mRNA hybrid studies were done showing which cells made this particular receptor, it seemed that nature was being awfully stingy with this form. That made it an interesting candidate for drug design because it should allow us to target a relatively smaller part of the brain rather than the usual approach, which ends up looking more like a shotgun blast than a sniper's shot. Now, that's when you made the discovery that this receptor was related in some way to eating."

"Discovery? Let me tell you a secret: It was pure luck. I was reading the original Yale study on this new subtype and I had this fantasy that this was the one responsible for the feeling of satiety. The only reason I had backing that belief was that it seemed to be concentrated in specific parts of the limbic system of the brain. We've got drugs to affect most of the other receptors, but none of them seem to have a profound effect on appetite."

Stephen was stunned. "You mean, when I started here on this project with you, there wasn't any actual evidence that it was the right target?"

"No." Jack laughed. "You didn't think we really knew what we were doing, did you?"

"I guess I never asked. I assumed that since you were paying me, you must have had a clue what you were up to."

"Welcome to my world, buddy. If there's one thing that we learned a long time ago, it's that drug design is often more luck than science. The computer certainly helps us shape new molecules to be tested as drugs, but figuring out what the right targets are is often a matter of luck. Besides, even if this receptor didn't control the appetite, it pretty much *had* to be doing something."

"I'm just glad you were right the first time. It's been much more exciting designing an appetite drug than yet another serotonin-based antidepressant. Anyhow, since no one had managed to purify this receptor to the point that they could do x-ray crystallography on it, we had to rely on the computer to deduce the 3-D structure of the molecule. The rest is a matter of history."

Jack nodded. "History aside, let me just run through it again. You designed a molecule which binds to the side of the receptor. Its shape helps it to improve the way serotonin binds to the receptor, effectively making the receptor more sensitive to serotonin." Stephen clicked a few times on the computer model and the Ascendiac molecule appeared, gliding towards the serotonin receptor. Then, the computer showed the two bound together, with a small extension from the Ascendiac molecule sticking up, near a pocket in the receptor itself. A serotonin molecule then floated in, fitting into the pocket with the Ascendiac finger seeming to hold it in place. "As the serotonin concentration in the midbrain rises after eating, the receptors fill up more quickly and at a lower serotonin concentration because of Ascendiac's help. The theory is that this will make people feel full sooner."

"Yup. We tried it in rats and their average meal size dropped by 35%. Then we tried it in monkeys and their meal size dropped by almost the same amount. They increased their activity levels slightly, leading to an improvement in the lean body mass to fat ratio, but without causing them to drop below a healthy level. Then the phase II human trials showed no significant side effects. Those patients were relatively fit, as phase II requires, but even they reported transient disinterest in inter-meal snacking."

"Do we know anything else about this drug?" Jack asked.

"I think the only other point is that it doesn't really affect the other serotonin receptors. The delta form has a positively charged amino acid which I've exploited for selectivity. The drug is about 100 times less effec-tive at binding to the other forms, according to the computer. The other benefit to this is the dissociation time, meaning that, once the drug binds to the receptor, it takes more than a day to fall off. This gives the drug a modest tapering effect which should help in case there's any tendency for rebound binge eating. It also means we can dose this once a day which is a big benefit for the patients."

Jack's phone rang and the caller ID showed his home number. He grabbed the receiver. "Hello, my dear, sweet, beautiful wife. Hang on a second." He took the receiver away from his ear for a moment, covering the mouthpiece. "Stephen, thanks a lot. I want you to take it easy for a few days, OK? Obviously, the early part of phase III is the most critical and I may need you at any moment. This is what we've been working towards for the last three years."

Stephen gave him a thumbs up and walked out of the office, beaming. *All those years of grad school really were worth it. This may end up being the treatment so many people are hoping for, and we are the ones who put it together. I always dreamed that, somehow, I'd find a way to make a difference.*

"Hi. Sorry about that, Sandy," Jack resumed. "What's up?"

"I'm not interrupting anything, am I? I can call back if you want."

"No, don't worry about it. Stephen and I were done anyway. Are you calling to remind me of something?"

"Actually, yes. It's Lisa's parent-teacher conference tonight and it starts at 6."

"*That's* what it was. I knew there was something I was supposed to do tonight, but I couldn't for the life of me remember what." Jack gave himself a gentle knock on the head for good measure.

"Well, that's why you're so lucky to have wonderful me as your wife!"

"You know, I was just going to say that." He chuckled. "Hey, has she been good this semester or am I going to get chewed out?"

"She's an angel and you know it. It wouldn't hurt if you spent a little more time with her, though. She still talks incessantly about the horse ride. Maybe you two can find a stable around here. I know there are some in north Jersey."

"That's a good idea, babe. Look, Ascendiac just started its phase III trial. Things are going to slow down here in a week or so, once they get the first wave of patients through. How about checking into that for me, and I'll pick a Saturday for us to go."

"I'll do that. Speaking of Ascendiac, I saw a spot on one of the morning talk shows about it. They didn't have any of the patients on, but they did interview a nurse from California who said she was working on the study and thought the drug looked very promising."

"That's more information than even I have! Wow, I can't believe we're this far along already. You know, if the drug is half as good as it seems in the lab, the stock options...."

ZBV.0972768009.G

delist unit# 15960763

xxxxx

Sandra cut him off. "Now don't start thinking like that, getting your hopes up. Just keep doing the right thing for the patients and the rest will take care of itself." She paused, then added, "Of course, I'll still love you even if you end up rich and famous."

Jack laughed out loud. "Yeah, you say that now.... Anyway, I'll be home in time for the meeting. What's for dinner?"

"I made some lasagna for you. We'll have to eat it when we get back from the school, though."

"Love you, Sandy."

"I love you, too, Jack. See ya' later."

They hung up, and Jack looked back at the computer screen which was still showing the model of the drug, receptor, and serotonin as it gently rotated in cyberspace. "My God, wouldn't it be amazing if this really turns out to be the cure for dieting and all the agony that goes along with it?" The magnitude of that concept sent a brief chill through him.

9.

Alison's third new patient for the day was a 19-year-old female named Susan who was sent to her with a diagnosis of generalized anxiety disorder, or GAD. As its name suggests, the primary symptoms of the disease are a diffuse, persistent state of anxiety. There are usually no specific phobias the patient can recognize, but rather they experience unease and apprehension which interferes with much of their daily activity. They may appear vigilant and tense, and their nervousness can even cause others around them to feel uncomfortable. Some patients respond well to short courses of benzodiazepines such as Ativan or Klonopin, but some patients relapse after the medication is discontinued. Since long term benzodiazepine use can lead to dependence, young patients are frequently referred to specialists who can help manage both the psychological and pharmaceutical treatment over the longer term.

Susan definitely did not appear at ease, sitting on the edge of the wooden chair in Alison's office and frequently scanning the room as though she were looking for something. Alison had offered her the highback leather chair most patients use, but Susan had said she thought it would be too confining. So, the interview was conducted in a soothing, slow manner with as few comments which could be interpreted as judgmental as possible. Although GAD is widely considered to be primarily a neurotransmitter imbalance disease rather than the result of a traumatic life experience, many patients present with several concomitant problems, and some of these can influence others. Alison was careful to explore Susan's entire psychiatric status to ensure that she had not missed any subtle, underlying stresses which could be exacerbating the GAD. After discussing her childhood, schooling, relationships, and social history, she was fairly certain that there were no hidden surprises.

"Well, Susan, I'd like to tell you what I think about your anxiety."

"Is it bad, doctor? I know it's bad, isn't it?" Her stereotypical pessimism was yet another unfortunate symptom of the disease.

"You know, I really don't think it is that bad. Let's look at a few facts first. You have been having symptoms like this for about a year, right?"

"Uh, I guess so."

"OK, now during that time you still managed to finish high school with good grades and you got accepted at a very respectable college."

"Yeah, but I didn't go and now they probably don't want me there anyway."

"Now let's be very concrete here. From what you've told me, your mom helped you send the college a letter exercising your right to defer acceptance for up to two years. Remember, you decided to do that because your symptoms were getting worse around that time. There's no reason to think they won't take you if you decide to go there within those two years."

"Oh, I hope so. Do you think they will?"

"I really do. Now, there is one other fact that is very important for us. Dr. Sanchez gave you some medication for two weeks, and you and he both feel that it helped you a whole lot. The only problem is that, once you stopped taking it, your symptoms came back."

"It just keeps getting worse and I don't know how to stop it."

"That's OK because I think I do. You see, Dr. Sanchez was worried about putting you on that medication for a long time because, after a while, it can have some bad side effects. The good news is that there are other medications which work just as well, but which take longer to start having their effect. Dr. Sanchez thought that you deserved to have one person help you treat just this anxiety problem, and I intend to be that person for you."

"Yeah...? Well, I... I guess that's really good, then."

"Fortunately, I have some of the medication here that you're going to need, and I can give it to you today. If it's OK with you, I'd like your mom to come in now so we can discuss your treatment together. Can I go get her?"

"Yes, that's fine, doctor."

Alison walked purposefully to the door and opened it. She saw Susan's mother in the waiting room and motioned to her to join them. "I was just about to tell Susan what we've found today. I agree with Dr. Sanchez that Susan has a case of generalized anxiety disorder which, as I'm sure he told you, is caused by a chemical imbalance in the brain."

Susan's mother replied, "He did explain that to us, yes."

"Good, so what I think we need to do is to get Susan on a reliable, effective medication regimen which we can keep her on as long as she needs it. Susan, I think there are three medications which have a role here, and I'm going to recommend two of them for starters. One is clonazepam, or Klonopin, a medication similar to the Ativan that Dr. Sanchez gave you. This is a relatively fast acting pill and it should help you feel better very soon. You'll only need about a week or so on that medicine, though, because I'm also going to prescribe buspirone, or Buspar, for you, which takes about a week to start working. Now this medication is very different in many respects from the other medicines you've had. It won't make you quite as tired as the other ones can, but it can be really effective in helping young adults who suffer from the sort of anxiety you have."

"Are there any side effects, doctor," Susan's mother asked.

"Well, yes, there are some side effects for almost every medication. If you want a list of them, your best bet is to read the paper that will come with the prescription. However, it's been my experience that the most common ones like a dry mouth tend to be minor and usually go away after a few weeks of taking the drug. Serious side effects are very rare, and while I can't tell you that Susan *won't* have any, I think the odds that she'll benefit from the treatment far outweigh the risks from this medicine."

"Yes, I see your point. I suppose that's not really a fair question, huh?"

"No, I'm glad you asked it because you clearly care about your daughter, and that's going to be very important to her as we help her through this." Alison opened her desk drawer and unlocked a metal box which was contained within. She took out a single dose package of clonazepam and handed it to Susan. "This is the fast acting medication I mentioned, Susan. I'd like for you to take this with some water from the cooler outside, OK? Then you and your mom can have a seat in the waiting room again, and we'll wait for the medication to start working. I think you'll start to feel better within an hour. If we're on the right track, we'll know today, and then you can go home confident that you're going to improve."

"I'm going to start feeling better today? Are you sure?"

Alison smiled warmly. "Well, I'm pretty sure, but that's why we're going to check."

"Right, OK. I got it." She stood and edged towards the door, hesitating briefly before reaching for the handle and walking into the waiting room, towards the cooler.

"Dr. Sonders, thank you so much," Susan's mother said. "We'll wait outside for you. Thank you."

"My pleasure. I really think she's going to improve on this medication regimen." The two women shook hands, and Susan's mother joined her daughter in the waiting room. Alison walked over to Pearlene to find out who was next on the list.

"Well, Doctor, I been calling this number all morning long, but no one's answered until about twenty minutes ago. Seems Mr. Riley has the flu real bad and forgot to call to cancel. He's not coming in today. Now I reminded him that we have a 24 hour cancellation policy, and I said he'd have to talk to you at the next visit to settle that. It's his first time doing that, you know."

"I guess I'll just have to have lunch, then. What am I going to do with all that free time, Pearlene?" Alison asked sarcastically.

"Actually, Doc, Sharon asked me to let you know she's nearly done putting in the information into the new computer system. She wanted to discuss it with you when you got the time."

"Sounds like that cancellation worked out in our favor then, huh? I'll be in the break room."

"Your lunch is in there already. I had them deliver it early today when I got through to Mr. Riley."

"What would I do without you, Pearlene?"

"Why, I 'spect you'd *starve*, Doc!" She gave a quick hoot of a laugh which made Alison smile, too, as she walked around back, where she found Sharon staring so intently at the computer screen that she didn't notice her enter. She was slightly startled when Alison spoke.

"Hi, Sharon, Pearlene said you wanted to show me the new billing program?"

"Oh, hello, Dr. Sonders. Yes, I was just looking at the results and... Oh, let me back up. As you know, this is just a demonstration version of the program, so it won't actually submit the claims you enter, it will just let you put the billing information in the computer as you normally would, then it prints out a summary of the billing data at the end, along with all sorts of analyses. So, what I did as a test was I got all the claims together from last month and I entered them into the system."

"You put an entire *month's* worth of billing in there? How long did that take you?"

"Not that long, really." Sharon was getting nervous, worrying that Alison was implying that she'd been wasting her time. "I think it took about ten hours or so."

"That's *amazing*. How long did it take you to sort through that much paperwork when you actually submitted the bills?"

"Well, you know, I guess I spend about 2 hours a day, give or take. Some days I don't work on it, though. Hmm. I guess when you look at it that way, it would have saved me some time."

"Good, because after all, that's part of the reason we're looking into this, right?"

Sharon nodded. "Yeah. So, OK, I put that in and then I ran the summary part. The computer found all sorts of coding improvements which would have meant about a 9% increase in revenue, and that's on the most conservative settings. The best part, though, is that it looks through the claims for any irregularities. For example, it keeps a list of the frequencies that different codes are used. If your billing falls outside the norm, it alerts you, making sure that you're not putting things in incorrectly."

"How'd we do?"

"Pretty well. The computer says we're in a low risk group for auditing, but it did question two follow-up visit codes. I have to check the Medicare books to see what the actual definitions are, but one of them may well be an error we need to fix. I think the other is simply a function of your patient population, so it's not really an error."

"That's terrific. Now, this works with other insurance plans, too, right? I mean, we don't see that many Medicare patients here."

"True, but Medicaid also requires the same strict adherence to the rules, so those patients also get covered. More importantly, though, it does work with Blue Cross, Aetna, and a few others. The computer found that, for last month, 82% of your patients would have been billed either electronically or from the program's printouts for those companies that don't accept electronic claims."

"Do you think it's worth getting, then," Alison asked. "Be honest."

Sharon sighed, feeling a little uncomfortable about making such an important and potentially expensive decision. She reconsidered the situation one final time, then stated, "Yes, if last month is any indication, the system should pay for itself in the first four months of the year."

"Perfect. That's just the sort of analysis I was hoping you'd do for us." Alison sat at the table and opened her lunch, a gourmet vegetable wrap from a local restaurant.

"Dr. Sonders, there is one other thing." Alison looked up and nodded, having just taken a bite of her sandwich. "I have an appointment this afternoon, and I was wondering if I could leave work a little early today, at about four-fifteen, or so."

"After such a nice job on this billing system, how could I say 'No?' Of course, Sharon, that's not a problem at all."

"That's great. Thanks!"

10.

I have got to get up here more often, Dave thought as he looked around the executive dining room at the plush accommodations and the exquisitely prepared, catered lunch. The room was usually reserved for members of the board and a few other high ranking officers, but Excella's monthly departmental business meetings were held here, ostensibly as a small token of appreciation for those who participated, though the real reason was that the officers didn't want to be hassled by having to dine in lesser arenas. Although the subject of the discussions was usually dry, even to someone with as much financial experience as Dave, today, he was truly looking forward to his five minute update. Each manager was expected to present an overview of the current state and near-term goals of his department. To keep the meeting orderly and as concise as possible, departments were assigned to seats, and the managers took turns speaking, working around the expansive table.

Today, Dave was so engrossed in thought that he entirely missed his cue. "Mr. Aswari, you *do* have the floor," one of the vice presidents chided.

"Oh, of course. Well, as you probably know, Ascendiac, our revolutionary diet aid pill, just started its phase III trial, with research sites in California, at Stanford Medical School, and in New York, at the University Medical Center. As a brief refresher, the medication works by enhancing the way a neurotransmitter called serotonin works in the brain. The effect is to reduce the appetite of the patient, helping them to eat smaller meals and to control cravings and snacking. Phase II trials proved the safety of the medication, and we are now beginning to prove its effectiveness as a weight loss medication. At last count, there were nearly thirty patients in the trial, and there were no notable problems reported. The clinical trial at Stanford was covered on one of the morning talk shows, and the research nurse they interviewed said she thought the drug was having significant results. Within two hours of the airing, Stanford's team had booked three solid weeks of candidate patient interviews, and the talk show promised to air an addendum tomorrow letting people know about the New York site, too. Gentlemen, this drug may be a miracle— a *cure* for compulsive overeating."

Dave paused for a moment to let the last statement sink in. Unfortunately, the enthusiasm he had for the project wasn't openly shared by the other attendees. He cleared his throat uncomfortably, then continued. "Our team's also working on several approaches to computer modeling for new drug discovery, with our first major development being Ascendiac. The near term will see further improvements in this system."

The chairman nodded politely as Dave finished his report. "Thank you very much, Mr. Aswari. We look forward to further updates as they become available. Hopefully for the shareholders, this will be Excella's first blockbuster drug. Next...."

Once the meeting had concluded, Dave headed back to his office, contemplating what the next step for him would be after Ascendiac. Laura, his secretary, interrupted the dream by handing him three phone message slips. "This one's from your mother. She said you should call her as soon as you can. The others sounded routine."

"My *mother* called? What did she say she wanted? Is she OK?"

Laura shrugged. "Well, she sounded more excited than anything. I don't think anyone's dying, if that's what you mean, but I didn't really ask. She just told me to tell you to call her when you got back."

Dave looked at the slip of paper and saw that the phone number she left was for her home, which he took to be a good sign. "OK. Anything else come up?"

"No, but I'm supposed to remind you that you have a routine conference call with the FDA scheduled for 4 p.m. It's an Ascendiac trial update thing."

"Good. I'll be inside, so call me about 10 minutes to four." He closed his office door and began dialing the phone while he fought back the dread of a thousand possible tragedies which could have prompted the unscheduled call from his mother. Dave routinely spoke with his parents at least once a week, so there was rarely a reason for them to contact him, especially at work. The call went through and his mother answered on the third ring.

"Hi, Mom? It's me."

"Oh, Davey! Hold on a second, let me get off with Aunt Sissy." Her voice certainly didn't convey a tone of badness, and as she put him on call waiting hold, he had a moment to recover from the tension. Finally, she returned. "You still there?"

"Yes, I'm here. What's happening?"

"Bobby was on TV! It seems his department has been working undercover to break up an organized crime ring that was selling illegal drugs, and today they arrested a whole bunch of people. The news report said, 'Assistant DA Bobby Aswari was the man primarily responsible for the big break in the case,' and they claim it was one of the biggest drug busts the city has ever seen. Even the Mayor was interviewed, and he talked about how important Bobby had been in the investigation!"

Dave was surprised by the news. He knew his brother had been working on the organized crime task force, but he hadn't mentioned anything about an impending raid. "Wow, that's great, I guess. They, uh, didn't say who the mob guys were, did they?"

"Mob? You think the *Mafia* was involved? I just assumed they were, you know, foreigners. It scares me to think he's going after Mafia people."

"No, Mom, I don't know anything about it! I guess I was thinking about the Mafia because of the crime ring comment. So... they didn't give any names?"

"Well, if they *did* say, I didn't hear it. Do you think he's going to be OK? I mean, these criminals sometimes go after the police, don't they?" His mother's pride had suddenly given over to maternal protective instincts.

"Uh, I don't really know, but I'm sure he can take care of himself. Besides, it's his job and it sounds like he's doing great things."

"Yeah, I guess he is," she conceded. "Remember how you two used to play cops and robbers? He always wanted to be the cop, trying to protect people from the bad guys. One time, *you* wanted to play the cop, and he ran inside, crying because he wanted to be the good guy. That's my Bobby, always looking out for people."

His mother's pride in her son brought back poignant memories for Dave, too. "Yeah, I remember what he was like," he said, as his voice trailed off. "I'll call him later and congratulate him. If you can tape the news tonight, I'm sure he'd enjoy seeing the report."

"Ooh, good idea," she agreed. "I'll have Dad put in a tape right now."

"OK, well, thanks for calling. I'll give you a ring tomorrow, as usual. Right now, I've got a few things I have to do."

"Yes, alright. Glad you called back, Dave. I love you."

"Yup, love you too, Mom." As he hung up, he heard his mother telling his father to find a blank video tape. Dave put down the phone and held his head in his hands for a moment, rubbing his eyes. He wondered if he could find out any more information about the arrests on the Internet, so he clicked on the web browser and began looking through the current news items.

The drug ring story was top on the list of regional reports, and it even had a photo of Bobby personally walking one of the handcuffed suspects towards a police car. As was customary, the suspect's head was hidden from view, but Dave could tell it was a Caucasian male. The story provided only scant details about the accused, but there was at least one inside source who suggested that the criminals might belong to a rogue branch of a major crime family. *Bobby, I hope you know what you're doing here. These people can be vicious, protecting their own at all costs.*

After another ten minutes of looking through various news reports about the arrests, Dave closed the web browser window, revealing the window that was hidden beneath. He was surprised to see that he had left the "Lightfoot" program running in plain sight of anyone who used his computer. Fortunately, Laura always kept an eye on his office, but if the wrong person stumbled on the security lapse and reported it to the FDA, it could easily cost Excella dearly in the phase III trial. He started to close the window when he noticed that the statistics had been updated since he started the program. He clicked "print" again, then quit.

The new status report showed that an additional fourteen patients had enrolled in the drug trial in the past four hours. Given the crush of patients after the network talk show story, Dave figured they should satisfy their study enrollment requirement by the end of the month. The weight loss trend was showing an even more impressive downward slope for the treated patients as they progressed through the week-long treatment arm. The only bad news was that two of the study patients were now listed as "lost to follow-up," a designation meaning that they failed to show for two consecutive daily evaluations, and they were unreachable at their primary and secondary contact phone numbers.

Patients who drop out of studies cause significant difficulties for the statisticians. Initially, studies chose to ignore patients who dropped out, simply erasing their information from the list of patients. However, this approach is potentially dangerous since such patients may actually represent a group with unrecognized similarities, thus tainting the results. For example, in early studies of certain pain medications, some patients dropped out of the study unexpectedly, and were lost to follow-up. The study results were examined, ignoring these patients, and the drug appeared to be safe. Before publishing the results, though, the study's authors decided to make a final effort to track down the patients by sending research assistants to visit the patient's homes personally. What they found was that many of the "lost to follow-ups" had actually been stricken with acute, life-threatening bleeding ulcers which were actually being *caused* by the treatment medication. Ignoring these people would have dangerously skewed the actual effects of the treatment.

The appearance of drop-out patients in the Ascendiac study caught Dave by surprise, and he started to wonder whether there was any significance in their departure. Then he realized that both patients were three days into the *placebo* arm of the trial, reassuring him that, whatever the reason they had for dropping out, it wasn't related to Ascendiac. As he contemplated the possible reasons for discontinuing the study, he breathed a sigh of relief before another though struck him. *What if the study coordinators see these dropouts, but because they're still blinded to the fact that the patients are in the placebo group, they panic? They could end up stopping the study because of this, only to find out it was a false alarm!* He furrowed his eyebrows as he shook his head slightly as he realized just how many people were involved in the trial who were outside his immediate control. *Don't worry, you guys, everything's going great.*

11.

"OK, Pearlene, I'm leaving now. You have a good night," Sharon announced as she walked past the reception area.

"Wait, before you go, Sharon, let me ask you something. Did you see that girl who was sitting in the waiting room this afternoon? You know, the one with her mother?"

Sharon paused for a moment, then nodded. "Yes, she was in the corner, near the door, right? What was she here for?"

"Well, Dr. Sonders told me she had a form of anxiety which made her nervous all the time. I'll tell you, she couldn't sit still, always looking around like something was about to happen, only nothing did."

"That sounds like a terrible way to have to live. The poor thing! Why was she sitting in the waiting room for so long?"

"Well, the Doctor told me that she gave her some medication to help her relax some. Gave it to her right here in the office, then told her and her mother to sit down and wait for it to work, and you know what?"

Sharon was hooked on the story. "No, what happened?"

"Well, I'll tell you, you wouldn't believe it. Less than an hour later, she looked just like a regular girl again. Night and day difference. Dr. Sonders told me to watch her to make sure everything was OK, and right before my eyes, she got all turned around and fixed up."

"Just from a pill?"

"Yes, ma'am." Pearlene winked. "That Dr. Sonders is something, huh?"

"She really is," Sharon agreed, as her mind reveled in the power of modern medicine. She headed for the door. "See you tomorrow," she said as she though about her own situation. *What I wouldn't give for that sort of cure for my weight problem. Something like that, where I could just take a pill and stop being hungry right away. If this medication trial I'm joining is even half that good, my prayers will have been answered.*

In the hallway, Sharon caught herself turning right, for the elevators, and doubled back towards the stairs. *No matter how good this drug is, I still need to exercise, and that's final.* Going down was certainly easier, but the small sense of accomplishment was still perceptible. The walk to the adjacent building was painless despite the gusty winds, but once inside, she chose to take the elevator to the third floor rather than walk so that she wasn't as winded when she arrived.

The University Medical Center's Drug Research Institute was a very busy location for phase II and III clinical trials. Trained office staff and medical personnel accepted several projects at once and generated a remarkable quantity of data which was analyzed both by their own people and by the collaborating pharmaceutical companies. A small poster for each of the drugs currently being investigated was hung outside the entrance. Each had the pharmaceutical company's logo, as well as a picture of the primary investigator involved in the study. Sharon paused to see that Dr. Todd Ulster, MD, was in charge of Ascendiac. The Polaroid head shot made him look more like an overworked graduate student, with a balding forehead, a bushy goatee, and distinct bags under his eyes. She hoped that meant he was up all night studying medical texts rather than out having another round with his friends.

About nine study drugs were displayed, spanning the entire spectrum of products from antihypertensives to sleep aids, to birth control. In order to maximize the study protocol compliance for every study, a specific team was assembled for each drug, allowing that investigator to become intimately familiar with just one medication at a time. This sort of product oriented approach won the center the respect of many prominent pharmaceutical firms, some of whom chose to wait for an opening rather than run the first stage of a trial at other medical sites.

Sharon entered the small reception area and walked up to the desk. She was slightly disappointed to see that the receptionist's name tag identified her as Merissa Toan, not Gheena, whom she had hoped to meet.

"Welcome to the Research Institute," Merissa announced. "Do you have an appointment?" Though polite, she definitely lacked Gheena's charming personality.

"Hello, yes, I have four-thirty appointment for the weight-loss study. My name is Sharon Keating." Merissa typed the name into the computer and found her on Ascendiac's list. "OK, you will be evaluated by Dr. Ulster. For now, please fill out this questionnaire and take it with you when you go to see the doctor. Have a seat in the waiting room and we'll call you when it's time to go in."

Familiar with the procedure, Sharon simply smiled and walked inside with the clipboard to find about a dozen other patients also waiting for their turn. She sat in the corner and started reading the first page of the questionnaire which was dedicated to routine biographical data and current addresses and phone numbers. She completed the spaces as required, then proceeded to the inside of the form which focused more on her weight history. The first question asked about her earliest attempts at dieting, and whether it had helped her attain her target weight. Poignant memories flooded her mind.

The pool party at Jennifer's turned out better than she had expected, since a few of the other girls also had shown up with not-so-revealing one piece suits. While she wasn't proud, Sharon was at least relieved to have seen that weight changes weren't strictly relegated to *her* body. Now she had to confront her eating problems, so she sat at the table with her mother and tried to work out a plan.

"I've never really tried to diet before, Mom, so you have to tell me everything I need to do." She felt tremendously determined, as though nothing could keep her from this goal. "Do I just stop eating snacks?"

Sharon's mother frowned. She knew that the real answer was much more of a long term affair, requiring vigilance and sacrifice all the time, not just for parts of the day. How could she explain this to her daughter, given the tenuous nature of their teen-parent relationship and the inevitable difficulties Sharon would have trying to stick to a diet? Choosing her words as carefully as she could, she said, "Shar, dieting to lose weight and keep it off is really tough. Now, I know you're a smart, dedicated young lady, and I really believe that you can set your mind to this and succeed, but nothing about this is simple. As we work on this together, I promise I'll stick by you and help in any way I can."

"Oh, what's so hard about it? Don't I just have to eat less?"

"Yes, that's part of what this ultimately comes down to. You have to eat less, and the food you do eat has to be good for you, too. Greasy, fried food, even in smaller portions, still adds to your hips. But the other part is to exercise more. You don't have to become a track star, but you do need to do more than talk on the phone and watch TV."

"So what's the big deal?"

Her mother realized that this was going to be much easier once Sharon spent a week or so actually following the diet. "Nothing, really, but it helps if you have a plan so that when you get home from school and you're hungry, you have an option other than letting your stomach get the best of you. The first thing, though, is to pick a goal weight. How much do you think you should lose, and when do you think you should lose it by?"

Sharon thought for a minute. "I guess I need to lose about 25 pounds by, maybe, the end of this month." Currently, she was 146 pounds and 5'5" tall, so she was shooting for about 120 pounds, the weight of one of her friends.

"Do you remember when the last time was that you weight 120 pounds?" her mother asked.

"Uh, not really. I mean, I haven't paid that much attention to it."

"I think you were in seventh grade then. Your body has changed since then, so trying to get back to that weight may be a mistake," suggested her mother.

"Why don't you ever like anything I do? If you just wanted to correct me, why didn't you just tell me what weight to be?"

The mood swings were starting again, so Sharon's mother paused for a moment, hoping she'd cool off. "Well, Sharon, remember: I'm trying to help you figure out how to help yourself. You can do anything you want, but the more of this diet plan you come up with, and the more realistic it is, the more chance you have of making it work. No one's saying you can't be 120 pounds. I'm just saying that you might want to try to pick a little easier target, and if... that is, once you're there, then see if you need to go more."

Sharon huffed for a moment, thinking to herself, then confessed "Yeah, I guess you're right. Maybe fifteen pounds is better."

"OK, let's make it fifteen pounds in six weeks. I think you can do that, and you'll see that it's a lot easier if you don't try to lose it all at once. Let me tell you, being really hungry all the time doesn't make you feel good, and if you don't feel good, then everything else is harder, too."

"What do you mean, 'everything else?'" Sharon was suspicious.

"The exercise, for one. But that's just part of it. Everywhere you go, you're going to see food. There are fast food restaurants, ice cream shops, parties, picnics, holidays, and samples in stores. You can't get away from it, but all that food adds up. Cutting out snacks and reducing the portions you eat at meals can help if you also control the urge to eat during the rest of those times, too. And the only way to get that kind of control is to feel good about yourself so that you can think, 'I'm a great, strong person and I'm just as happy *not* eating that as I would be if I took one.'"

Sharon looked straight at her mother and admitted, "That part's going to be hard because I sometimes feel like there's no hope for me, and I might as well just eat what I want." The pitiful honesty ripped at her mother's heart as she sympathized with Sharon's plight.

"I know the feeling, Shar, but you'll do it. Like I said, I'll be there to help you, OK?" They both fell silent for a minute. "Now, let's make a plan here. First, stick with cold cereal or oatmeal for breakfast. I like eggs, too, but they have way too much fat."

"I can do that."

"Yes. Now lunch is a little harder. You usually buy lunch at school, but we should try packing you a lunch so you can have a little more variety and a lot better quality. Tuna fish is good if you don't put so much mayo in it. Cold cuts on a sandwich can be OK, but only a slice or two of cheese. We can buy a week's worth of lunches at the store, and every day you should also take some fruit or vegetables. Apples were my favorite, but oranges, carrots, celery, or peppers taste good and hold up in a lunch box just fine."

"Ugh, a lunch box? I don't want to bring one of those! Can't I just use a bag or something?"

"Of course, a bag is fine. I can get a whole package of brown bags to use. Now, after school you can plan for more fruit or vegetables, or, what I liked to do, was to eat pickles or pretzels, but only after I exercised. Since it's nice outside now, you should think about running or biking. Start slowly and work your way up to a thirty-minute workout. When it gets cold, you can do aerobics or something."

The plan took another hour to complete, but Sharon pledged to stick with it. There were rough times, most of which led to fights with her mother, but she always eventually admitted that she was sliding back to her old ways and her mother was simply trying to help her stay the course. By the end of the six weeks she was running at least 20 minutes every day (sometimes 30), and she felt better than she had in recent memory. Much more importantly, though, she had reached her goal of fifteen pounds by the middle of her fifth week, and had seemingly leveled off at seventeen pounds by the end of the sixth. Her mother attributed the plateau to the increase in her leg muscles balancing the loss in fat.

"Miss Keating?" The voice came from ahead of her, and it took an instant to remember where she was.

"Yes, that's me!" Sharon responded as she filled "14 years old" and "yes— lost seventeen pounds in six weeks" in the appropriate boxes. "I haven't finished the survey yet."

"No problem," replied the study nurse who had called her, "just bring it with you and you can work on it inside." She followed the nurse into the examining room to wait for the doctor.

12.

The Palo Alto one-bedroom apartment was beginning to smell like a garbage dump as the food carelessly left on the table rotted, putrefying in the warmth of the dark kitchen. This didn't seem to bother the apartment's tenant, a 31-year-old Web page designer named Zachary Powell, despite the fact that he was usually fastidious when it came to neatness and hygiene. Even his computers were suffering from neglect, covered in an array of empty food containers and opened packages of Ring Dings melting on the monitors. The local cockroach population had just zeroed in on the address and they were busily expanding their ranks.

Zack stared blankly at the wall of his bedroom, only dimly aware of the surroundings. His body, never the source of pride or joy for him, now lay unwashed and unshaven, neglected, in bed, for the third straight day. This morning, he gave up making the arduous journey to the bathroom when nature called, overcoming that most rudimentary training which began early in childhood. The curtains were drawn tightly shut against the mid-afternoon sun, but even the nearly perfect weather of northern California could not penetrate the dense, gloomy pall that was draped over him.

He was no stranger to the blues, having spent much of his life on the fringe of social circles, rather than in them, as he would have preferred. In high school, dating was a problem because he was overweight, but not the jolly sort of overweight that eases the interpersonal interactions. He was big, and he stayed big despite desperately wanting to be average. He tried sports but he couldn't play, and when he tried dieting, he found himself even more depressed than when he simply let himself go, eating until he was at least sated.

In college he met a classmate who seemed cut from the same mold. She was too self conscious to be comfortable with others, but she found solace in food which became like a drug to her, helping to fill in the places where she longed for other things. The two dated for several months, exploring the world of sexuality and relationships which they both craved but feared they would never experience. In the end, though, despite the aphorism, misery doesn't love company, but rather it smothers it. Those were dark days, but they were worlds apart from today.

Two weeks ago, Zach's one-man company finally caught a break when he signed a contract to create and maintain a website for a large commercial vineyard in the Napa valley. The deal would last at least three years, and the income was enough to cover his living expenses plus a small surplus. Now, all the one-time contracts he made would be icing on the cake rather than the last minute lifesaver to prevent his eviction for one more rent period. As he celebrated alone at his favorite restaurant, he decided that it was time for his life to change, too. He would find a way to be the man he'd always dreamed of: the man who wouldn't stand out in a crowd.

An ad in the newspaper caught his attention, and he called the number to find out more about the new weight-loss drug being studied at Stanford. *This is what I've been waiting for,* he decided. *All my life I've dealt with my problems by overeating, but now I can fix that. I'm going to break free of this.* He fit the study perfectly and began the trial with unvarnished optimism despite the fact that he wasn't sure if he was taking the study drug or the sugar pill. *Who cares what's in it? I feel good and I'm already starting to feel less hungry.*

As the days went by Zach had found a whole new side to his life, and with each came an array of previously unseen of color and promise. His energy level increased and the pounds slowly started to melt away. For the first time in memory he didn't feel like finishing a meal. The cabinet full of snack foods stayed full. At the end of the week, twelve pounds lighter, Zack looked in the mirror and said, "It's a damn miracle. If this isn't a cure, I don't know what is."

The switch to the other pill was painless. In fact, as far as he could tell, he felt just the same and he was still losing weight, but it would not last. By 36 hours on the other pill, he started having cravings for snacks, and the old habits silently returned in force. Halfway through a box of Twinkies he realized to his horror what he was doing. The new world that had grown up around him suddenly collapsed on itself, leaving its mark on the way down. As though a blind man had been given the gift of sight for a week, then had it taken away, the loss was worse than if he'd never known what his life could be like.

His mind, which, in Web design, had been quick and skilled, creative and analytical, suddenly focused on one repeating, inescapable, spiraling thought. *I'm worthless.* It was a black hole, pulling everything around it into its infinite mass from which nothing, not even the bright light of the previous week, could escape.

Abruptly, Zach lurched out of bed and pulled the nylon drapery cord off his bedroom window. *Fine.* The alarm clock hit the floor as he climbed onto the nightstand and tossed the cord over one of the exposed beams, tying the dangling ends in a makeshift noose. *I'm worthless.* He stepped off the nightstand and hung.

13.

The clock inched past five p.m., and Jack knew he had to leave so he wasn't late for the parent-teacher conference. It was times like this he was glad he'd decided to move across the border to New York state. His commute was reliably 25 minutes, a vast improvement over the unpredictable crossing of the New Jersey border on the Garden State Parkway. He took one last look at the computer screen to see the latest update on the Ascendiac trial. Thirty-eight patients were now enrolled, nearly 50% more than they had just a few hours ago. The screen also reported that two patients had been moved to the "lost to follow-up" category, although the "official" version of the data acquisition program which Jack was using did not provide information regarding which arm of the study those two patients were in.

Seems like the study's working, Jack thought. *A couple of drop-outs are expected in voluntary studies, especially when it's a weight loss program. These people are so used to miracle claims and failed results that they probably just assume that this stuff doesn't work. The ones who get the placebo first must figure that it's simply another case of an empty promise, so they get frustrated and leave. Maybe that's something we need to look at more closely. If we spent more time teaching the patients about the two arms of the study and the fact that they may get chosen to get the sugar pill first, they'd be more likely to finish both weeks.*

He shrugged at this thought and decided he'd discuss the issue with Dave tomorrow, since any changes to the patient consent and teaching would at least have to go through him, if not the FDA. He turned off the office lights and headed for the parking lot, slightly amused by the fact that this was the earliest he'd left work in recent memory.

Driving was always a passion, and his burgundy 1992 Porsche 911, which he'd bought used in 1996, was a gift he'd been promising himself since he graduated medical school. The classic style was pleasing to the eye, but his real interest in the car centered around the venerable horizontally opposed "boxer" six-cylinder, air-cooled, Porsche engine. It was a marvel of German engineering and the primary reason he didn't live any closer to work than 25 minutes. A brisk commute through the slightly twisty back roads never failed to rejuvenate him.

The engine was finicky, though, and it required at least five minutes of idling to begin to warm up, otherwise it was prone to stall. Consequently, as he sat in the snug driver's seat and listened to the motor whir unevenly, anticipation of the ensuing drive grew. After the requisite time, the temperature gauge began to move, so he eased the car out of its spot and drove through the gate. The traffic was still light as the New York City rush hadn't reached that far, making the trip just that much more pleasurable. When he arrived home, he saw he had ten minutes to spare, so he killed the ignition in the driveway and walked inside.

Lisa heard him drive in and was waiting in the kitchen when he arrived. "Hi, Daddy!" she called as she ran over to give him a hug.

Jack bent down and hugged her, then stood up. With a very serious face he said, "Wait a minute. Aren't you the girl who's in trouble at school?"

"No! I was good!"

"Are you sure? Your teacher isn't going to yell at me, is she? I might get scared, you know." He frowned playfully.

Lisa giggled. "No, Miss Brummel is going to give you a gold star because I'm so good! I even got extra credit for the book report I did."

"Oh, *that's* right. You're the *good* daughter, not the bad one," Jack said as he nodded thoughtfully.

"*Daddy!* I'm the *only* daughter."

"Really? The only one? Well, you must be the good one *and* the bad one, then." He shook his head.

"You're silly!" Lisa concluded as Sandra entered from the dining room.

"Kid's right about that, Jack," she said as they kissed.

"Hey, those shoes are great. How come I've never seen them before," Jack asked.

"Oh, these old things?" Sandra said jokingly. "I've had them since, oh, this afternoon, I guess."

"I suppose this means I'll have to take you out to dinner some time this month so you can wear them again, eh?"

"Yeah, like that will ever happen." She rolled her eyes, then said more seriously, "OK, well, we might as well go. Here, Lisa, put on your jacket."

As she put her arms through the sleeves, Lisa asked, "Are we taking your car or Mommy's?" The back seat was a tight fit, but Lisa knew that her Daddy liked to drive his car, so she always wanted to ride in it with him.

"We can take mine, but only if you're *sure* Miss Brummel isn't going to yell at me."

"I told you. I *promise!*" She folded her arms in mock annoyance and for an instant, Jack thought she looked exactly like her mother.

"Come on, you two," called Sandra. They climbed into the Porsche and started off for the school. "Alright, quick refresher. Lisa's teachers are Helen Brummel and Tim Randolph. The principal is Andy Fairbanks."

"Is there going to be a test?" Jack asked. "Can I take notes?"

"Hey," Sandra said, "I know how bad you are with names and I'm just trying to help. Any more news on your drug?"

"They told us in school that drugs are bad," Lisa announced from the back seat.

"And they're right," Jack assured her. "What Mommy meant to ask was whether our new *pharmaceutical* is doing well, but grown-ups sometimes use the word 'drug,' when they mean 'pharmaceutical' because we can't say that word too many times!" He made some nonsensical sounds to emphasize the trouble he'd have, causing more giggles from his daughter. "But you're right, sweetie, the drugs that your teachers told you about *are* bad and they can hurt you and your parents."

"I keep forgetting how tricky that topic can be," admitted Sandra.

"Well, to answer your question, we've got about forty people enrolled so far, and they've still got a few hours of daylight on the Left coast. No worrisome questions from anyone yet, so no news is good news. We've got a few drop-outs, but nothing out of the ordinary. I was trying to figure out a way to keep people from leaving so early in the study because I think some of it may be avoidable. Especially in these weight loss studies, when people are randomized to the placebo arm first, I think some of them get frustrated and quit, figuring it's just another easy fix that doesn't work. If our teaching was more focused on that mindset, maybe we'd retain those folks, too."

"They quit during the first week? That's not showing a lot of resolve. No wonder dieting doesn't work for them."

"In all fairness, some of them have tried every diet in the book. Who knows how many months they've stayed on them in the past. Besides, I don't really know *when* these people dropped out. It could be during the treatment arm, but I'm just speculating. I won't know for sure until after the study is complete and the information is unblinded. For now, it's top secret, and only the computer knows who had what pills. No one else can see so that there isn't any accidental bias."

"Daddy, what's 'bias?'"

"Good question, honey. Suppose I said that we'd flip a coin to decide if you got ice cream for dessert tonight. Heads, and we have ice cream, tails and we don't. So I flip the coin and it lands on the floor. Now you have to decide if the coin went high enough for the toss to count, OK?"

"How high is high enough?" she asked.

"That's up to you to decide, and whatever you say will determine if it's a good toss. Now, I toss the coin and don't show you which side is up. Since you don't know what the result is yet, your decision about the coin's height is unbiased. You don't know if saying it was high enough is a good thing or a bad thing, so you'll be fair. But, if you *know* the coin landed tails, your answer could now be biased. You may say it's not high enough because you want me to toss it again, hoping it will come up heads. If you, for some reason, *want* one result rather than another, then you would be 'biased' towards one decision."

"I think I get it. If I want ice cream, then I'll call a do-over if I see it comes up tails because I'm biased."

Jack smiled. "Exactly! You're very smart."

"I know, Daddy!" she exclaimed as they parked at the school.

"OK," Sandra kidded as they climbed out of the car, "now let's just hope your teachers say the same thing!"

14.

The news from his mother about the arrest had annoyed Dave, but he decided to find out the facts for himself before speaking with Bobby. He turned on the stunning, 52" flat screen television which he'd purchased two months ago and browsed through the TiVo recordings to find the most recent newscast the machine had recorded.

In the late 1980's, Nicholas Negroponte, the engineering visionary who directed MIT's multimedia research and development think tank, predicted that, within the foreseeable future, computers would be able to observe our television-watching habits to learn our program preferences. They would be able to predict what shows would interest us, then they would scour the broadcasts, grabbing suitable material from the hundreds of channels which were fed to them. Negroponte called this process "broadcatching," but at the time, it sounded more like an episode of the Jetsons than the natural evolution of the VCR. In the late 1990's, though, a company called TiVo produced the first major consumer-oriented device to perform exactly this task, and for its owner, the machine changed forever the way that television was used.

Dave's TiVo found that he watched several news programs every evening, so within a week, he could come home, pick up the remote, and start any of the major newscasts at his convenience. Commercials, sports updates, and human interest stories could be bypassed quickly, allowing him to condense an hour's worth of reports into a little over twenty minutes. Efficiency was the name of his game, and TiVo allowed him to bend the TV to his will.

Tonight he was looking specifically for coverage of the arrests, so he scanned through the ABC network's six o'clock program until he saw his brother's face. The story was essentially the same as his mother's version, although the reporters had gotten the names of several suspects from the police. They were identified as being part of a dissenting faction of a well known organized crime family, much as the Internet report had speculated. The accolades from the Mayor regarding Bobby's contribution to the case were the final straw for Dave. He clicked the mute button and picked up the phone, careful to choose the corded one rather than the wireless to maximize the security of the call. He dialed Bobby's home number but got the answering machine. He waited to leave a message.

"Bobby, this is Dave. I saw the report on television and I wanted to talk to you about it."

There was a click and a beep from the machine. "Yeah, it's me," Bobby said. "I was just screening the calls. Lots of people wanted to talk, especially the reporters. I can only stand so much fame, you know?" He sounded smug.

"Fame? Is that what you think this is about? I want to know... How did you break this case, huh?" Dave's patience was thinning rapidly, and the tone grew angrier with each word.

"Now calm down, Dave. Jesus, what's got into you? You want to know about this case? Take a guess, genius. You told me the trial looks good, so these guys are happy. They threw me a bone, that's all. Besides, I did them a favor by cutting out some dead wood for them. One of the perps is suspected of killing a kid."

"They did *you* a favor? What am I doing helping you? This isn't supposed to be a jackpot here, it was supposed to get you out of an obligation and that's all. Honestly, I don't see what the problem would have been just taking out a loan to cover the debt. Losing that sort of money in a casino is embarrassing, but it wouldn't cost you your job. Cutting deals with these criminals certainly could."

"You just don't get it, do you? I'm not in this to be an assistant DA all my life. If I keep my head down and win a few good cases, I can get promoted, but it's all publicity and politics from here on up. Some day, I'd like to run for office, but how could I explain a gambling debt to the press? A story like that would end my political aspirations forever."

Dave thought about this for a moment. "Well, you could have come to me for the money."

"First of all, you were buying your house when this started and I knew you didn't have that sort of cash just floating around. And second, I got myself into this, so I'm getting myself out. You're more like an insurance policy so we don't get screwed on the stock deal. Anyway, this is like taking candy from a baby, but no one gets hurt. The stock goes up, they get out and make their share, and I leave this skeleton in the closet, where it belongs."

"As a lawyer, you've got to know that insider trading is a crime, and that would kill any hope of a future for you. Besides, what are you going to do if the FDA decides not to approve us?"

"What do you mean? I thought you said this was in the bag already. Why would they do that?"

"How the fuck should I know?! There's no sure thing in life, and you're in over your head already. You might as well get in bed with your Mob buddies because if this doesn't work out, I don't know how you're going to talk your way out of it. I mean, I can tell you if you need to bail on this stock so you don't take a bath, but that's all. If things don't work, they may get lucky and still pocket a few dollars, but it won't be what you promised them. Then what are you going to do?"

"I guess I'll just have to make sure it doesn't run into any problems," Bobby said dryly.

"How? Do you think you have an inside line on the FDA? Let me tell you, these guys don't play the sort of games you're used to. Even big companies can't sway their opinions, and if you think you can flash a fancy law degree and make a deal, you're out of your mind."

"Maybe the pressure needs to be placed somewhere closer to home, then, Dave. After all, I wouldn't want *your* reputation to be harmed by all this. I'm assuming you never mentioned to Mom about your little "Mrs. Robinson" affair with Mrs. Urich, next door."

"What is that? Are you *threatening* me?"

"I've got to watch out for myself, you know."

"Well, you'd better start doing that right now, then." He slammed down the phone. His hands, curled into tight fists, were still shaking, but he couldn't tell if it was anger or fear. The whole situation seemed so surreal that Dave could barely believe it wasn't part of a B-grade movie. Now, with his brother's ego starting to control his personality, the stakes were being raised again. He sat on the sofa, illuminated by the bluish glow from the television, and rubbed his temples. *Jack, this thing better fly because I don't know how I'm going to be able to deal with you and him if you're on the wrong side of this equation.*

15.

March 11th arrived, and for Sharon it was the first day of the rest of her life. The 10th, with all its intrinsic meaning, had been a depressing milestone, but that day was behind her now, and the future, it seemed, could only look brighter. The snooze bar bought her an additional nine minutes of bed time before she had to face the morning mirror. As she lay there, eyes closed, listening to the early traffic through the closed window, she found herself thinking about the experimental weight loss medication she was now taking.

Or am I taking it? I might be getting the sugar pill now. I wonder if I'll know. I guess I could weigh myself every day, but then again, my weight seems to fluctuate all the time. They said this medication was supposed to make me feel less hungry, but I think I'm the same as I usually am in the morning. Oh, this whole sugar pill or medication thing is really annoying. I wish they could just tell me so I could decide if it's worth staying on. Well, either way, I'm going to stick with the diet this time. I know I can do it, and I am putting my foot down.

She pulled back the covers and walked towards the bathroom, not waiting for the snooze timer to nudge her out of bed. In the bathroom, despite her ritual of avoiding a full-length look at her nude body, she sneaked a peek as the shower ran. She knew she was carrying at least 35 extra pounds and none of it could hide without clothes, but she stared directly at her image for a moment, silently acknowledging this fact.

You know, I can almost see the thin me in there, just waiting to come out and blend in with the crowd. This whole diet thing isn't going to be so bad no matter how you look at it. I just have to remember, every day, that I'm in here, and I'm coming out to play this summer. I've done much more difficult things in my life, such as live with this weight problem and the humiliation I feel every day. Losing that albatross will make every day of the rest of my life that much easier.

Despite the disappointment she felt when she saw her body, Sharon smiled today because she knew the woman inside her could see that she wasn't afraid. Then, sarcastically, she thought, *Geez, I wonder if I'd always be this chipper if I always woke up without a mild hangover.* Today, instead of the Motrin, she opened the medicine cabinet and took out the nondescript white bottle labeled "Study Drug A, #14403. Take one in the morning and one at night." Inside were the mystery pills, each slightly yellow, with a script 'E' stamped on one side. The yellow seemed to be a sugar coating which hid the flavor of the medicine within. Sharon held one up, briefly considering whether she should suck the coating off to determine what the inner substance tasted like. Then she realized that the term "sugar pill" probably wasn't literal, and the company likely chose some other chemical for that pill to stop people from cheating on the study. With a brief shrug, she tossed the pill in her mouth and swallowed a sip of water. It tasted exactly the same as the one they gave her at the study office yesterday.

She completed her morning cleansing ritual, dressed, and headed into the kitchen for breakfast. *I wonder if I should try to eat a smaller breakfast today. If I'm getting the sugar pill, I still should work on dieting, right? But they said they wanted me to eat normally.... Well, I was going to start a diet yesterday, so I'll just make that my "normal" eating habit, and if I lose more weight because of the pills, so be it. Either way, I'm going to do this.*

Out came the cereal bowl, spoon, and Frosted Flakes from the pantry. She saw the box of donut holes which usually accompanied Tony the Tiger, but she tried to ignore them today. *That can't be a good habit. I guess I need to get rid of them.* She threw the donut holes in the trash, then got the milk from the refrigerator. *I've got to remember to buy skim next time.*

By now, the gnawing in her stomach had grown to a growl and she noticed her resolve slip just the slightest bit, so as a safety, she poured some cereal in the bowl, then returned the box to the pantry. *Otherwise, I'll just sit here and eat the whole package, so cutting out the donuts won't have been worth a thing.*

Although the change was barely perceptible while she ate the cereal, by the time she finished, she really *wasn't* looking for more. She sat at the table, feeling full, and wondering if it was a psychological effect or the real thing. *I definitely was hungry when I got up, so that argues against the pills being the drug, but now I'm not that hungry even though I had only half of what I normally eat, and I'm full. I know I promised myself I'd make good on this eating thing, but could I have done that much on my own?* She tried to make herself want more food, but it didn't seem to work. *I wonder if this is what it's like not to have a problem with overeating,* she thought in amazement. *I had a normal-sized breakfast and I'm, well, not hungry any more. That would be a godsend!*

The drive to work was uneventful, except for the fact that Sharon didn't even notice that she wasn't already planning her morning snack. She had spent the time trying to figure out what other improvements she could make to the new billing program. There were so many features that could be customized to tailor the data input windows for a specific office's needs that she found herself completely wrapped up in the possibilities. When she got to the office elevators, she pressed the up button before remembering that she was going to be walking instead.

Another habit I've got to break, she chided. One night hadn't changed the number of steps, however, and when she finally arrived at the fourth floor, she was thoroughly winded. She walked unevenly into the office and sat in a chair next to Pearlene's window.

"Oh, hi, child," Pearlene said. "I knew someone had come in, but I was in back looking for a new pen. How are you doing today?"

Still panting, Sharon replied, "You know, Pearlene, I'm doing great. Today is a whole new day, right?"

"Well, now if that ain't a good attitude, I don't know what is." She smiled. "Of course, you're still *sounding* all worn out, you know."

Sharon tried to chuckle between breaths. "Yeah, I'm going to get those stairs one day. It's just going to take some time, that's all." She looked at Pearlene seriously for a moment while she considered what she'd say next. After a pause, she continued, "The other day, I turned twenty eight and a half. I've been dreading that day for my entire life."

Pearlene shook her head. "You? Worried about getting old? Well, let me tell you, you're just a pretty young thing, dear!"

"Yes, I know that it's not that old, but it's sort of a day that I picked out a long time ago as being an important date in my life. I wanted to have some idea of where my life was going by then. I guess it started because I figured it would take a certain amount of time to meet a man and marry him, and I wanted to, you know, be married by the time I was thirty."

"Now, you mustn't rush these things, God's got us all in His plan, you know."

"Well, I hope that's the case. But what I'm really thinking about now is trying to lose some weight. I've been heavy for most of my life, and like most women, I've tried all the diets and exercise plans out there, but I never seem to have any success. I don't know what's gone wrong in the past, but this time, things are going to be different. I made it through March 10th, and that was a big thing for me, but in a good way. I'm going to get in shape, for real this time." As she finished this sentence, a patient opened the waiting room door and walked towards Pearlene's reception window. Sharon, deciding she'd said enough for now, changed the topic. "Does Dr. Sonders have a busy schedule today?"

"She's got a meeting this afternoon over in the medical school. I think she's going to give a few lectures to the students this year, and they want to have some sort of organizational meeting, according to my book. Rest of the day is business as usual, without lunch again."

Summoning her remaining strength, Sharon stood. "Well, I'll be in the back. I had some ideas for the new program on the way in today, so I've got to read up on it. If it can do everything they say, I might be putting myself out of a job!"

"Oh, you know we'd never let you get replaced by a computer!" They both laughed, then Pearlene turned her attention to the newly arrived patient.

Sharon walked into the back office and started making a pot of coffee. When she took the grounds out, she saw the package of cinnamon rolls she'd put there late last week. *Oh, I can't have one of those*, she thought. Then, after a moment's pause, she realized, *Actually, I don't even want one. I still feel full from breakfast. This has got to be a miracle, this drug. There's no way I'd be looking at that box without wanting one right now.*

She filled the coffee carafe from the water cooler, poured it into the machine, and started the pot. As the first drops fell through the filter, she sat at the computer and started exploring the built in tutorial, searching for the commands to modify the active features and thinking not at all about food.

16.

"Dr. Sonders, your next patient is here a little early," Pearlene announced over the phone intercom. Alison was typing on the computer, entering her office notes from the previous patient, a nine-year-old girl who was having concerningly frequent nightmares after she was a passenger in a relatively minor car accident. Alison was helping her manage the post-trauma stress symptoms primarily through traditional psychotherapy. She stopped typing for a moment to answer Pearlene.

"Thanks. Please ask her to take a seat. I'll be ready in a few minutes." The intercom clicked off, and Alison looked back at the screen to begin reviewing what she had written so far. Instead, she found herself thinking about her eighth birthday again, and the trip to New York to see the Nutcracker Ballet.

The evening of the ballet finally arrived and her father had come home from work an hour earlier than usual to get ready for the trip. Alison was waiting for him, already wearing the blue sweater that Tammy had given her, along with her black skirt, just as she planned. "Hi, sweetheart," her father said jovially as he hugged her. "Why are you all dressed up tonight?"

"Because tonight is the ballet!" she replied, pushing herself away in horror. "You didn't forget, did you?" Alison was completely fooled by her father's sarcasm. Before she got too worked up, he quickly corrected the misunderstanding.

"No, of course I didn't forget! I came home extra early so we can get there on time, silly!" He laughed, and so did Alison, who resumed the prematurely terminated hug.

"Remember, you promised to wear your special tie for me."

"Oh, I remember my promise," he said with an extra dose of satire. When she was much younger, Alison had noticed one day that he was wearing a tie she had never seen before. It had abstract pastel shapes on it which, when viewed correctly, actually depicted a horse race, although at first glance (and often at second glance), it appeared only to contain meaningless patterns. Unlike most of his ties, this one was cotton and it only matched one of his shirts, so the main reason Alison had never seen it was because it didn't go with much. Nevertheless, in an effort to add a little excitement, he proudly proclaimed that it was his "special tie," only to be worn under very specific circumstances.

This explanation had made much more of an impression on his daughter than he had anticipated, though, so now she would ask if he was going to wear his "special tie" each time they had a dressy engagement. Once the shirt wore out, the tie was effectively orphaned, so whenever Alison asked whether he'd wear the tie, the answer was a gentle "no, this isn't special enough," or some other, similar excuse.

The New York trip, however, ranked pretty high on Alison's list of important events, so he realized that there was not going to be an easy way out this time. He didn't have the heart to reveal to his daughter the shocking mundaneness of this vaunted garment, so he agreed he'd wear it despite the fashion *faux pas* it would entail. If nothing else, the saga had been a valuable lesson about the acuity and tenacity of a child's memory.

"Where's Mommy?" he asked, hoping she might have made some plans for dinner.

"She's downstairs ironing your new shirt."

"What new shirt?"

"We went to the mall today and got you a shirt to match your tie. Mommy said that you needed a special shirt to go with the special tie."

He smiled to himself, realizing that his wife's excellent taste wouldn't permit such a transgression, especially during their first family trip to the Met. "Why of course! How thoughtful of her. What color is it?"

"It's light blue. Mommy took your tie to the store and found a shirt that was just right." Alison winked at him, meaning that she approved, too.

"I'm sure it's not as pretty as your blue sweater, though."

"No, it's not *that* pretty."

Alison's mother emerged from the basement staircase with the newly pressed shirt. "It may *not* be pretty, but it's *perfectly* pressed." She gritted her teeth for comic emphasis. "I forgot how tough these Egyptian broadcloth shirts can be to iron."

"I guess the tie will have to be perfectly knotted, then, eh? Uh, is there something here to eat before I get dressed?" he asked.

"Alison and I had sandwiches, and I made you a turkey, ham, and Swiss on rye. It's in the fridge."

"You're the best." He kissed her cheek, then retrieved his dinner. Alison lingered in the kitchen while her mother went up to the bedroom to dress.

"Daddy, how long does it take to get to New York?"

"Well, it depends on how you get there," he answered between bites. "If we tried to drive now, it would probably take about an hour because there is a lot of traffic. But if we take the train, it should only take about forty minutes."

"Why is the train so much faster?"

"Well, the train tracks don't have traffic on them. There's just one train at a time, so it always takes about the same amount of time to get to the city. Late at night, when there's less traffic, driving would be faster, but it's more work than sitting on the train and letting someone else drive."

"The train sounds like a pretty good idea."

"I suppose it is, and I think you'll like being on it."

"Do you think the ballerinas ride the train?" Alison wondered.

"I think some of them do, sweetheart. Maybe we'll see one after the show and you can ask her."

"Really? Do you think I could meet one?" The excitement was growing by leaps and bounds.

"I don't know, but we can try, OK?"

"Oh, that would be wonderful!" The prospect of meeting a real ballerina was something Alison hadn't even considered until now. She immediately began wondering what she could ask her, but the possibility that she might speak with one seemed overwhelming. She was completely absorbed by this prospect, and her questions to her father temporarily ceased.

The train ride into the city was pleasant and much easier than the drive at that time of night. Since he wasn't familiar with the specifics of the New York subway system, Alison's father had spoken to a friend at work who told him which lines ran north to the Met. They arrived with plenty of time to spare, allowing Alison a chance to explore the cavernous lobby filled with that night's elegantly dressed patrons of the arts. She was sure this was Heaven on Earth.

Abruptly, the computer screen flickered, dragging Alison back from the dreamy memories of childhood as the screen saver replaced the text of

Alison's office note with a colorful display of cascading shapes. The transition reminded her that she still had work to do apart from analyzing her own development and memories. Fortunately, the computer switched to this mode after only five minutes of inactivity, so Alison still had time to complete her notes before the start of the next patient's scheduled appointment.

With one last introspection, she realized that the memory of that birthday present still brought a smile to her face, but she was sure there was some other, less obvious reason that she was now reliving this part of her life. However, that reason wasn't readily forthcoming, and her patient caseload currently took precedence over curiosities about her own formative years.

She finished writing, saved the notes to her computer's drive, then opened her office door and beckoned to her next patient.

17.

"It's always something," Charles "call me Charlie" Calhoun muttered to himself as he hung up the cell phone. At a mere 31 years of age, being the property manager for PeopleFirst Rentals seemed like the perfect job when he applied, but a few months of action proved that assumption wrong. The company managed mostly two- to four-family rental units, and it tended to attract an upscale high-tech clientele, a dramatic switch from his previous job in the high-rise building downtown. He was anxious to distance himself from the constant overdue rent issues and the dilapidated physical structure, so he eagerly accepted the new offer, feeling almost guilty about receiving a pay raise *and* nicer working conditions.

Within two weeks, however, it became clear that, though the problems were different, the stress and hassle involved in dealing with people remained unchanged. Instead of getting called because an entire floor was suddenly without water, now he got called because someone's hot water was a little too hot. Either way he needed to track down the problem, but now he had to deal with a multitude of small issues and frequently demanding tenants who would carp about the high cost of living and the fact that, for that much money, there shouldn't be *any* delay in addressing their complaints.

Yesterday, in the latest crisis, he got a voicemail message from a tenant complaining that her neighbor was becoming a nuisance because his apartment smelled like a rotting garbage dump. Charlie put that one squarely on the list of things to check out... someday. Today, though, the same tenant was now saying that she had seen two cockroaches in her apartment and she was sure they were coming from that neighbor. In the last building, only seeing a two roaches in a day would have been a major victory, but different standards now applied, so Charlie found himself driving through the neighborhood streets in the company pickup truck, looking for the trademark orange mailboxes which marked the building as a PeopleFirst Rentals address.

He arrived and parked on the street next to a two-hour limit parking sign, carefully checking his watch to ensure he didn't acquire yet another $25 ticket. The complaining tenant lived on the second floor, according to the phone message, so Charlie slid his 5'6", 215-pound frame out of the driver's seat and walked to the bed of the truck. He rummaged through the contents, looking for a box of roach trays which he eventually found and stuck under his beefy arm. The sweat from his armpit had already begun to soak into the box when he got to the top of the stairs and was greeted by the rancid odor of decaying food. It didn't take long to figure out which of the two apartments the complaint was against, so he knocked at the other door and waited for the tenant to answer.

A diminutive Asian woman, no older than 25, Charlie figured, eyed him briefly through the chained door. "Are you from PeopleFirst Rentals?" she asked without an accent. Charlie figured she must have lived in the States all her life.

"Yes, ma'am," Charlie replied, trying to be polite. By now, the tenant's complaint seemed reasonable even to him, so he genuinely wanted to help. "Are you Jessica Tang? I heard you had some roaches?"

"Do you have ID? I had a problem once, so I'd just like to see your ID first."

"No problem." He reached into his back pocket and took out his wallet. He owned three identical shirts which he wore on a rotating basis (though the rotation was sometimes less than daily) so the picture looked exactly like him. The tenant nodded, then unchained the door and invited him in. "Where did you see the bugs, Miss Tang?" he asked as he returned the ID to his wallet.

"Call me Jess, please. They were here, by the door. I think they came from the other apartment."

"Probably did. Seen them anywhere else in here?"

"No, just here."

Charlie looked around the main rooms briefly, but he couldn't even find a crumb on the floor. This tenant obviously took great pains to keep her place neat and clean, so it was pretty unlikely the roaches were actually hers. Satisfied that she was not to blame, he told her, "OK, well, I think they probably *did* come from next door. I brought a box of roach trays for you to put here, just in case some decided to move in." He took the box out from under his arm, then realized that it was fairly moist. Embarrassed, he tried to wipe it on his leg without much success, so he sheepishly offered the dry end of the box to her. "Uh, just put these under the sink in the kitchen and bathroom, then one or two out here. I don't think you'll need them for long."

"What are you going to do about the other apartment?"

"Well, the tenant sure is responsible for keeping the place neat and orderly. I'll see if they're home, but if they're not, I'll leave a note for them to call me immediately, and I'll come back tomorrow with a key if I have to."

"It's a guy," she offered.

"Who? The other tenant?"

"Yes, I think he said he is a computer programmer or something, but he never struck me as being a messy person. I met him a few times and he always seemed nice. His name is Zach."

"OK, well, do you know what hours Zach works? Is there a time he's usually home, or anything?"

"I think he works from home. I've seen him around at all sorts of times. I'm a student myself, so I'm home during the day sometimes, too."

"All right, well I'll check if he's there now, and otherwise I'll leave him a note. Don't worry, I won't tell him that you called us. This is pretty obvious, so I'll just say I was here for routine maintenance and I saw the roaches."

"That's really nice. I was hoping there would be a way to fix this without making it sound like I'm complaining about him." She smiled thankfully.

"No problem. Everything else OK?" Charlie inquired.

"Um, yeah, everything else is fine."

"You just call me if you need anything, then. I'll see if this Zach guy is home now." Charlie nodded goodbye, then let himself out, casually stepping on a stray roach as it scurried for cover on the concrete land-ing. Just the few months away from their constant presence was enough to re-sensitize Charlie to how unpleasant those bugs actually were. He wiped off his shoe, then knocked on Zach's door several times, but no one answered. Out of curiosity, he tried the handle but the door had a self-locking mechanism which prevented his entry. He shrugged, then returned to the pickup truck to find one of his "official notice" signs, on which he noted the date and time of his visit as well as the need for the tenant to call his cell phone number immediately. He added a line saying that the apartment would be entered in 24 hours if he hadn't received a response.

When he got to the top of the stairs again, the smell hit him anew. "So much for nice," he grumbled, "this guy's living like a pig." He posted the sign on the door then walked back to his truck. He wrote down the apartment address and number on a memo pad which was attached to the windshield so he would remember to bring the keys with him tomorrow in case the tenant failed to respond to the notice. "There better be a good reason for this, 'cause I'm not a friggin' maid service," he said to himself as he pulled away from the curb.

18.

Jack had spent the morning in the corporate library reading through one of his favorite textbooks on molecular biology. With the Ascendiac trial ongoing, he was loath to start another drug project in the event that he needed to devote time to keeping the trial on track. So, he chose to relax in the relative isolation of the library stacks, refreshing his knowledge of viral genomics. Since his first course in college, he was fascinated by the sheer engineering beauty of viruses, organisms which, while not alive in the strictest sense, have nonetheless evolved to be capable of protecting and propagating their own DNA more efficiently than any other known entity, with virtually no resource wasted. Most "higher" organisms such as plants and animals use a single, independent sequence of DNA to code for a single gene, the same way the single groove on a record encodes a single song. Viruses, however, can pack multiple genes onto just one sequence, taking advantage of various tricks that have evolved over millions of years. Thus, a single groove on a record could encode a song if played in its entirety, but also a political speech if only part was played, and even, perhaps, a Shakespeare soliloquy if played in reverse. Their versatility never ceased to amaze him.

Feeling refreshed and a little guilty for being idle for the morning, Jack returned to his office to find that very little had happened in his absence. Of course, his cell phone was with him the whole time, but he didn't even have phone messages that needed to be dealt with. Feeling slightly lost, he sat at his desk and woke up his computer. The Ascendiac trial data window was still visible and it showed him the latest updates on the trial. More than 50 patients had been enrolled so far, over the course of 11 days, and he still had yet to receive a phone call regarding a problem with the study.

Then the bottom portion of the data window caught his attention. The number of "lost to follow-up" patients had grown as well, totaling 6. Although the number was still small, it now represented more than ten percent of the enrolled patients, a considerably larger fraction than he was hoping to see. A troubling inquietude came over him as he stared blankly at the screen, wondering if the changes were significant. On the one hand, as he pointed out to his wife, the study population may be less reliable than most when it comes to weight loss, but at the same time, if they ever hoped to win approval, any deviation from the norm had to be thoroughly investigated internally, before the FDA caught wind of the anomaly.

He weighed his options, but none seemed particularly appealing. Dave would almost certainly blame the patients, which was definitely the easiest explanation and the one which would draw the least attention. Stephen, though a brilliant protein researcher, didn't have the experience with clinical trials to offer much advice. Jack himself was acquainted with some of the folks at the FDA and they would definitely have the expertise and experience to evaluate the findings given the fact that dozens of dieting drugs had been evaluated by the agency, but involving them would be letting the cat out of the bag in a way that could jeopardize the trial permanently.

After a few minutes of deliberation, it occurred to him that he could call the Stanford research site and speak with the site director there. Those folks evaluated many investigational drugs every year, so Jack reasoned that they must have a handle on how many people would be expected to drop out of this kind of study. They would be relatively unbiased in the sense that a successful drug brought them notoriety and more business, but a botched research project could cost them in terms of reputation and law suits.

He clicked on the e-mail program icon at the bottom of the screen and looked through his archived messages for the one which contained a list of the study site coordinators. Re-reading the terse memo annoyed him because, despite mentioning the locations, it never once said that the study had actually begun, renewing the feeling that the drug trial had been started behind his back. He found the name Joel Williams, MD MPH, next to the Stanford address and phone number, so he picked up his phone and dialed.

A moment later, a pleasant sounding woman answered the phone. "Hello, Doctor's office," she said.

"Hi, this is Dr. Finnegan calling. I was trying to reach Dr. Williams. Is he available?"

"I think he just got back from lecturing at the medical school. Is he expecting your call?"

"No, I don't think so. I'm one of the developers of Ascendiac, and I was calling to speak with him about the trial."

"Oh, OK, from the Excella company, right?"

"Yes, that's us!" Jack replied hopefully.

"Well, let me see if he can talk now. Please hold a moment." The line went silent briefly, then an instrumental rendition of a popular song Jack couldn't quite identify cut in. Before it got to the chorus, the receptionist was back. "Doctor, I'm going to transfer you."

"Thanks," Jack said, but he wasn't sure if he'd said it before she'd disconnected the line.

A moment later a deep, slightly raspy voice came on. "Hello, this is Joel Williams. To whom am I speaking?"

"Hi, this is Jack Finnegan from Excella Pharmaceuticals. I developed Ascendiac and I have been following the progress of the trials on line."

"Oh, right, with the computers," Joel observed. He sounded to Jack like a man in his late fifties, and he suspected, as was true of many physicians, that he never really became comfortable with computer technology. "Seems like an interesting drug, I must admit."

"Really? Why do you say that?"

"Well, of course, the data are blinded here, but my staff seem to think that most people are getting results during one week of the trial. The consensus around the office is that there is a marked reduction in appetite, and if that turns out to be the week they're on the study drug, then you've got a real winner. Patients seem to tolerate both arms of the trial well, too. I haven't been alerted to any unusual side effects so far."

"That's great news. I, uh, guess you're not concerned about the drop-out rate, then?" Jack unconsciously held his breath after he asked this question.

Joel was silent for a moment, and Jack's muscles began to tense as he waited for the blow. Finally, Joel asked suspiciously, "Why? Is there something you haven't told us yet? I know you guys are only focused on the bottom line here, but I thought I made it clear to your board that we require *absolute* openness in these trials. If you haven't been honest about this drug, you'd better come clean now. I don't want any of my patients put at risk just to line your pockets...."

Though Joel's tone had become slightly irritated, Jack relaxed considerably since he knew the answer to that question already. "No, actually we don't have any reason to think that the drug has problems. To tell the truth, I've almost been a little worried that we haven't seen *anything* wrong with this yet. The whole impetus for my call is that, so far, the only thing that we've seen that may be a little out of the ordinary is the 'lost to follow-up' rate. I figured it might be related to the study population, given that many of these people have probably been yo-yo dieting for their whole lives so they might drop out on the control arm figuring that it was another ineffective scam."

"Well, I'm glad to hear that. Frankly, we've been burned in the past with drug trials, so when I get a call from the company, I tend to keep up my guard. As far as the drop-outs go, I suspect that's exactly the problem. People start on the placebo arm and they don't see a change so they leave. Until we look at the unblinded data, that's just a theory, mind you, but I haven't heard any real complaints of side effects or anything so far. We're looking at several drugs right now, though, so I can't say for sure that I know all the details about this one. There are two graduate students heading up the data collection, though, and I think they're both very much on the ball. Let me talk with them today and I'll get back to you, OK?"

"Sure, that would be a tremendous help. Like I said, I don't expect to find anything, but if there's a trend here, I want to be sure we find it on the leading edge, rather than the lagging. If the study design needs to be tweaked, it's much easier to do that now compared with making changes afterwards."

"Yes, that is definitely the case. Now, I'm certain I have your number here somewhere, but why don't you give it to me again and I'll call you either today or tomorrow. I think these two students come in at night to collect the day's data, so I might not see them until eight or nine o'clock your time."

Jack recited his office and cell phone numbers, then added, "Calling me tomorrow is perfect. Thanks again for the excellent work you guys are doing."

"Well, I have to admit that the press we got yesterday made my job a whole lot easier. Our phone has been ringing off the hook for your drug, and the increased patient traffic inevitably helps fill our other studies, too. I'll call you later."

"Thanks." They hung up.

The reassuring conversation helped him relax a little, but the uneasiness still remained. He wondered if he should at least share his concern with Dave now that he'd discussed the issue with one of the study coordinators, but there was a double-edge to that approach. Dave might feel threatened because a potential problem which no one else had noticed was being discussed outside the company before the facts were known. On the other hand, if word got back from the site that he'd called without informing Dave, that could cause problems, too. It was a delicate situation with undesirable consequences on both sides. In the end, Jack could only rub his temples and hope for the best.

19

Merissa was working at the Drug Research Institute's reception desk again when Sharon appeared for her 12:45 daily check in. She wondered if she'd ever get to meet Gheena, whose enthusiasm seemed so important when she made the decision to try the drug study. "Oh, hello," Merissa said, looking up from a magazine. "You're here for a follow-up, right?"

"Yes," Sharon replied.

"What study was it? Ascendiac?"

"Yes, that's the one," Sharon said, feeling only slightly wounded by the fact that she was pegged as being on a diet drug trial.

"OK, you'll need to see Jim, the research assistant. It should only take about five minutes. Please go to room 14, around the corner and to the left. Leave the door open when you go in."

"Thanks." She walked down the short corridor until she found the door with the appropriate number. It was a small room with an examining table, a desk and chair, and a gooseneck lamp. She sat on the edge of the table and waited for about three minutes, when a cheerful young man, about six feet tall, 185 pounds, and wearing a white lab coat with and ID, entered. He glanced at his clipboard before introducing himself.

"Hello, I'm Jim Parnot, one of Dr. Ulster's research assistants. You're Sharon Keating?"

"Yes, I am. Nice to meet you." They shook hands.

"Good. Well, I have a few quick questions, then we'll have you put on this gown to be weighed. You started the trial yesterday?"

"Yes, in the afternoon."

"All right. Have you taken your medication since then.... I guess that would be two pills by now?"

"Two, yes. One yesterday and one this morning." Jim seemed to note each answer on the paper borne on his clipboard.

"Good, and have you noticed any changes, either desirable or undesirable, which you might attribute to your treatment so far?"

"Well, I don't think I'm eating as much food as I usually do, but I don't know if that's because I decided to diet, or because of the drug. I think I'm less hungry, though." Jim continued to write on the form.

"You're less hungry between meals or all the time?" He allowed a momentary pause before explaining, "They're standard questions. I know they seem a bit stuffy."

"Well, I guess just in between meals. I was pretty hungry this morning, but I ate a smaller than normal breakfast and felt full. I didn't even start to think about a coffee-break snack today. In fact, I barely noticed that it had gotten to be lunch time. I had a couple of bites of a sandwich and I felt full again."

"So you feel you have more of an early satiety, or fullness, than a suppressant of your appetite?" He looked at her for the answer.

She thought for a moment, then replied, "Yeah, I guess that's right. Does that mean I'm on the drug, then?"

Jim smiled knowingly. "Actually, I've heard all sorts of things from people. None of us have been told whether you're getting the drug or the placebo. Have there been any side effects you've noticed."

"No, not really.... You mean bad things, right?"

"Anything you've noticed, either good or bad."

"Well, for what it's worth, I've felt a little more energetic today than usual. I don't know if it's because I feel good about dieting or what, but... well... you asked, so there it is." Sharon frowned, thinking about how that sounded while Jim wrote on the form.

"OK, anything else?"

"Not that I can think of, except I don't remember ever not feeling hungry before. I mean, if I can stay like I am today, I'd never end up overeating."

"That's great. I hope you're one of the ones on the medication, then, because it sounds like you're achieving your goal." He smiled, but she wondered if he'd ever know what it was like to be overweight and out of control of his appetite. "Do me a favor and put this gown on. You can leave your underwear on, but take off everything else, including your shoes. When you're ready, just open the door, OK?"

"Sure." Jim stepped out and Sharon took her clothes off and put on the gown, initially with the opening in the front. However, she realized that it would never close properly this way, and it took her a moment to realize that it was designed to be worn in reverse. Once properly covered, she opened the door to the hallway and saw that Jim was at the scale weighing another patient. Sharon felt extremely self-conscious in the revealing hospital clothing, managing to take little solace in the fact that the other patient was at least 50 pounds heavier than she was. The other patient stepped off the scale and headed into her examining room while Jim motioned to Sharon to come over.

She walked down the hallway, growing more uneasy with every step. It wasn't often that she faced a scale alone, much less in the presence of a young male with a keen interest in the reading. She would gladly have run in any direction, and her mind was futilely working overtime to discover a way out. Before she found a solution, she was standing on the cold metal, watching Jim shift the weights along the graduated bar. "Good," he said when the arrow end finally settled midway between the stops. He noted the reading of 175 pounds on the clipboard record.

Nervously, Sharon observed, "Well, that's a little less than yesterday, right?" She knew that her initial weight was 177.

"Actually, each measurement is entered into the computer, and we don't get to see the list on any given day. All the information will be analyzed at the end. But, if it is, that's wonderful, although I'll caution you that people's weight normally fluctuates by as much as a pound or two each day. A several-day-long trend is much more important, but that has to start somewhere! You can change back into your clothes now, and I'll come by in a minute."

Sharon realized that talking about her weight was even more uncomfortable than not talking about it, so she forced a quick smile then retreated to the exam room immediately. As she dressed, she tried not to think about the embarrassment of standing on a scale in front of a stranger but that tactic wasn't exactly working. Instead of the usual downward spiral of emotions, though, she found herself looking at the situation from a different point of view. *Hey, he's a professional and he's used to seeing overweight people. I'm not proud of my body, but that's why I'm here, after all. I'm trying to fix this problem, and this fear of the scale can just be another incentive for me to stay on the diet.* She cocked her head slightly at this last thought, struck by the upbeat nature of it. *Wow, I like the way that sounds. Usually, I'd be running for a package of cookies and the TV remote at this point, wouldn't I?*

The knock at the door startled her. "Are you ready," Jim asked?

"Uh, yes. Come on in."

"OK, since this was your first follow-up visit, it took a little longer than the rest should require. Each day, we'll ask the same questions about side effects, number of pills you've taken, and so on. If you notice things that you want to tell us, you may want to write them down because we'll try to make this as quick as possible, and it's easy to forget things in the process, but we really want to know exactly how you feel about this medication. Also, there are two computers in room number one, at the end of the hall, which you can use to give us completely anonymous feedback of any sort you like. It could be about the checkups, the medication or weight loss, unexpected effects of the medication... whatever." Jim took out a stack of index cards from his pocket and fanned them out, face down, like a deck of playing cards. He smiled as he said, "Pick a card... any card, but don't show me," trying to sound like a street magician.

"What is this for?" Sharon asked as she reached for a middle one.

"That has a username and password on it which will allow you to remain absolutely anonymous when you log into the computer. At the end of the study, just tear up the card and throw it out. You don't have to use the computers, but if you want to, they're available to you and we want you to feel completely comfortable talking to us about this study."

Yeah, but I wish you could find a way for me to feel even marginally comfortable getting weighed for the study. "Thanks, I will. Are we done?"

"Yup. See you tomorrow!"

20.

The phone call he'd had with his brother continued to concern Dave, and he'd been rehashing it all day in an internal monologue. *God damn it, Bobby, why are you acting this way? You could solve your problems so many ways, now, but you decide to play games instead. I just don't understand the threats, either. I've always been there for you, and the thanks I get is blackmail? Christ, I should let you make your own bed this time. Threaten one of them and you'll end up under a thousand pounds of New Jersey trash.*

The real victim here is going to be Mom, anyway. If anything happens to you, she'd never get over it. At least she'd probably be able to cope with my affair, though I'm sure she'd want to move away from the Urichs, and that means she'd have to give up the house she raised her family in. I wonder if she'd ever understand what happened between us that summer, when Frank was temporarily stationed in Mexico and he left Patty home, alone. His stomach still knotted up when he thought about facing his mother with this little tidbit.

I'm sure just hearing that you willfully broke the law would be devastating for her. She still thinks you're the eight-year-old good guy who could never do wrong, so that would shatter her world. I guess the only way this is going to work is if that damn drug works out. I was great when I was dealing with the stress of hundred-million -dollar hedge funds, but now, trying to keep you out of trouble by betting on this drug is taxing my limits. I just don't know how much control I have over the situation. Anything could happen, and people like Jack only respond so much to pressure. At least I've got an inside line on the raw data, but I don't even know how that's going to help.

The phone beeped, indicating that his secretary was calling in to him, so he grabbed the receiver. The whole situation with his brother still had him irritated so he snapped at her before he realized what he was doing. "What is it now?" he asked.

Laurie, used to his mood swings, simply ignored him. "Sir, I have Mr. Nettle, the Vice President, on the line."

He still hadn't fully separated himself from his monologue. "Huh? What does he want?"

"I don't know, but you might want to try to be polite to him." It was a risky reply, but she decided to throw a little attitude back at him to see if he came around.

"Oh, yeah. I'm sorry, I've been thinking about something else. OK, I'll take it. Thanks, Laurie." He sounded sincere so Laurie accepted the apology as she put the call through.

"Dave? How are you? It's Bob Nettle," he said without pausing for a reply. "Listen, I just wanted to say that I think you guys are doing a great job with this Ascendiac project. Really, it was a good update today at the meeting."

It was obvious he'd called for a more important reason than simply to offer a compliment he could have made at the meeting. "Yes, it's pretty exciting," Dave agreed.

"Right, well, I just wanted to let you know that, because of this drug, we've been negotiating a sort of merger with another pharmaceutical company. I can't divulge the other party just yet, but it's what you'd call a household name. It would mean a lot for our shareholders... and a guy like you... if you play your cards right. You could make out pretty well if this goes through, let me tell you."

"That's great news, sir," he offered, still waiting for the other shoe to drop.

"Yes, yes it is. So, well, we just wanted to make sure you knew how important this drug is to the future of our company here. I'm sure you want it to succeed, just like we do, and I trust that if there were, say, any issues with the drug, you'd let us know... discreetly, of course."

So that's it. You're trying to make sure I'm playing for your team, too. It's not enough that my family needs this thing to work. Now I've got a merger hanging in the balance and this guy thinks I have some control over the study?
"Well, we haven't seen any problems yet," he said noncommittally. He considered leaving the uncertainty there, but decided it might end up increasing the pressure from above. "But, if something were to come up, I'll definitely call you first, OK?"

"I think that would be a prudent move, Dave. I'm glad we had this talk. Keep up the good work, and with a little luck, you'll get to enjoy the stock rocket with the rest of us!" He hung up.

I guess I was that single-minded, too, when I was trading. At least a stock spike might make your loan problems go away, Bobby. Of course, that's assuming you're smart enough to pay up and stop dealing with those guys. God, I hope you've got that much common sense. Your apparent political aspirations and spectacular, high-profile drug bust thanks to your mob friends aren't exactly all that reassuring, though.

Perpetually sifting through all the angles, Dave's mind drifted back to the dilemma he'd face if Jack turned against the drug for some reason.

21.

Sharon was still reading about the intricacies of the new billing software when Pearlene poked her head through the door. "Haven't heard a peep from you all afternoon, girl. I don't recall ever seeing you like this. Are you moving in here or something?"

Much to Sharon's surprise, she found it was after five o'clock. "Wow, I didn't even notice the time. I've just been so focused on this program that I lost track."

"It's that exciting, is it?"

"I don't know, really. I mean, it's just a program, but it seems to have so much promise for us. If we get this thing running right, we could turn around the whole billing process. I guess I never realized how much satisfaction I could get from being in charge of a big project like this."

Pearlene smiled. "Well, it sure has gotten hold of you. Except for sneaking out around lunch time, I don't think you left this room all day. Maybe all that exercise is starting to have an effect on you!"

"Yeah," Sharon said thoughtfully, "that and the whole diet thing. I really think I can lose weight this time, and I'm going to keep it off once it's gone. I know I can exercise some, and if I eat less and keep only good food around, I'm sure I can beat this weight problem. I have this wonderful new conviction that I can succeed at this, and I guess that attitude is carrying over to work as well."

"Sounds like you got yourself some religion there."

"It's something like that. I'm a little afraid that I'm going to find out that it was just a brief phase again, and tomorrow I'll be back to my usual self, but I just don't feel like that's the case this time. I can remember the first time I tried to diet and how certain I was that I could just change my habits. That never lasted more than a few days, though, before every meal, every *hour* became a struggle. Even when I didn't know I was thinking about food or being hungry, I'd find a bag of chips in my hands. Now, all of a sudden, it seems completely natural, like I'm just going to do it right this time. I haven't had any cravings, and I have all this energy by no hunger."

"Well then you go, girl!" She wagged her finger and smiled at the cliché. "I do hope you make it this time. If there's anything I can do to help, you just let ol' Pearlene know, right?"

"That's really sweet, but you've been a tremendous help already just by talking to me."

"Oh, go on now."

"No, really. I've been through this a hundred times before with my mother, so we have too much history for her to be a good supporter this time. I still need to talk with someone, and I spend so much time here with you that it's a big boost to my self-confidence, knowing that you're just around the corner if I need you. So far, I'm doing pretty good, but this is just the beginning of a long process and I know there will be tough times ahead."

"Well, then, you just make sure you come and talk to me any time you need to, OK? You know where to find me!" She chuckled. "And, as you can see, I've got my share of weight problems, too, so if this works, you promise you'll tell me all your secrets, right?"

Sharon considered telling her about the diet pill but she figured there would be plenty of time to talk about that later. "Yes, I will," she replied. "Now, let's get out of here before I start reading again!" They considered stopping in to tell Alison they were leaving, but her door was closed, so they figured she was busy with work. In the hallway, Sharon hesitated for a moment before deciding to take the elevator with Pearlene. *I suppose I'll just have to skip the stairs tonight. Maybe I should start walking after I get home, like around the block or something.*

The two parted at the garage, and Sharon climbed the stairs to the third level, where her Explorer was parked. *Guess I need to stop at the grocery store. I don't think I've got any low-fat food at home. Maybe I should use the Waist Cincher's approach to make sure I get a balance.* This thought brought back memories of her first encounter with commercialized dieting programs.

By the summer of eleventh grade, Sharon had seen fifteen pounds come and go twice. She'd manage to get on a diet for a few weeks with decent results before her subconscious would sabotage her efforts, making her crave foods she had forbidden for herself. Pizza and chocolate were the perennial spoilers, and it seemed that each time she tried to give these up, she ended up eating even more of them when her resolve finally broke. This time, with another summer beginning and the autumn, with the high school Senior Shuffle semi-formal dance party coming in less than five months, she felt renewed pressure to find the body she wanted.

A newspaper advertisement for the Waist Cincher's group caught her attention one Saturday morning as she was getting ready for her summer job as a cashier. Her mother was about ten feet away, folding laundry, when Sharon said, "Mom, I need to talk to you."

Of course, with such proximity, the two could easily have had a conversation, but this request was actually a plea for undivided attention, and her mother knew it. She suspected what was on her mind, even before she saw the paper. "Sure, honey," she said as she put down the shirt and sat at the table. "What's up?"

"I hate being fat. Every time I get on a diet and lose weight, I end up gaining it back, plus more. You help me get started, but after a while I start craving some of the food that I have to give up, like pizza. Eventually, it's all I can think about, and if I give in and have a piece, I can't stop again. It's like it just starts a chain reaction, so a little suddenly becomes a lot."

She had heard this talk at least twice a year recently, but it never got easier for her to hear how painful the struggle was for Sharon to control her weight. Trying to stay supportive but neutral, she asked, "Well, do you have any thoughts on how we can break the cycle?" She suspected it had something to do with the full-page advertisement in front of her.

"Well, they say here that their group helps you to stay focused on the dieting part, but you can eat whatever food you want. How do you think that works?"

"I've never been in their program," her mother cautioned, "but I understand that they have a sort of point score for each type of food. I think what happens is that you get a certain number of points each day, and you can use them however you want. I think the points keep your calories down, and the meetings are a way to make sure you stay on the plan."

"That sounds like a good idea, doesn't it?" To her mother's ear, her voice contained a dangerous level of optimism.

"It must work for some people because they have been around for a long time, now. I think you pay a weekly fee for the meetings, but you've got a job for the summer, so if you want to try it, I think you should. Of course, I'll be here for you, too, if you need me."

The first group meeting was to be held in the grade school auditorium on Sunday night and Sharon was excited by the prospect of being among others who were fighting the same battle she was. The registration process took about ten minutes and twenty dollars, but the rewards would be immeasurable, she thought. Once the new members were checked in, everyone gathered in groups of about eight, arranging their chairs in circles. A moderator, who was also a client, led the self-help session, encouraging each person to discuss their successes and lapses in the previous days' dieting.

The first to speak was a new recruit named Eric, a 38-year-old divorcé who never really succeeded in getting back into the dating scene. He had slowly accumulated 75 pounds over the course of his six-year marriage but had failed several attempts to "work out some and eat better." The moderator asked him to discuss the most difficult failure he had in dieting, and he described a scenario all too familiar to the rest there.

"The worst thing I did was probably last week, which is really why I came here tonight. About three weeks ago, I bought another gym membership, this time at one of those chain gyms that has workout classes and stuff. Anyway, I had been pretty good about going to the beginner spin class, and I was even starting to work out afterwards. I was trying to keep the eating under control by keeping water and raw vegetables around, along with those rice cakes, and for the first time that was working, too. Then, you know, work got busy in the middle of the week and I ended up missing lunch one day, so I was really starving on the way home. I don't even remember deciding to stop, but the next thing I knew, I was at the drive through ordering a fried chicken dinner. I ate it in the car on the way home which is something I had sworn I'd never do again, but it didn't even start to satisfy my appetite. I realized what I had done, and that made me frustrated and depressed, so I ended up eating even more, until I realized that there was no way I was going to make it alone." The entire group was nodding in sympathetic agreement by this point.

To Eric's left, 52-year-old Becky told the group she had been a member for just over a year, and she was asked to evaluate her progress over the last week. "This week was better than last," she confessed. "I had a little relapse when my candy craving got the best of me, but I managed to get things under control again. You just can't believe your eyes when you look down to find two Kit Kat wrappers on the sofa when all you wanted to do is watch TV. It's like my hands are under someone else's control at times. That happened several times last week, but I made sure this time that I didn't buy *anything* like that at the store. You know, you buy treats for the grandkids for when they come over, but they never last that long. Anyway, I'm still twelve pounds less than when I started, but my goal was to lose 40, so I've got a long way to go. It seems like an endless tug of war, with one step forward, then two back." Again, nodding consensus from the group.

Tales of dieting anguish continued, and in the end, everyone felt that they were pretty much in the same boat. The moderator then discussed the weekly recipe recommendation which was designed to add a little variety to everyone's eating habits while allowing them to keep that day's point score under control. The new members also got a fifteen-minute overview of the point scale before adjourning.

As she remembered it, Sharon's experience was similar to Becky's, after a few months worth of meetings and food point tallies. In the end, even with the support of fellow dieters, the real rub was keeping the food intake within the allotted points. Inevitably, even with the allowed variety, a few extra slices of pizza would shatter the diet, and the ensuing disappointment because of her failure would push her further along the overeating path.

It always comes down to that, doesn't it? I guess that cycle of hunger and depression sort of overtakes you, and you go down from there. If I can stay away from that, I'm home free, and so far, so good! She found a parking spot at the local supermarket and headed inside to find the low-fat, low-calorie solutions that would carry her home to a victory over her weight.

22.

The Palo Alto morning sky was overcast, which was somewhat unusual given the generally fair weather. Even ominous clouds on the horizon only rarely resulted in a significant amount of rain, with most of the precipitation falling in short bursts which Charlie could just wait out in the truck. Nevertheless, today he decided he might as well bring an umbrella, so he found one in the back of the coat closet and tucked it under his arm. It was 8:00 a.m. and he was starting his morning rounds, driving from one building to the next to make a brief inspection of each. Through what he considered surprisingly good fortune, he managed to start the day with a clean voicemail box— Not so much as a single complaint about a leaking faucet had been phoned in during the night. In itself, that seemed to promise at least a peaceful start for the morning, so for a change, he thought he'd reverse the usual route today, checking the buildings in the opposite order. As he was contemplating this, he was struck by another thought: *Man, you've really got to get a life if reversing your route is what you consider "adding a little excitement to your day!"* Shaking his head sarcastically, he climbed resolutely into the pickup, then winced when he saw the note reminding him to bring the key to Zach's apartment.

"Damn, I knew I forgot something," he said to no one in particular as he climbed out and trudged back to the apartment to retrieve the key. *So much for the empty voicemail being a good thing. It means that guy never called back so I have to track him down.* The keys were on the table next to the door, exactly where he'd left them. *Another failed "perfect plan" for making that foolproof. It almost never rains here, but today I had to decide to bring an umbrella so I forget the keys instead. That's you, buddy... Charl-E Coyote, Super Genius.* He pictured himself as the brown and tan Looney Toons character holding a cartoon version of his umbrella over his head to block an anvil which was falling from the desert cliff above.

Most of the calls he got in his current job related to complaints about the buildings and fixtures, so Charlie hadn't yet needed to intervene in a dispute between tenants. In contrast, at his previous job he would get calls about people having raucous parties almost every week, and in the interest of sanity and peace, he often tried to work out a settlement before someone would dial the police. When matters were less pressing, he found that most tenants responded to a written notice which he taped on the apartment door. He would usually get at least a phone call back from the tenant to tell him where to stick his complaint, but Charlie had become a skilled negotiator, so he'd wait for the yelling to settle down then he'd work out some sort of compromise. Occasionally, people would ignore the door notes because they were moving out soon and figured there wasn't anything he could do to compel them to keep things in order. That, Charlie had decided, was a grave mistake. *You guys always forget about your generous security deposits, don't you? That lease gives me a lot of leeway, and apartment cleaning by Charlie is pretty expensive, you know.* Still, since it was easier not to deal with conflict, he hoped that there would be a simple solution. He checked the revised itinerary and saw that Zach's apartment building was now second on the reversed list, so he'd know soon enough how much trouble this guy would be.

Cross-town traffic was a little heavier than usual because of the threat of rain, but Charlie eased the pickup through the pristine streets, thinking about how nice life would be if he were completely in charge of one house. *Maybe it's time I should start saving some money for a down payment on a place of my own. As it is, I get a great deal on the monthly cost from PeopleFirst Rentals, but I might not work for them forever. I bet I could put away a few hundred a month, then the next time PeopleFirst decides to dump a decent single or duplex, I could make an inside offer. I guess I'd be losing out on a good rental deal but I'd be building up some value in the house. Or, maybe I could rent out the house and stay in the apartment, although I'm not really sure I want anyone messing up my place the way some of these guys mess up the rentals.*

He mulled the possibilities as he turned the final corner to the first property. It was a four-unit place with a medium-sized front yard and a driveway on the side where he stopped the truck but left it running. Walking around the building, he decided that a little rain would definitely do the lawn some good, as it was slowly turning an unhealthy greenish-brown color. It also looked like it was getting longer than usual so he made a quick note in the log book to check on the landscaping and automatic sprinkler schedules. He couldn't recall offhand which company was responsible for this lot, but sometimes the guys got backed up for one reason or another, so he'd have to give them a call later to find out what the story was.

Nothing else appeared out of order so he wandered over to the truck just in time for the first drops of rain to catch his attention. *Ah, got lucky this time. I actually* will *use the umbrella after all!* He smiled smugly as he backed out, onto the street. A fine pattern of water was already collecting on the windshield so he turned on the lights and wipers as he pressed on towards Zach's apartment building. He started thinking about a house again when the image of the young female neighbor of Zach suddenly flashed through his mind. *Jess... I think she said her name was Jess. I have to make sure I follow up on the roach problem next week. Once those bugs move in, they can be hard to move out. Hmmm. She said she was some sort of student, didn't she. I wonder what she's studying.* Charlie wasn't sure if it was her gentle smile, petite size, or the fact that she was polite to him even though most tenants would have accused *him* of causing the roach problem, but whatever the reason, he had taken a liking to her and he decided he was going to make absolutely sure she didn't get bothered by the roaches again. *This Zach guy better not give me a hard time about the garbage dump he's created.*

There was a parking spot on the street about two houses away, so he backed the truck in and noted the time in the log book. The rain persisted, but it was still fairly light, so he decided to take the unopened umbrella along for safety. As he approached the outside staircase, the stench from the apartment caught up with him. *Ugh, how can people live like that? Even New Jersey's not* this *bad!* He tried to breathe through his mouth while he climbed the stairs, growing more annoyed with each. Several roaches scurried for cover as he approached the door to Zach's apartment, and Charlie flattened one with his shoe just for good measure.

The note still hung on the door, apparently untouched from the previous day. *This guy must be out of town or something, but even if he is, why leave things such a mess?* He knocked on the door loudly. "Hello! This is the landlord. I need to come inside." Not hearing a reply, he put the key in the lock and opened the door, allowing an overpowering wave of warm, humid, fetid air to flood the landing and cause Charlie to gag uncontrollably. He drew a slow breath through his mouth once the gagging stopped, then stepped gingerly inside. The apartment was dark and hot, with most of the blinds shut, but as his eyes adjusted, Charlie could see the multitude of bugs running around on the floor in front of him. There seemed to be several containers of old food strewn around the kitchen along with other garbage lying on the floor and tables. *What the hell is wrong with people? Who'd leave their home a mess like this, whether they expected to come back that night or not?* He scanned the apartment, looking for the light switch when he noticed the silhouette of the person who seemed to be standing in the far room. "Hey," he asked nervously as his hand searched the wall, "what are you doing there?" He found the switch which turned on the overhead lights in the living room, casting enough illumination into the bedroom for Charlie to be able to answer that question for himself.

"Oh my God!" he stammered as he started towards the hanging body. His first instinct was to try to help the man, but once he got a little closer, it was clear that he was very dead. Charlie was only dimly aware of his own racing heart and sweating palms as he fumbled for his cell phone. It slipped through his grip, dropping onto the carpeting with a dull thud, and as he bent down to pick it up, the umbrella fell from his arm onto a group of roaches which were congregating nearby. His stomach turned as he hurried out of the apartment and dialed 911. The fetid smell still surrounded him on the landing, though, so he staggered down a few steps to find cleaner air. He barely noticing how hard he was breathing, but it definitely caught the 911 operator's attention.

"Hello... Are you OK? What is your emergency?" the operator asked.

"I need help. There's a guy here. He's... I think he's dead." Charlie tried to keep himself together but shock of seeing the body had pushed him to the edge of panic.

"Can you tell if he's breathing?" she asked.

"What? I... Well, I didn't check... But I think he's been dead for a while. He was... well it looked like he was hanging from a rope or something."

"OK, sir, where are you now?"

"Uh, it's 147 Mountainview Terrace. It's an apartment."

"OK, well if you're pretty sure he's dead, then there's nothing you can do for him. It might be a crime scene, so stay out of the apartment and wait for the police."

"Yeah, OK, I'll wait out here." He was still breathing heavily as he turned off the phone and steadied himself against the railing, still trying to comprehend the gruesome scene. *He hung himself. That's why the roaches were there. He wasn't away, he was* dead. He said that out loud to himself several times until another thought overpowered that one. *I wonder if Jess is OK?* He started up the stairs again to see if she was home when he saw a police car with its lights on approaching the apartment. "Hey, over here," he called to the officer, who waved in acknowledgement while he retrieved a crime scene box out of the trunk of his car and ran to the stairs.

"Are you the one who called 911?" asked the officer, whose name tag introduced him as Paul Mackenta. Before Charlie could answer, the smell from the apartment caught up to him. "Oh, man, I guess that's the apartment, huh?"

"Yes," Charlie answered as a wave of nausea washed over him. He panted for a moment as the feeling subsided. "The guy's in there, too." The officer started up the stairs and Charlie reflexively followed. "He's in the bedroom there," he said, pointing inside while keeping back on the far side of the landing.

"All right, sir, stay out here, OK. I'm going to take a look inside, then I'll be back." As the officer walked carefully into the apartment, Charlie turned and knocked on Jess' door. He waited for a moment, but there was no answer. The silence worried him, but he could only hope she was just at work or school or something. The smell from the apartment was suffocating him again, so he climbed down the stairs to the fresher air to wait for the officer. Before Mackenta came out of the apartment, though, another squad car arrived on the scene, and the officer who climbed out had apparently already made radio contact with Mackenta.

"Hi, I'm Officer Davery. Are you the man who called 911?"

"Yes, I called. I work for the landlord." Davery pulled out a notepad as he proceeded with the interview.

"Good. What's your name?" He was already writing as he asked the questions.

"Charlie Calhoun. Uh, Charles, really. I mean... people call me Charlie."

"OK, Charlie. I just need to ask you a few questions. What happened here?"

"Well, yesterday I got a call from one of the tenants. Her name's Jess. She lives across from the apartment up there. She said she had some roaches and she thought they were coming from that guy's place. She thinks his name is Zach. Anyway, I left him a note asking him to call me but he didn't. Today, I came by to find out where the roaches were coming from and I saw the guy in the bedroom. At first I thought he was standing there, but then I saw the rope around his neck."

"Did you do anything in there? Move anything?"

"No, I don't think so. Just got inside and turned on the light and there he was." Mackenta finally emerged from the apartment and joined the two at the bottom of the stairs. The smell seemed to follow him down, and he was still breathing through his mouth as the slight breeze slowly removed the odor.

"Looks like you did all you could, sir," he said to Charlie. "That man's been dead for a while, at least a couple of days, I think." Then, to the other officer he said, "I called homicide. Looks like the victim took his own life, but I didn't see a note. With that smell, though, it's not a place I want to spend a lot of time in right now. I'll leave it to them to figure this out."

Davery nodded. "Thanks, Paul. Let me ask a few more questions while we wait for the detectives." He turned back to Charlie. "So you work for the landlord? What do you do?"

"Well, I manage some of their buildings. PeopleFirst Rentals is the company."

"You were here yesterday you said, but you just left a note. Did you notice anything about the place then? Any broken glass, broken doors, that sort of thing?"

"No, just the smell and some roaches. I didn't see anything else. I talked to the tenant who complained, but that's about all. Knocked on Zach's door but no one answered, so I left the note." Charlie shook his head as he realized how close he had been to the dead man the previous day.

"Do you know the name of the tenant by any chance?"

Charlie was still thinking of Jess, so he missed the point of the question. "Yeah, her name is Jessica Tang."

"Jessica? Who's that? The one who complained about the roaches?"

"Right."

"OK, do you know the name of the victim? The guy in the apartment?"

Charlie realized his mistake. "Oh, his name. Uh, I should have looked it up in our records but I didn't think of it. Jess said his name was Zach, but that's all I know. My log here is just organized by building, but the tenant list is separate."

Paul interjected. "His mail was addressed to Zachary Powell. Do you recognize that name?"

Charlie thought for a moment before shaking his head. "I don't know off hand, but I can check with the office. They have a list."

Davery then said, "That won't be necessary right now. We'd like to have a phone number where we could reach you in case we have any other questions about the building, though."

"Sure. You can call me on my cell phone. Just follow the instructions for the emergency contact and it will put you through to me. I'm the building manager and the phone's turned on 24/7." He gave the number to the officer as Jess came running up the street.

"I saw the police. What happened," she asked, trembling as she considered the possibilities.

Feeling relieved to see she was all right and wanting to break the news to her gently, Charlie answered. "Well, Jess, I came by today to find out why that apartment is full of roaches, but when I got inside, I...." He trailed off, unable to think of an easy way to explain the situation. "Uh, I found that Zach... was dead."

"Oh, God, that's terrible! How can it be? What happened? He wasn't... *killed*... was he?" The possibility that a murder had occurred next door struck a note of fear and her face reflected the horror within.

"No, it looks like he did it himself," Charlie said.

"*Suicide?*"

Charlie nodded solemnly.

Davery, who was talking with Paul, finally realized that Jess was the neighbor Charlie had mentioned. He stepped over to her, notebook in hand. "Excuse me, Miss, did you say you live here?"

Jess nodded as she began to sob gently. "Yes, my apartment's up-stairs."

"Your neighbor... His mail is addressed to Zachary Powell. Is that his name?"

She nodded immediately. "The name's definitely familiar but I really just knew him as Zach, though." The shock was causing her to tremble as she spoke.

"Do you know anything about him? His personal habits, problems he had, anything like that?"

"Not really. He kept to himself mostly. I know he was a computer programmer or something. He always seemed nice until just recently, when the apartment started to smell and the roaches appeared. Other than that, I couldn't tell you much. I only saw him a few times even though we lived so close." Her voice started to crack.

"Did you happen to notice anything out of the ordinary, except for the smell?"

"No, He seemed just fine, then one day last week his apartment just started getting worse. I never even thought to check on him." She broke down in tears.

"OK, Miss. Thank you for your help. The detectives may have some more questions for you when they arrive. Just do us a favor and stay here for a little while if you don't mind."

The rain picked up for a moment, just enough for Charlie to realize he'd lost his umbrella. When he realized he'd dropped it in the apartment, he froze, wondering how he'd explain to the police that he *had* changed something at the scene. Nervous, he approached Davery. "Uh, I just realized something I told you might be wrong."

"What's that," Davery asked, checking his pad.

"Well, I think I dropped my umbrella in there when I was trying to call for help. I didn't realize it when you asked if I had changed anything."

Davery closed his pad again. "Umbrella, eh? Well, don't worry about that. We'll get it for you later."

The rain was starting to run down Jess' face, next to the tears, and Charlie realized he could offer her at least a little shelter for the time. "You can sit in my truck if you want. It will keep you dry for now."

"Thank you," she said between sobs. "I need to sit down anyway. I can't believe this. I mean, I went to the store thinking this guy was just an inconsiderate slob, but I was so wrong. He needed help and I didn't even know it." Charlie opened the passenger door for her and she climbed inside while they waited for the detectives.

23.

"Pearlene, when is that student supposed to be here?" Alison was initially flattered to have been asked by the recruitment committee to interview a prospective medical student, but when she realized that the interview was scheduled in the middle of a busy day, she was starting to have second thoughts.

"She's supposed to be here in five minutes, doctor. You're running a little early today, I believe."

Alison checked her watch. "Oh, I guess I am. I hope she's on time because the afternoon's going to be tight as it is."

"I think she'll be here. I called Missy a few minutes ago and she said they was right on time. Why not have your lunch now? It's in the back."

"I've said it before. I don't know what I'd do without you!" She walked back to the break room to find her lunch on the table across from Sharon, who was eating a sandwich and some carrots while she was leafing through a large three-ring binder.

"Oh, Dr. Sonders, how's your day going?"

"Hectic, Sharon. Remember, back here, you can call me Alison."

"Yeah, sometimes I just forget. What's got you busy today?"

"I agreed to interview a medical student. I mean, she's a college student looking to go to medical school. At the time I thought it would be an honor and a chance to help someone who *didn't* have a psychiatric disorder make a decision about their future." She found that Pearlene had ordered her a chef's salad for lunch today, and she began eating it. "But now that the day is here, it seems like it's going to be impossible to squeeze the half-hour interview into the day."

"Did Pearlene know about it? She usually makes room for everything, although I'm not sure how she manages to do it."

"Yeah, she's probably got it figured out. I guess part of what's been bothering me is also stuff about my history. You know, decision I've made along the way. Medical school was a pretty big one, and sometimes I have my moments of doubt."

Sharon was genuinely surprised by that comment. "You're kidding? You? I mean, you're so good with the patients, it seems. You help so many people every day. I can't imagine what some of them would do without you."

"Well that's kind of you to say, but there are dozens of people in the city who are at least as capable as I am. They'd all survive. And don't get me wrong— I love my work, but, as you well know, it takes up a lot of my time. I wonder what it would be like if I had chosen a different path. When I was a child, I wanted to be a ballet dancer more than anything, and when I was eight, my parents gave me tickets to see a real ballet in Lincoln Center."

"Dr. Sonders?" Pearlene interrupted. "The student is here to see you. Should I have her wait in your office?"

"Yes, I'll be right in." She took a last mouthful of lunch.

"Did you enjoy it? That ballet, that is?" Sharon needed some sort of closure.

"The performance was beautiful. I always appreciated that trip." Sharon nodded in appreciation, but Alison knew there was too much more to the story to fit into one sentence. She smiled as she headed back to her office.

The student was dressed in conservative blue suit with a white blouse. Her hair was neat and she wore only a small ring on her right hand. Medical schools are still largely run by aging, conservative doctors, so every book will tell you that your best bet is to maintain an appearance that is as conformist and unimaginative as possible. Alison was well aware of this image and she was all too happy to dispel it. The student stood as she entered the room, so Alison walked over to her, shook her hand warmly, and introduced herself. "Hi, I'm Alison Sonders."

The student's hand was cold and clammy, and she nervously responded, "Hi, Doctor Sonders. I'm Katherine Steitz."

"Well relax, Katherine, I'm a psychiatrist, or, as we call them in the business, a head shrinker." She made quotation mark signs with her fingers when she said this. "Have a seat and let's talk. They didn't tell me anything about you. They think it helps keep us honest, I guess. Where are you from?"

"I'm a senior at Mount Holyoke college in Massachusetts."

"OK, that's great, but I'll assume that you got the interview here because you're qualified from an academic standpoint. I want to know a little about you as a person. You know, stuff that makes you different from all the other people we see. Where did you grow up?"

"Oh, I'm originally from Pennsylvania, in a town called York."

"Sure, I know York. That's Amish country, isn't it?" Back in medical school, Alison had spent a long weekend there visiting one of her classmates who was doing a rotation in a local hospital. Although she hadn't been in York long enough to get a good sense of the local culture, she definitely recognized the friendly, blue-collar nature that pervaded the town.

"Yeah, and Caterpillar, York Barbells, and Harley Davidson country, too."

"How did you like living there?"

"It's home, you know. I think a lot of people don't really appreciate their home until they leave. I know I thought it was a terribly closed-minded place, and I still think it is, but since I've been in college, I can appreciate some of the benefits of the rural community as well."

"Have you traveled much?"

The question caught Katherine by surprise and she was embarrassed to admit she hadn't. "I guess I spent a lot of summers working, so I didn't get a chance to travel."

Alison nodded. "I know that feeling. I only got to see Europe for the first time two years ago. It's worth the trip, though. What sort of work did you do during the summers?"

"When I was in high school, I worked at my dad's company. He has a landscaping business in town, and I'd help him do the billing during the summers when things were most busy. During the winter it was slower, so Mom could handle most of the paperwork. Then, when I got older and I started thinking about going to medical school, I decided to work somewhere that was more medically oriented. I volunteered at the hospital in town while I took an EMT training course. The ambulance corps was always looking for a few extra people so that the regulars could take vacation. I filled in for their shifts and I learned a lot about taking care of patients. Not so much the medical stuff, since that's more for the hospitals. What I got to see was how scary it is to be a patient. Fortunately, most of the calls we got weren't serious, but the patients didn't know that. They just needed help and they turned to us to take care of them. Our job was to make sure they got to the hospital safely, but in the mean time, we had to comfort and reassure them and their families. It was an amazing experience to be able to do that."

"Wow. That's wonderful. You're the first person I'm officially interviewing, but I've talked to dozens of prospective students over the years. I can't tell you how many of them keep rambling on about 'Helping people,' without having a clue as to what that means. You're way ahead of the curve by recognizing that a lot of what we do is give people the strength to work through crises. That's one of the most important parts of the job, but no one even teaches that in medical school, and some people don't *ever* learn it."

"It's been a great experience for me, really."

"Well, what else can you tell me about yourself? What do you do for fun?"

"I love painting, actually. My favorite subjects are outdoor scenes with people and nature coming together in some way, but I've done all kinds of stuff. I studied a little of it in college, but it was mostly for my own entertainment and to fill up some requirements."

"Have you ever had anything displayed in a show?"

Katherine chuckled as she answered. "Actually, the only stuff that ever got shown was a six foot by eight foot original piece I did. It was oil on metal, and it has been on display for a few years now... on the side of one of my dad's trucks!"

Alison laughed out loud. "I hope you got paid a hefty commission for it!"

"Actually, my dad wasn't exactly keen on the idea at first, but it turned out really nice and he ended it using it in his advertisements, too. That was payment enough for me."

Alison talked to her for a few more minutes, making sure she used the allotted time even though she had already decided that Katherine would be an outstanding candidate for the school. Pearlene called in on the intercom as the end time neared. "Well, Katherine, I'll tell you that I'm definitely impressed by you. I'm sure you're aware that the admissions process is largely a giant lottery because we get so many good candidates applying each year. But, for what it's worth, I'm giving you my highest recommendation. You are exactly the type of person we'd love to have here, and I truly hope you can join us. Here's my card. If you have any questions, feel free to call me. And if you decide to go somewhere else, feel free to stay in touch. I think you'll make an excellent doctor some day."

The two women stood and shook hands again. "I've heard that before from my family, but it really means a lot coming from an actual physician. I'll definitely let you know what happens in April, when the acceptance letters go out. Thanks for a great interview." She smiled and left, and Alison sat back in her chair, deep in thought. *She's lucky she kept her painting hobby in her life. I wonder how things would have been different if I had stayed with ballet.* In her mind, she was again at Lincoln Center.

"Daddy, why did the lights just go out?" The hall lights dimmed briefly again, and Alison worried that there was about to be a blackout.

"That just means they're going to start soon, so everyone should go to their seats." They had been standing in the lobby watching the people gather and they had lost track of time. "Hon, do you have the tickets?"

Alison's mother pulled them out of her purse. "Of course. You're the only one who forgets tickets!"

"Hey, that was eleven years ago, and it turned out the play was terrible anyway," he replied in a mock hurt tone.

"Yeah, I know it was just a scam to get me to the drive-in instead." She winked at him.

"Come on, you guys. They're going to start!" Alison was pulling her father's hand as she tried to drag him to the door. The usher checked the stubs then directed them to the eighth row, center section. A tall man was sitting in front of the left seat, so Alison sat between her parents, affording her a terrific view of the stage. She was so excited that she could hardly control her emotions. "I can't *believe* we're going to see a real ballet! This is so awesome! It's the best present ever! When are they going to start?"

After what seemed an eternity, the theater lights faded and the orchestra began while the curtains were drawn apart in a gentle arc. Alison tried to take everything in, but there was too much to see— the scenery, the lights, stage. She nearly missed the entrance of the first ballerina, but once the figure emerged on the scene, her eyes were riveted. It was exactly as she had dreamed. The graceful figures seemed to float across the stage in perfect form, defying gravity with every leap and twirl. It was mesmerizing, and even her parents found themselves entranced by the performance.

When the show was over, Alison diligently reminded her father that they were going to try to talk with one of the ballerinas. "Oh, honey, I don't know if they will have the energy to talk after that long performance." His intentions were good when he had suggested that to her, but now that he saw the size of the audience and the plethora of ushers, he had second thoughts about whether they would be allowed backstage.

"Can we just ask, Daddy?" She looked at him with her beautiful blue eyes and for a moment, he wasn't entirely sure she hadn't learned how to use them as a weapon against him. "If they say 'no,' we can go," she added solemnly.

"Well, OK, I guess we can ask one of the ushers. We'll be right back," he said to his wife as they walked towards the stage. A pleasant-appearing, middle-aged woman was standing by the stage-side exit. "Excuse me, ma'am," he started. "I'm sorry to bother you, but my daughter, well, she just loves ballet, and she was wondering if there was any way – if it's not a bother, that is – that she could talk with one of the ballerinas for a moment. She thinks she wants to be a ballerina herself, you see...."

The woman interrupted him. "Oh, we get young ladies here all the time who want to meet the performers. Most of them love the attention. Let me see if there's anyone back stage who would like to meet you. What is your name, sweetheart?"

"Alison," she said with pride and anticipation.

"Wait right here, will you?" The usher stepped through the door and returned a minute later with a young woman who appeared to be about 32. She was still wearing her tights and leotard as well as part of her costume.

"Hello, Alison," she said. "I'm Cindy. I heard you want to be a ballerina. Is that right?"

"Yes," Alison replied cautiously. "Can I ask you a question?"

"Sure, dear, what is it?"

"Why are you so thin. Are all ballerinas that thin?" She was looking at Cindy's arms, some parts of which were muscular, and other parts were bony. Up close, Alison thought she didn't look as pretty as they all looked on stage.

Cindy laughed nervously. "Most of us are. We have to be very careful to stay thin and in good shape because performing is hard work. The dieting is pretty tough when you start, but you can eventually get used to it. It's all worth it, though, when you see the audience and you put on a good show. Hearing the applause at the end and seeing everyone standing there, clapping— it's a great feeling."

"How much do you have to practice? I take lessons two days a week and I practice at home for an hour almost every day."

"That's a great start," she said enthusiastically. "Right now, because we're in the middle of a performance, we spend about four hours a day, plus the show. In the month leading up to the show, though, we spent at least eight hours a day rehearsing and practicing. Of course, most of us have part-time jobs, too, because it's hard to afford rent around here on that salary alone."

"Are you hungry all the time?" Cindy's slender appearance was still troubling to her.

"Well, sometimes. But you find ways to be less hungry. I mean, it's not like I have much of a choice. If you're not thin, it's pretty hard to get a good job in a city like New York."

"Do you like dancing?"

"I love dancing," Cindy replied. "but more like the kind you do in clubs. Ballet is like a combination between work and art. We make our bodies into a form of art, and that is very rewarding, but there is very little freedom of expression. I have to do exactly what the director tells me to do, even if I think it would look better some other way. It's my job to make my body perform precisely the way the director wants, and that takes a lot of work. In the end, though, I think the results are beautiful and I'm very happy to be here."

Sensing that the conversation should end, Alison's father cut in. "Well, thank you so much for a wonderful performance tonight. I know we all loved the show and we both really appreciate that you took the time to talk with us."

"Yes, thank you for talking to me," Alison echoed.

Cindy smiled. "A lot of girls come here because they love ballet, but only a few will go on to become ballerinas. I just hope everyone who doesn't at least continues to love the performances. Good luck to you." She turned, thanked the usher, then disappeared through the door.

Alison was clearly disappointed by the meeting. "Let's go home," she suggested. Her father knew that there were things he could tell her about being a professional athlete or performer versus the enjoyment of watching their talent, but he figured she was old enough now to work on drawing her own conclusions. Cindy's almost ghostly appearance was a surprise to Alison, and it would take her some time to come to terms with that. For now, rather than embark on a long, complicated discussion, he chose a more fatherly approach.

"Hey, how about some ice cream when we get home? We can stop at the 24-hour store on the way back."

Although it didn't clear her mind of Cindy completely, it was an effective tactic. "OK, but I get to pick the flavor!" She giggled a little and he squeezed her hand gently as they walked through the aisle to her mother.

I guess things would be a lot different if I'd pursued dance.... I'd be unemployed! There's no way I could stand that sort of dieting and abuse. I wonder if that's what drew me to psychiatry? I know I always found those sorts of self-destructive attitudes fascinating. Maybe that ballerina was the reason I decided to try to treat people with exactly those problems. She tried to remember if there was a defining moment in medical school that pushed her to her specialty, but nothing particularly stood out. *I bet that's been part of it all along. I never really did get over the way that poor woman looked, standing there after a strenuous workout, flat-chested, with thin arms and legs riddled with veins, telling me she didn't mind dieting. She was probably bulimic, now that I think of it. I know it changed how I felt about ballet, but isn't it interesting that it probably made me aware of how some people treat themselves.*

Alison realized that it was time to get back to work. She clicked Pearlene's intercom button and asked for the next patient.

24.

Instead of getting harder each day, this time the diet seemed to take care of itself without constant willpower and denial. Sharon had become so focused on the billing work that she only found herself hungry when Alison's lunch would arrive, reminding her that it was time to take a break. Work wasn't the only thing that was benefiting from her success, either. Her self-confidence was at an all-time high recently, and she was feeling pretty good about her prospects of slipping into the normal body size that she'd coveted for so long. Even the study check-in today wasn't as intimidating as yesterday. It was nearing 5:00 p.m. and she was finished with a major topic in the computer manual, so she decided to take a break and call her mother, who was supposed to be leaving with her father early the next morning for a long weekend vacation.

"Hello?" came the harried voice at the other end of the line.

"Hi, Mom, it's me."

"Sharon? Aren't you supposed to be at work? Is something the matter?" Her mother always found ways to be concerned, and something as simple as an unexpected phone call would be enough to make her nervous.

"No, Mom, everything's fine. I'm at work, and I know you're leaving tomorrow for your trip so I just wanted to say 'Hi,' before you leave."

"Oh, that's nice of you, dear. I'm trying to pack right now, but your father isn't sure what it's supposed to be like down there. I don't know if I should bring mostly spring or summer clothes, or what."

"You're going to North Carolina, right?" Her father was addicted to golf, so they frequently traveled to places known for their courses. "I'll check on the computer for you and let you know what the weather shows."

"I already know. Your father's been watching the Weather Channel for the last four days, trying to figure out when he should reserve tee time at that one club he likes so much. I want to know what everyone *else* will be wearing so I can go with the flow!"

Sharon laughed. "Yeah, nothing like being a conformist, right?"

"No, that's not it at all. I just don't want to embarrass your father in front of his friends. We're supposed to meet Martha and Thomas and some other couple there so the boys can play a round."

"I've always liked that pink outfit you got, with the little bit of lace around the cuffs. That seems like it would cross the winter-spring boundary nicely, and it's dressy enough to wear out with the right shoes and a necklace. Why not take that?"

"Hey, that's a good idea. I think it's still in the other closet so I didn't see it when I was packing. Anyway, what's new with you?"

"Actually a few things. I've got a project here at work that's pretty important, and I'm really enjoying working on it. It's a whole new billing program for the office, and I think it's going to revolutionize how the work is done. It takes a lot of setting up to get it to work efficiently, so I'm spending a lot of time learning the intricacies of the software."

"That's wonderful, Shar. You always stuck with things until you were happy with them, so I'm sure you're going to get this program working just the way you want." Sharon could hear a bit of pride in the way her mother spoke, and it was touching.

"I certainly hope so. But the bigger news for me is that I have decided that I really have to get in shape. This time, I'm serious about it. I know I've tried a thousand times before, but this time there's a little difference. The other day was my twenty-eighth and a half birthday. I know I never mentioned it, but ever since I was about sixteen, that day seemed like it would be the end of the world for me if I were still single."

"What are you talking about, Shar? You're not even thirty yet, and nowadays, thirty is still young."

"Yeah, I know, but as a teenager, it seemed pretty logical. It probably sounds silly, but at one time, it seemed so far away that I couldn't imagine the day would ever come, so I sort of made it a deadline for myself so I'd have time to get married before I was thirty. Anyway, that's not exactly the point. I picked out this one day years ago, and now, suddenly, it was here. I realized that I couldn't let it be a bad thing, though, because I'd spent so long being afraid of it. So I decided that this was going to be the day that changed my life for the better. I'm going to get in shape, do the best work I can at my job, and enjoy my life as it is."

Her mother knew she was treading in dangerous water, having gone down this road countless times before with her daughter. The roles were always the same, with her offering unconditional support while her daughter tried again to fight nature. She figured there was no sense changing her approach now. "Well, Shar, you certainly sound optimistic, and, like I just said, I know you can stick with anything you set your mind to."

"I know, but this time it's a little different. Whoops. Can you hold on a second? Pearlene wants me." She held her hand over the phone to answer Pearlene, who had stuck her head in the break room.

"I'm sorry to bother you, dear," Pearlene said. "I just wanted to say 'Goodnight.'"

"Oh, if you hold on a second, I'll walk down with you."

"Sure thing. I'll be in the waiting room."

Sharon uncovered the phone. "Anyway, I'll tell you more about this when you get back. I hope you have a nice trip, though, and tell Dad I called, OK?"

"Of course, Shar. You know we both love you and we're proud of you."

"I know. I love you guys, too. Bye now." She hung up, feeling good about the fact that she was able to talk with her mother about her new diet plan without having to rely on her for help. This was going to work, she decided, and she was going to stick to the diet even after her time on the study medication was through. The resolve was empowering and she felt like she could walk on air. A quick look around the room confirmed that the computer was properly sleeping, the manuals were stacked on the desk, and the current billing paperwork was meticulously sorted for the day, so she found Pearlene waiting outside.

She must have had a smile on her face because Pearlene said, "You know, child, you look like you won the lottery. How come you so happy after a whole day of work when you barely even took a lunch break after your appointment today?"

"I'll tell you on the way." The two women walked to the elevator and waited for a car. "I haven't really told anyone about this yet, but I feel like I can talk about things with you, Pearlene. You always see things from a different perspective than I do, and it's really helpful to hear your opinions."

"Well isn't that nice of you to say. Now, what's on your mind?"

"It's about my diet. I've been trying almost all my life to be thin. Actually, the truth is that I've been trying all my life just to be average. Social stuff, like dating and all, has always been hard for me, and now that I'm getting closer to thirty, I really want to be able to enjoy that part of life, but my weight has always kept me isolated in a way." Pearlene was nodding empathetically, being overweight herself and knowing all too well what it meant to be part of a group that was considered socially disadvantaged. "Anyway, so the other day I turned twenty eight and a half, and that was a day I was dreading since I was a teenager because it only left me a year and a half until thirty. I realized that, if I was going to change my life, I had to start now."

"Now let's not start saying you're old because I *knows* what that make me!" She chuckled.

"No, it's not that, but I really thought my life would be different than it is so far, so I decided that I was going to get on a diet and make it work, for good this time. Of course, I've said that a million times before, but this time the whole March 10th thing made it that much more important. As luck had it, on my way in to work that morning, I saw a poster on the wall near the elevator announcing a study the Medical Center is sponsoring to test a new diet medication called Ascendiac."

"Don't tell me you signed up for an experiment! You're letting yourself be their guinea pig?" Pearlene's forceful response took Sharon completely by surprise. She'd been apprehensive about exactly that, but she had managed to suppress her fears enough to sign up for the study. Now, her confidence was suddenly shattered.

"Uh... Yes, I did, I guess. I mean, they said it's safe."

"Sure they did." Pearlene waved her hand dismissively. "They also made you sign a form saying you wouldn't sue them if you got hurt, didn't they?" Sharon hadn't read the entire consent form she'd signed, but she was pretty sure that was the essence of it. Embarrassed, she nodded. "Yes," Pearlene continued, "they don't want to get their money taken away from them if they poison you by accident. You don't see them trying to experiment on their own families, do you? Just us poor folk who get fooled into trying things they tell you will change your life."

"Well," Sharon started, trying to save a little face, "they said I would only be on the medicine for a week, and the other week I'd take a sugar pill. It sounded like it might be OK."

"A week! For a diet pill? How much weight could you lose in a week? Enough to take a chance like that? What happens after a week is up but you still need to diet more? They'll tell you that you're on your own, that's what."

"But I've already decided that I'm going to stay on the diet this time, no matter how hard it gets," Sharon replied.

"Then what you need that pill for, girl? If you're going to lose the weight on your own then you just do it on your own. You take a week of their drug just to show them it's safe, then you spend the next year dieting all by yourself. I'm telling you, just give it back and tell them you don't need their pills."

"They offered me $400 if I finished the two weeks, though."

"Oh, it's so safe they think they need to *pay* you to use it, eh?"

Sharon frowned. "You know, you've got a point there, Pearlene. I was a little nervous about this whole thing when I first called them, but then I started the medication and I felt great and I wasn't so hungry all the time. I guess there's no reason I couldn't just give the bottle back and keep going on my own, now. Like I said, I'm going to make this diet work this time for sure."

"That's right, girl, You just walk right in there and tell them to experiment on someone else."

Sharon's great mood had evaporated by the time they'd reached the garage. "You know, I guess you're right, Pearlene. A week isn't enough time to lose any real amount of weight, and I'm on my own after the study no matter what. I've got so much confidence that I can do this that I suppose I don't need the medication after all. I hate to be a quitter but I never really thought about the risks like you said."

"Oh, I'm just looking out for you and Doctor Sonders. Lord knows we need to keep you out of trouble so you can run the office for us!" The two women hugged briefly, then parted.

25.

The police had been courteous all morning, but the stress of the situation was wearing Jess' patience thin. Charlie had been there for almost two hours before they decided they were done questioning him, and she was glad when the detectives finally took a break from her for a while so she could try to collect her thoughts. Not five minutes after they left her apartment, however, her cell phone rang.

"Jess, hi, it's Al. Where are you? We've been looking around for you all morning." Like Jess, Al was a student, and the two had been working together on their most recent project for almost five weeks. Jess found team research work tedious because she always seemed to get paired up with people who spent more time trying to avoid work than simply doing their share. This time was no exception.

"I'm at home, Al," she said, annoyed that he was bothering her when she needed some time to herself. "I'm sorry I didn't call, but there is a problem here. My neighbor was found in his apartment this morning. He killed himself. The police have been working for hours and they've been asking me all kinds of questions, trying to figure out exactly what happened." She was particularly blunt in the hopes that it would shock him into feeling a little sympathy for her situation. It seemed to work.

"Oh, that's terrible. Were you friends with him?"

"Actually, I kind of was. I didn't know him well, but we had talked some from time to time. Recently, his apartment had been smelling terrible and we started to get roaches, so I called the landlord. That's how they found him, and that's why I didn't make it to work today."

"Yes, I understand, of course.... I'll let everyone know what happened. Do you think you'll be in tomorrow?"

"Probably. I just need a little time to get over the shock of the whole thing."

"You know, if there's anything I can do...." He trailed off before making any actual commitment.

"I appreciate that, but I really just have to rest today."

"Sure. There's kind of a new project we have, but I can put the list in your box." He was still angling to delegate some of the work despite Jess' obvious preference not to think about that today. "Joel wants us to track down the study drop-outs for some reason. I guess he's worried that there might be a reason they've stopped taking the drug. Anyway, I divided the list by zip code because we might have to go door to door to find these people. I have a lecture to be at in half an hour, so I'm not going to get to any of these names today. I'll just put your half in your mailbox here and you can work on it tomorrow, too, OK?"

"Fine." She was irritated and she was not doing a good job hiding it. "I'll see you later, Al."

"Right. Get some rest tonight, Jess."

Why? So you won't have to do any extra work, right? "Bye." She hung up, shaking her head. The smell from Zach's apartment had permeated every room now, but she was already becoming desensitized to it. She wished that same thing would happen with Al, but he still managed to find ways to get under her skin. *At least, after the news story, we're getting a lot of new patients for this study, so we'll finish it soon and I won't have to work with him again. This degree better be worth the annoyance of dealing with Al every day.* She tried to think of something more pleasant about the project and she realized, of course, that the real reward was the benefit that the drug brought to medicine as a whole, and the Master of Public Health mentality resurfaced in her again. *I guess these studies have a lot of good in them, too. Even this diet drug thing, while not a cure for cancer, is kind of neat, especially when people see they're losing a little weight and they've never been able to do that before. It will be good for their health and for their psyche. Hopefully we'll find that most of the weight loss was occurring during the drug phase of the study, and the Excella company will have a new tool to combat obesity, an undeniable major public health problem in this country.*

At that moment, Jess saw a stray roach run across the floor and under the kitchen cabinet where she hoped it would find the roach tray. It was a grim reminder of the events leading up to today.

26.

The alarm clock was louder than usual this morning, and the sudden sound startled Sharon. Last night, she had lain awake in bed contemplating what to do about the Ascendiac study. On one hand, she desperately wanted to stay on the diet, but on the other, Pearlene had made some very convincing arguments about why she should lose the weight without the drug. Every diet she'd ever tried and quit before reaching her goal haunted her, one by one, like the ghosts in the Dickens story. All she was left with in the morning was a catalog of previous failures and her own newfound commitment to succeed at all costs, despite having skipped last night's dose of the medication.

Groggy and disoriented, she stumbled out of bed and found the bathroom light which instantly revealed her body's reflection in the mirror. She squinted at it, afraid to see the perpetual overeater she knew lurked inside. To her surprise, she saw only herself, though maybe just a bit thinner? She turned to one side, then the other, making sure it wasn't simply an illusion. The change was subtle for an outsider, but in her eyes, the difference was stark. She actually *was* losing weight, and she had yet to have a craving for any kind of food whatsoever.

"I can do this, I *can* do this!" she told the reflection. She felt hungry this morning, but not more than yesterday, while she was taking those pills. "Maybe they were the sugar pills after all," she suggested to the mirror. "Maybe I really *have* overcome that voracious monster inside! Pearlene was right. I'm not going to cover up the symptoms any more, I'm going to cure myself for good."

High on confidence, she showered, took one more look at her figure in the steam-covered mirror, then dressed. As she poured her breakfast cereal, she was especially careful not to exceed the portion limit she'd set, but when she was finished, she had the same sense of satiety that she'd experienced yesterday.

The drive to work was uneventful even though there were patches of rain during the trip. Sharon always kept a spare umbrella in her truck for such occasions, and as she parked in the garage, she decided she'd need it today. Walking along the avenue, she began to wonder what she would tell the people at the Medical Center about her withdrawing from the study. She hadn't had any adverse reactions to the pills and it wouldn't be fair to make something up, she thought. Telling them that a friend talked her out of it made her sound too much like a pushover, and accusing them of experimenting on her sounded almost paranoid. *I guess the truth is that I need to do this on my own, for me. The pills may help for a week or so, but where will I be after that? This is too important for me to be relying on an experimental drug which is going to be taken away from me before I'm ready, and I don't want to have to sign up for a lifetime of medication just to be thin.*

She rehearsed the reasons in her mind as she approached the Green building. Inside, she punched the "up" button before remembering to take the stairs. The elevator doors opened to reveal an empty car. Seeing that she wasn't inconveniencing anyone, she left the waiting elevator and climbed the two flights. Inside, she encountered a receptionist whom she hadn't seen before. The woman appeared to be in her late twenties, with a creamy, smooth complexion, deep brown eyes, and bright white teeth that contrasted strikingly with her dark skin and full lips when she smiled.

"Hello, my name is Gheena. Welcome to the Drug Research Institute. How can I help you?"

"So you're Gheena. I'm so glad I got to meet you. My name is Sharon, and I had called you the other day asking about the Ascendiac study."

Gheena frowned slightly, trying to remember that phone conversation from the dozens she'd handled since then. "Oh," she said as her face showed a glimmer of recognition. "You work in the next building, right? I remember you now. What can we do for you today?"

Sharon, who was temporarily distracted by this meeting, turned red as she remembered why she had come. "Um.... Well...," she started. "I guess I'd like to talk to one of the research assistants if that's OK."

"Certainly, Sharon. I think room 5 is open. Just walk around here and peek in. If there isn't anyone in there, have a seat but leave the door open and someone will be with you."

"Thanks," she said as she walked inside feeling painfully guilty. Room 5 was, indeed, empty so she sat in the chair and began having second thoughts about withdrawing. *I hope they don't argue with me. I'm not sure I could deal with that right now.*

A few minutes passed, and Sharon noticed that her hands had gotten cold and clammy, and she felt like she was starting to sweat. *Where is this guy? I don't want to wait any more to do this,* she thought in desperation. Just then, Jim walked in.

"Hello, I didn't see a paper outside. Are you currently in a study?" It was clear he didn't recognize her yet.

"Yes, I'm in the Ascendiac study. My name is Sharon Keating."

"Oh, right, I remember you now. Did you have an appointment this morning?"

"Well actually, no. I was supposed to come in around one o'clock, but I needed to talk with someone sooner than that. I want to stop being in the study. I brought back the pills I didn't use." She produced the bottle from her purse.

"Oh, OK," he said hesitantly. "Was there a problem? If there was any specific reason you wanted to stop, we'd really like to know. You can tell me or, if you prefer, you can enter it into the computer. Either way, it's very important that you give us as much feedback as possible. Obviously, we hope you'd reconsider, but all of our studies are strictly voluntary." It was clear he was disappointed, but he had no intentions of putting up a fight. The Institutional Review Boards which must approve all medical studies are extremely strict about allowing patients to withdraw at any time, for any reason, and it is a policy well known to all researchers. Violating this would almost certainly mean the end of any hope of being involved in future research efforts.

Sharon was simply relieved to hear that she would be allowed to withdraw. She tried to explain her motives but she found it more difficult than she had anticipated. In the end, she asked that she be allowed to summarize her feelings on the computer. Jim assured her that all her responses would be kept confidential. He accepted the returned pills and wished her well.

She found the computer room at the end of the hall and sat down in front of a terminal. In her purse, she found the card she'd been given with the username and password on it. Once entered, the computer presented a few stock questions regarding the study she was in and how many days she'd been enrolled. Eventually, she got to a free response window and she began explaining her reasons for leaving. Each sentence she typed brought back more memories of previous dieting schemes, from the group sessions to the fruit diets to starvation periods. One particularly difficult afternoon came to mind....

"More fruit? I can't stand this any more!" she shrieked, tears streaming down her cheeks. "I don't give a shit about graduation. I have to eat something!"

Her mother hadn't seen her this agitated before, and it scared her a little. She desperately hoped there would be something helpful she could say, but her maternal intuition told her differently. Still, staying silent would deprive her daughter of a much needed target to allow her to vent some of the anger. She braced herself for the onslaught, then offered, "I know it's really hard, Shar, and taking a little break from time to time makes these diets tolerable. I think it will be OK if you eat one regular meal."

"Sure, what do you care if I quit, right? *You're* not trying to fit in a graduation dress." The remark was cutting, but her mother tried to remember that this was helping dissipate her daughter's pent-up emotions.

"That's where you're wrong, dear. I really *do* care how you feel. If there were anything at all that I could do to help you, you know I would. I just think that it's not quitting if you take an occasional break from the diet. Everybody needs a break from time to time, and if you do it in a way that doesn't lead back to old habits, then you may find the long term easier to deal with. Sort of like giving yourself a reward for being good."

"Then how am I going to be in shape in time if I keep giving myself rewards? I don't know what you're thinking, because the only way to lose weight is to diet all the time."

"Sharon, you're not listening to me. I know that you're upset, and I know how hard this has been for you. But if you think about it for just a minute, you'll realize that one meal isn't going to make you gain or lose ten pounds, right? I mean, sometimes it's just the right thing to stop what you're doing and catch your breath. Then tomorrow, you just get back on track and keep at it."

This levelheaded reasoning fortunately managed to sneak past Sharon's frustration and anger long enough for her to pause and consider her mother's advice. "Damn it," she started, albeit in a softer tone of voice. "Why is this so hard? It's just not fair, Mom. Why can't I just be like everyone else who eats normal food and fits in normal clothes?" She had started sobbing now, and her mother gently put her arm on her shoulder for comfort.

"I don't know why you got stuck with this problem, Shar. I mean, everyone has their cross to bear, and I guess this is going to be yours. But you've got a strong will and you're a good person, so I know that you'll beat this problem, one way or another. It may never be easy for you, but I know you can do whatever you set your mind to. Just remember that you're not a quitter, and that there's no shame in taking a break from things so you can check your perspective and regain your strength."

Sharon looked up, through her puffy eyes. "Yeah, I guess I'm not going to change in one day, for better or worse. I keep forgetting I have some time and I should pace myself for the long term. I'm sorry I yelled at you."

Relieved that the situation diffused itself, her mother responded in her most soothing voice, "I know, dear. I know."

Sharon finished the free response part of the questionnaire and stared blankly at the screen for a moment as the image of her consoling mother faded. Explaining her reasons for withdrawing from the study was cathartic, and by the end, she'd convinced herself that she had, in fact, given back something to the drug company with her narrative. She hit the 'send' button, logged out, and walked back to the reception area, feeling her steely dieting resolve growing stronger inside her with each step.

Gheena saw her and asked, "Did you get what you needed, Sharon?"

Smiling as she considered her new found self esteem, She replied, "Yes, actually I did. Thanks again, Gheena," as she walked out the door.

Climbing down the two flights got her heart going faster again, but she was starting to feel less short of breath with each mini-workout. By the time she'd reached Dr. Sonders' office, though, she was again puffing heavily.

"Hi, Miss Sharon," Pearlene greeted in a particularly cheery voice. "Still at it with those stairs, eh?" Pearlene was feeling guilty for having come off so strongly against the study yesterday, and she was desperately hoping that Sharon hadn't taken things the wrong way.

"Morning, Pearlene," Sharon replied between breaths as she sat down heavily in one of the chairs. "I want to thank you for being honest with me yesterday. The different point of view.... It was a big help."

"Oh, I hope I didn't offend you. I really should have stopped myself, but me and my big mouth, well we just got carried away!"

"No, really, I think you were right. No matter how good that drug might have been, I have to do this for myself, for the rest of my life. I told them this morning that I'm leaving the study. I even gave back the pills. I know I can do this on my own, and I really feel great about it." She'd regained her breath and got back on her feet. "You've got to keep being my cheerleader, though, OK?"

"'Course I will!" Pearlene promised.

Sharon smiled in acknowledgement as she headed back to her desk. She sat in front of the computer and waited for it to power back up. After about fifteen seconds, it looked like it had crashed, so she pressed control, alt, and delete and waited for the system to reboot. *I can't believe that I still don't feel hungry. Not that I want to go back to the way I was, but I wonder if maybe that was the study medication I had gotten, and the appetite change was actually the drug working for me. Still, I haven't taken it since yesterday morning, so shouldn't it have worn off by now anyway? Whatever. I still need to get a regular exercise routine going, and I probably should work out a weekly low-fat menu for myself, including some snacks in case I start to feel hungry in between.* The computer screen finally showed the familiar icons, so Sharon started the Web browser and searched for some suggestion on diet menus. She spent the first twenty minutes printing out various recipes before turning her attention back to the billing software.

The next time she thought at all about food was when Pearlene carried Dr. Sonders' lunch delivery into the break room.

27.

"Yes, Dr. Rheinberg, I've been keeping an eye on the Ascendiac data, too," Dave assured as he discussed the ongoing study with the head of the FDA New Drug review board during one of their unscheduled phone calls. As much as it galled him, he wished Jack could have been in the room with him to provide some scientific support. "We also noticed that the 'lost to follow-up' percentage was higher than we had hoped, but we believe it may be related to the study population. After all, most of these people have spent their adult lives going on and off diets. We are fairly certain that these numbers reflect this fact, rather than some underlying issue with the medication itself."

New drug applications receive intense scrutiny from the FDA, and no two approval processes are exactly alike. Even if a pair of drugs are virtually identical, the Agency may arbitrarily require extra steps to prove the safety of one versus another. There are several reasons for the discrepancies, but one of them is simply that there is no one process which can determine reliably how safe and effective any given drug is. As time and experience increase, new side effects appear and new methods of testing are created, with each raising the bar for the next approval process. The FDA cannot simply ignore new facts just because a similar product was approved in an earlier, less sophisticated era. Allowances are also made based on the intended use for the medications, permitting less rigorous and lengthy testing of drugs whose need is perceived to be particularly urgent. The most obvious examples of such "Fast-tracked" drugs were many of the novel anti-HIV agents which were approved in a matter of months, compared to the usual years for other drug. At the opposite end of the spectrum, the FDA tends to be extremely conservative when investigating lifestyle drugs such as Viagra, Botox, and Ascendiac, all of which stand to generate large fortunes for the owners, but which are difficult to consider essential for wellbeing. In these cases, missing a potentially serious side effect or drug interaction because of excessive haste greatly tarnishes the FDA's reputation and dangerously skews the risk to benefit ratio.

Dave's eyebrows raised, wrinkling his forehead in exasperation. "Yes, we do have someone looking into those patients, and our chief investigator is personally in charge of all the reported adverse events." He rubbed his temples slowly while he listened to Rheinberg's commentary. In front of him, the computer screen was still showing Lightfoot, and he scanned the updated information as he waited to respond to the FDA's director. The computer reported that fully 83% of the drop-outs were in the placebo arm, a fact which Dave was certain meant that the problem was clearly not with the drug. *Damn it, I wish I could just tell this jackass that the drug is so good that people can't stand* not *having it. I'll bet some of them drop out then rejoin under a different name just to get another week of medication. If Rheinberg could only see these numbers!*

"I really think it's simpler than that, though," Dave started. He paused while Rheinberg responded. A little more disappointed, he continued. "I suppose you're right. I do feel pretty certain about the reason these people stopped the study, but speculation isn't as good as hard data. OK, how about we track these people down and ask them what happened. We can even follow up with people who complete the study, say, two or three weeks later. Do you think that would help solve this problem? I'd really like to find a way to keep as many of the data points as we can." *I don't need this to drag on any longer. If he slaps another requirement on us, it could be an additional year before we come to market. That's not going to help me very much, and Bobby's starting to worry me a little. If I tell him there's going to be some setback, God knows what he'll try.*

"Well, I was thinking more along the lines of a phone interview for the follow-up. Look, I can put some ideas down on paper and fax them to you, say, tomorrow. That will give us some time to brainstorm, and hopefully we can address these concerns for you immediately. Believe me, we want this drug to be safe and effective, above all else." Another pause. "Right, we'll have that to you by tomorrow, then. Thanks for calling." He pressed the switch hook, then dialed Jack's office.

"Jack, it's Dave," he said. "Listen, Andy Rheinberg just called because he is wondering about the drop-out rates for the Ascendiac trials. He is pushing for us to do something to find out why the patients left the study. I tried to explain to him your theory about these people being lifelong diet quitters, but he thinks we need more information so I tossed him a bone. I told him we already planned to do a post-study surveillance, so we need to push up the time frame for your little study." Dave listened for a minute as Jack agreed. "I'm going to be busy until 3:30. Be in my office then and we'll write out a brief proposal. I need to fax him something tomorrow." Another pause. "What don't you understand about this? I really think we need to give them something small but safe, so they don't decide to start another time-consuming arm of this trial. Just be up here this afternoon and we'll hammer out a plan." As he hung up, he could feel the veins in his head start to bulge as his frustration built. As much as he enjoyed the pressure, getting squeezed by upper management, the FDA, his brother, and a do-good researcher was beginning to erode his patience.

Meanwhile, Jack had been in his office with Stephen when the call from Dave came through. Tapping on his computer screen, Jack said to Stephen, "I wish we knew what was making those people drop out. It just makes me a little nervous seeing almost twelve percent of the patients not following through with the study."

"I don't know," Stephen replied. "Maybe I haven't been involved with enough clinical studies, but that seems sort of reasonable to me. Anyway, you're the one who suggested that it may have to do with the patient population we're recruiting." Stephen's cold was improving rapidly, but the v's were still hard to tell from b's.

"Yeah, I guess. It's just frustrating not being a part of this thing. I'd love to get my hands on a few of these study volunteers and talk to them just to find out what went wrong, what made them leave. I've never felt so isolated from the results before. Then again, I've never felt like I had so much riding on a damn study like this."

"I'm with you on that one, Jack. We put our hearts into this drug and if it works, not only will it be a huge cash cow for us, but for half the U.S. population, it will be a whole different approach to an old problem. For what it's worth, my advice is to work on something else for a little while. Staring at the computer will only drive you nuts. I was planning on heading over to the cafeteria for some lunch after meeting with you. Why don't you come along? I've been poking around with a new project and I think I've got enough of a handle on it that we should talk."

"Really? I thought we were going to lay low for a little while. You know, kind of take a break."

"Like I said, staring at the computer screen will drive you nuts. I needed something else to work on so that I didn't spend all my time thinking about the study. Once we enroll about half the total number of patients that we need, then some of the trends will make sense and I'll start watching the numbers regularly."

"Well, I'm glad one of us is staying sane. I'll make a deal with you. You tell me about your new project so I can forget this Ascendiac thing for a little while, and I'll buy lunch. I haven't been to Oscar's in a while and today's a perfect day for it."

"You mean that bistro on the other side of town?"

"Yeah, that's the place. About a year ago, I met the owner there after work one day and we started talking. They have a nice bar, you know, and Dave was supposed to meet me for a drink, but he was a little late. Anyway, Oscar, the owner, actually grew up in New Jersey, but he spent four years in France learning to cook. Someone in his family — his aunt or something — died and left him this house in town, along with some cash. He turned the place into a restaurant, bought a liquor license, and he's been doing quite nicely since then. The lunch menu has mostly the same stuff as the dinner menu, so it's really good quality. Besides, Dave wants to have a meeting at 3:30 to figure out how to handle the FDA on the question of the drop-outs, so we've got plenty of time to shoot the breeze there."

Stephen put his arm behind his back and winced. "Oh, twist my arm a little harder, please!" he said, mockingly. Then, as he feigned wiping a tear from his eye, he parodied, "You had me at 'free food.'" They both laughed as they walked out the door.

28.

"Oh, Jess, I heard about your neighbor," Patty said. "How are you holding up?" Patty had been Joel Williams' secretary for more than seven years, and she made a concerted effort to get to know all the graduate students who worked their way through the research center at Stanford. On any given month, there were generally eight who were involved in various medical research projects under Joel's auspices, and they changed every two to four months. The rich diversity of personalities intrigued Patty, making the job attractive enough to keep her there despite the often tedious task of running the office.

"Patty, thanks for asking. It was a real shock yesterday, and I just needed some time to sit at home and come to terms with things. Plus, the police had a number of questions about Zach, most of which I couldn't answer. It took them the better part of the day just to collect all the facts, though, so they kept coming back to me to see if I knew anything about his work, his family, his personal life, *et cetera*. I'm still a little drained, but I figured that getting back to some routine might help me."

"That sounds pretty reasonable, but if you need more time off, just let me know. I'm sure Joel could make some arrangements for you."

"It's a very thoughtful offer but I think I'll be OK. Thanks, though. You're the first person who offered to help. Well... I guess that building manager guy was nice, too. Anyway, I think I'll be fine. I didn't really know the guy personally. It was more the shock than anything."

"Well, Joel's in his office if you came to see him. Do you want me to call in?" Patty picked up the phone in anticipation.

"No, I just came to get my mail. Al told me that we're trying to track down the study no-shows now, and he put a list of names in my box."

"Right, you're working on that diet drug study. I know Joel talked to someone from the company the other day, and I think that's who actually wants to know why the patients have dropped out. Does it seem like a lot of them are?"

"More than average, I guess, based on the norms for prospective studies, but I don't really know how many is too many. If we can contact them, it will definitely make the study more useful, though." There were several pieces of paper and mail in her box, so Jess started sorting through them to find Al's list.

"I'll let you get to work, then. If you need anything, just call me. We look after one another here, you know."

Jess gasped. "Oh my *God!* This better not be a sick joke. It's him. Jesus, it's *him.*" Her voice was high and loud, and her hands had started to tremble.

"What's the matter? Who is it?" Patty asked nervously.

"Zach.... It's his address, too. This is the guy from my apartment! I need to see Joel."

At that moment, the door to the inner office opened up. "What's happening out here?" Joel asked insistently.

"This guy who's on the no-show list. He's the one from my apartment who killed himself. He was in the Ascendiac study!" Jess handed him the paper, pointing to Zach's name and address.

"*This* guy is the one who..." His voice trailed off as he tried to find the words. "I mean, I don't know what to say. Do you think he was taking the medication when he did it?"

"I don't know," Jess replied. "I think they said he was dead for a couple of days, and he hadn't been in to the study center for a couple more, according to this sheet." Her stomach turned when she thought about the possibility of a connection between the study drug and Zach's demise.

"OK," Joel finally suggested. "Why don't you see what you can find out about the other people on the list there. Maybe Al has some information, too, so talk to him first, then start calling around to see if you can get any leads. I still expect that most of these people are fine, but they just decided to stop the study for some reason, like they went on a business trip or something. Call me if you find anything, or at least in two hours to let me know how it's going. I'm going to call the manufacturer to see what they know."

"Do you want me to get them on the line for you?" Patty offered.

"Sure. Do you still have the name of that guy who called.... Jack, I think? See if you can get him for me. Jess, we haven't had any other reports of serious side effects so far, right?"

"No! I would have told you immediately if we had. I've only talked to a fraction of the patients personally since most of them are handled by the study nurses, but so far, it's all been good news. You know, though, I don't know if anyone wrote things in the computer that they didn't tell us. Who has access to that information?"

"I don't even know. I guess Excella has it, but maybe we're supposed to as well. I'll ask them about that, too."

Patty had found the number and started dialing. After a moment, she shook her head. "The voicemail picked up, but he left a cell phone number on the greeting. Should I call that?"

"Keep it handy, and try his office number again in half an hour. Jess, you find Al and figure out what he knows so far, then call me here." She nodded and left.

"I'll tell you, Patty, I hope these guys have been open with us. If they know about a problem with this drug but they pushed it through to phase III anyway, I'll personally make sure the FDA never considers a new drug application from them again." He stopped and took a deep breath. "Of course, I guess all this could just be a terrible coincidence, too. This guy might have been on the placebo for all we know, and he could have been depressed, too. Dieting and depression certainly *can* go together. Hey, can you find his clinical information for me? I'd like to see his weights, how long he was in the study, his pre-study evaluation... anything we've got on this guy and on all the other drop-outs." Patty was already dialing the receptionist at the study center as he finished the sentence, so Joel returned to his office to plan the next move.

About twenty minutes later, Patty called in to tell him she was transferring a call from Jess. He picked up the phone and asked, "Well, what did you find out?"

Jess sounded concerned. "I just got over to the study center to find a woman and her daughter talking to the receptionist. They were asking to see someone about Ascendiac, so I said I'd be happy to help. I took them to a consultation room where the mother started telling me that her daughter had begun the study last week and was doing really well on the first set of pills. She was losing some weight and her appetite was almost down to a normal level, according to her. The two of them were amazed because apparently the daughter had been dieting on and off for most of her adult life. Oh, the mother's a nurse of some sort, too."

"Uh huh," Joel acknowledged.

"Anyway, so they switched study arms at the end of the week, then on Tuesday, the mother hadn't heard from the daughter for two days so she got worried. She went to the apartment to find the daughter curled up in a ball on the sofa, surrounded in snacks and junk food wrappers, crying to herself. She kept saying she's a failure because she couldn't keep to her diet. She'd been binge eating for two days, and was now apparently having an emotional breakdown. Her mother said she'd had bouts of depression before, especially around some of the fad diets she'd tried, but nothing had been quite this severe. She found a bottle of Prozac in the medicine cabinet, apparently from the last episode of depression, about a year ago, and somehow managed to get the daughter to take some."

"What happened?"

"Well, she stayed there with her until today, trying everything she could think of. This morning, the daughter was apparently a little more cooperative, so she brought her in here."

"What did the daughter say about all this?"

"She didn't say much, and she really looks depressed, actually."

"Was there any indication that she was thinking about suicide or homicide?" This was a standard, textbook question every third year medical students learns to ask depressed patients. Although it had once been believed that discussing suicide might make patients more likely to commit the act, it was eventually shown that the majority of depressed patients will readily admit to having suicidal ideations. Once the subject is broached, patients become much less likely to act on their impulse and will often agree to safety contracts, wherein they pledge not to harm themselves without first alerting the health care provider to their intentions. Although on the surface such an informal verbal agreement seems relatively powerless, safety contracts have been conclusively shown to save lives and suffering by establishing a clear lifeline of communication in times of dire need.

"The mother didn't say anything about suicide and the daughter wouldn't even make eye contact, much less answer questions."

"Alright, I think she needs to be admitted to the psych ward for her own safety. I'll call Mort Stern who is a friend of mine and have him meet the mother and daughter in the ER. No, wait. I have a better idea. I'll have him come over there and see them first. What room are you in?"

"B as in boy," Jess replied.

"I don't know what's going on here, but we can't let this girl out of our sight for now because if it's related to the drug, we're going to be responsible for her." The thought of one suicide was bad enough, but letting a second one slip through his fingers would be considered gross negligence. "Go back to the room and tell them that Dr. Stern is going to see them, then stay in the room until he gets there. Afterwards, get back to your list and keep looking for other problems."

"What do I do, Joel?" Jess asked nervously.

"About what?"

"If the daughter... you know... tries anything? I'm not a doctor...."

"If she's depressed, she's probably not going to get violent. Most of them don't. Just sit with them and make sure they don't leave your sight. Not for the bathroom, not for a phone call, not for anything. She may be all right, but I'm not willing to take any chances. Mort will be there soon."

He hung up, struggling to piece the story together in his own mind. Thinking aloud, he reasoned as he drummed his fingers on the desk, "She has a history of depression, especially when she falls off a diet routine. She was losing weight last week, which sounds like the active arm of the study, then a few days after the switch, she breaks the diet and ends up almost catatonic on the sofa. She takes Prozac for two days which supposedly gets her back on her feet, but that's way too short a time for it to be the Prozac working since it takes at least two *weeks* on that drug before you start to see results." The drumming had gotten intense enough to start to hurt his fingers, so he stopped. "If there's a connection between her recovery and the Prozac, the timing doesn't make much sense to me." He dialed Mort's pager, entered his number plus *911 to let him know it was urgent, and waited for the response.

29.

Stephen closed the car door firmly but gently and walked around the back as Jack climbed out. "Well, I'm sold," he quipped. "There is no substitute for Porsche. Hey, thanks for lunch, too."

Jack smiled. "Glad to have the company. I don't know why we don't take breaks like this more often."

"Because of all the work, remember?"

"Oh yeah," Jack replied slowly in an exaggeratedly surprised tone. They both laughed. "Well, I'm heading up to see Dave. I'd ask you to come, too, but I doubt it would pay to torture both of us. Keep thinking about that new project you've got. You're onto something there."

"Alright, but call me if you need anything."

Jack arrived at Dave's office at 3:30 on the dot and bid a warm hello to Laura. "Someday, when I'm an important guy here, promise me you'll defect and be my secretary!"

"Oh, stop," she protested. "You know flattery will get you everywhere!" She winked as she dialed in to Dave. "Mister Aswari, Doctor Finnegan is here, sir." She added a little extra emphasis on the word doctor. "OK, I'll let him know," she said as she punched the "disconnect" button. "Dave says to wait out here, he'll be with you soon."

"Guess that means I have more time to try to win you over!" They both chuckled.

Inside, Dave was staring at the computer screen, attempting to comprehend all the Lightfoot data before his meeting with Jack. Although the drop-out rate was substantial, the confidential data showed clearly that the majority of people were actually leaving from the placebo arm, about two or three days in. Each case looked almost identical, too, with significant weight loss on the drug, then the crossover to placebo, then the drop-out. He couldn't understand why someone would be within five days of collecting a cash payment when they quit, but the data didn't lie.

These people are not leaving because of some problem with the drug! They were quitters, and dumb ones at that. Whether they're gaining weight off the drug or they just don't like being their same old gluttonous selves, they're screwing up this study for no good reason. All the other indices were promising, with an average weight loss during the drug arm of six pounds. That's nearly a pound a day, and none of these people had a strict diet to follow! I can't believe we have to keep these results secret when it's so clear what's happening.

His frustration was slowly growing into an irritation with the scientific community at large. *These guys make such ridiculous, bullshit rules because of some imagined risk of bias. I'm an adult, for God's sake. I can see the information without having it cloud my judgment. All this secrecy so that the end is one big surprise is just a waste of energy. If they looked at these numbers now, they would probably approve the drug on the spot.*

He thought for a minute about how he could let the information slip out without causing Jack to cry foul and jeopardize the whole study. It seemed like a simple thing, but the more he considered telling him, the more he worried that Jack would blow the whistle and kill the entire project. For Dave, a man who succeeded in the financial world where knowledge was power, being hamstrung because he *had* information was particularly galling. He thought through a number of different scenarios in which Jack would anonymously receive a copy of the data, but every time it looked the same. If Jack figured he knew too much, he'd open his mouth and complain about improper scientific technique. Then they'd be writing follow-up studies for the FDA until the cows came home.

Trapped, he called Laura. "Send him in," he said curtly as he hid the window containing Lightfoot. Dave decided it was important for him to appear to be in control but mildly annoyed by Rheinberg's request, although not so annoyed that Jack would feel like he was hiding something. He turned to the computer and started typing just to look busy when Jack entered. "Hi," he greeted curtly. "Have a seat."

"So, exactly what do we have to do for these guys?" Jack asked. "They don't want us screwing up the study now, do they?"

Dave was taken aback by this unexpected attitude. If Jack thought that Rheinberg's request was inappropriate, then maybe the situation wasn't as challenging as it had first appeared. He decided to push the envelope a little to see what Jack was thinking. "I don't think that anyone is trying to screw things up, Jack. I think Rheinberg just wants to make sure we're not missing anything important in this higher-than-average drop-out rate. Anyway, I thought you were the one who first showed an interest in this post-study follow-up stuff."

"I am, but that's exactly the point. It's supposed to be *post-study* follow-up. See, if we start looking into these people officially, during the study period, we can run into a real problem. Let's say that there is some sort of trend, like that the drop-outs all said they were binge-eating once they switched arms of the study. Well, we can't tell from the blinded data if they switched from the drug to placebo or from placebo to drug. No... that's too simple an example." Jack paused, stroking his chin as though in deep thought. With a dismissive wave of his hand, he continued. "Anyway, if there were a worse side effect than binge eating, it would be even easier to see, but let's say the FDA decides that the trend is important to them, and they want to know whether the patient was getting drug or placebo at the time. Now we're sunk. To answer that, we'd have to unblind the data, which taints the original study."

Dave was admittedly a little lost by the whirlwind explanation, but he was glad to see the passion in Jack's argument. "So what can we do?"

"Well, I definitely don't think we should jeopardize the study for this. I mean, we've got some good press for Ascendiac and we have built an excellent patient base already, so it would be catastrophic to make any moves which could be interpreted as indicating a potential problem with the drug. I desperately want to know why people are dropping out, but we have to be very careful about how we collect and classify any information."

Thinking about the Lightfoot data, Dave asked, "Would it matter if we knew that people were leaving from just one arm of the study? I mean, if most of the drop-outs were, say, from the placebo side, would that change things?"

"Maybe, but it's hard to say. In order to find that sort of thing out, we'd have to open the blinded data, and that would essentially kill the results." Jack caught himself thinking about the trust fund he wanted to set up for his daughter with some of the Excella stock profits. He knew it was wrong to let greed interfere with his work as a researcher, but the Ascendiac reward seemed so close that he found himself resenting the FDA for their excessive caution in light of a seemingly imagined and frivolous concern. "How much information does Rheinberg actually want from us?" he asked pointedly.

"I don't know. I suggested that we'd try to call the drop-outs and ask them why they left." Dave suddenly found himself sorry he'd even offered that.

"What if we just called them to make sure they're OK. We could... I don't know... say we felt bad that they left without getting any money for their efforts, and offer them forty bucks to take a written survey about the drug. I know it's a little more direct than what I suggested the other day, but I didn't expect the FDA to be involved like this. We could then tell Rheinberg that everyone we contacted was OK, but we wouldn't have to open the written surveys until the study was over. Hell, we wouldn't even have to *send* the surveys until then, and that way we could keep the results clean."

"Do you think that would work? I mean, will Rheinberg buy it?" Dave was beginning to appreciate the benefits of Jack's cautious approach to protecting the integrity of the study data.

Jack shrugged. "I can only image what they might be looking for. People drop out of studies all the time. Why *they're* particularly worried about this one, I don't know. We provided multiple ways for the patients to tell us how the drug is working and whether they're having any problems, including a completely anonymous computer feedback system. How important could anything we're missing actually be?" Jack's cell phone started vibrating, but he didn't notice it at first, as he was still wrapped up in the discussion with Dave. The third ring caught his attention and he pulled the phone off its clip. He didn't recognize the number and he debated briefly whether to answer it. He shook his head to Dave, indicating that it was a nuisance he'd have to endure. "Hello, Jack Finnegan."

"Jack," the voice on the phone said. "It's Joel Williams from Stanford again. We need to talk." Joel proceeded to describe the events of the day, starting with the suicide and moving on to the woman and her mother in the study office. Jack grabbed a sheet of paper from Dave's desk and started taking notes which he used to let Dave know the details of the conversation.

After a few minutes, Jack spoke. "This could be an important finding, Joel. It could also be coincidence. I'm not trying to minimize things, but we need to figure out what to do with this information now. You said that the woman had a history of depression, right?"

"That's what Jess told me," Joel confirmed. "She apparently had some episodes during other dieting attempts."

"OK. What about this Zach guy? Do you have any medical history on him? Did he leave a note or anything?"

"Nothing yet. We were going to pull his file when the other woman showed up in the clinic with her mother. The new patient screening form isn't that detailed, though, as you know, so I don't expect to find much there."

"What's your gut instinct about this, Joel?"

"I've never seen a suicide in one of our patients before, and we've studied almost every antidepressant out there. I'm concerned, to say the least. On the other hand, when we study psychopharmaceuticals, those patients are under the care of a psychiatrist, so they have some support. I suppose this guy could just have been an overweight, depressed person who was going to do this with or without the drug. I can say even less about the woman, since she's already got a history of this sort of reaction. Right now, though, any link to a drug effect seems circumstantial at best."

"I'm inclined to agree with you on that, especially because this drug is so selective for one type of receptor and we haven't seen any real side effects in the pilot study or from the electronic feedback we're collecting now. What do you think we should do?" Jack was being careful to keep Joel's opinions the focus of the discussion given his earlier misgivings about the motives of pharmaceutical companies.

"Well, we could consider stopping the study, but that would really set us back. I think we need to find everyone else who stopped participating and find out how they're doing in case there is some kind of trend here. We probably need to screen people for depression, too, so that we can see if that's a risk factor. I think we need to do that, at a minimum."

"I agree," Jack replied. "Look, we're supposed to talk with the FDA today anyway, so we'll let them know that we want to do some surveillance follow-up by phone to investigate the drop-outs. Your people are already doing that, which is a great start. If you send me the list of names and contact information, we'll start trying to track them down with you so we can keep the FDA informed of our findings. Obviously, if either of us finds an important trend, we'll have to make more aggressive changes."

Joel thought for a moment, impressed by the fact that the drug company was considering going straight to the FDA with this potential problem. Their apparent openness reassured him. "That sounds very reasonable. It's probably all just related to the fact that overweight patients are more likely to have depression, but I know I'll feel better if we do something to confirm those suspicions."

"So will I. Oh, and when you send the names, maybe you can suggest some screening questions we can add to the new patient screening forms to get a psychiatric history."

"I'd be happy to. Thanks again, Jack." They hung up.

"Nicely handled, Jack." Dave said. *Sounds like somebody finally decided to play for the company team after all. It's about time you started thinking about the future, Jack, and how much this drug is going to mean to us... and to Bobby.*

Jack's mind was on an entirely different problem, though. "Jesus, Dave, what if we're wrong and there *is* a connection?"

30.

What time is it? Sharon felt a gnawing sense of irritation all afternoon, and it was finally reaching a crescendo which she could no longer ignore. She clicked on the clock icon at the bottom of the screen but she only felt worse when she saw it was only 3:19. *Today is dragging on forever! I can't believe I've been working on this stupid program for three days now and it still isn't finished.* She buried her face in her hands, feeling the frustration ooze through her pores. *Damned useless computer. This is such....*

She sat straight up in the chair, her face white with fear and the harsh sound of her gasp still audible in the room. *What the hell is happening to me? Am I really that mad at a computer? Yesterday I couldn't have been happier with this thing but now, all of a sudden, I'm ready to lose it?* She tried a few cleansing breaths and it seemed to relax her enough to release the death grip she had on the chair's arms. *OK, Shar, just the stress of this whole diet thing. I must have been suppressing some of that so I could keep the appetite under control. Just let it go and things will be fine.*

A minute passed and she was feeling almost normal again. *Get yourself together now... Work is going fine... We all knew the project would take a while... Only a couple of hours to go today, no big deal... Hey, I'm still not thinking about food, either... Guess that's good, too... I'm on the diet and it's working just the way it should... Let's just take a quick walk then settle back down.*

She stood from the chair and made her way out to see Pearlene, who had just checked in the last of Dr. Sonders' patients for the day. "How goes it on the front line?" Sharon asked in as cheery a voice as she could muster.

"Making along, you know," Pearlene replied. "Everything OK with you? I was starting to think you'd never leave that office if I didn't come get you out for the day!"

"Well, I think that level of intensity was getting to me. I finally felt like I needed to stretch my legs for a minute." Then, in a lower tone meant to keep the discussion private, she said, "Truth be told, I was just sitting there at the computer and I felt this surge of anger. It came out of nowhere, but I just couldn't take the billing program work any more. Stranger thing is that, a minute later, it was gone. I don't know what came over me."

"Oh, child, we can all see it. It's stress. You've been fretting about getting older like you said, and it gets to wearing on you. A woman turning thirty is a big thing. You just found a way to worry about that a little early is all. When was the last time you just relaxed and did something fun for a change?"

"Uh, I don't know. But I keep thinking that I have to keep an eye on the diet now, so I'm trying to establish a new routine for myself so I don't get sucked back into the old habits."

"Maybe that's true, but you can't let it make you crazy, either."

"You're right, Pearlene. I haven't been out for a drink in a few days, and it's really the best chance I have to meet people outside of here. I can call Sue and see if she can meet me tomorrow, after work."

"That sounds like a fine idea. You'll have something to look forward to, and it will also give you a reason to wear something special, you know? Nothing like wearing a special outfit now and again so you feel like you look your best."

"You're a mindreader! I was just thinking that I could wear a new pair of shoes I just got to match my Talbot's blouse! I've been holding on to them for just the right time, and this is it." She couldn't help feeling like she was talking about a prom dress, but she *had* been thinking about high school recently so it was on her mind. Whatever the case, a little socializing was just the thing to keep her on track and remind her why she was not going to fail the dieting this time. "One other thing, now that you've fixed my life again. What's Dr. Sonders doing after this last patient? Is she going to be in the office or does she have somewhere to be?"

"I think she's planning on working in her office for about an hour before she's giving a lecture at the medical school. Do you want me to schedule some time for you?"

The request was a spur of the moment thing, and Sharon was already feeling a little guilty for imposing. "If it wouldn't be a bother, I'd like to talk to her for a few minutes, in her office. It won't take long and it would be a big help."

"I'm sure she'd be happy to see you. I'll let you know when she's done, OK?"

"Great." Sharon returned to the break room and sat in her chair again. *What was that? You know you can't bother your boss for personal reasons! Well, you shouldn't, at least, but I guess it's OK if you're just asking for some advice. I mean, it's not like I'd be asking her to treat me or anything.* She wrestled with the options for another moment before deciding that it probably would be acceptable to ask a few questions, but that's all. Then she turned her attention back to the billing program, and the three remaining chapters on how to add the proper modifiers to enhance specific billing codes.

Sharon managed to maintain her composure for the rest of the work day, and she was nearly back to enjoying the progress she was making on the billing project when Pearlene appeared at the door. "Dr. Sonders said that she'd be happy to chat with you, if you still want. I'm going to leave now, so you two will have plenty of privacy." She smiled and turned around, allowing Sharon to accept the news without having to come up with an awkward explanation as to why she wanted the meeting. Pearlene had suspected it was about the same aging issues she'd raised with her, so it seemed appropriate to leave the specifics alone.

"Thanks! Have a good night!" she called to Pearlene. *All right, just stay calm and keep it short. You're not there to bother her, remember.* She walked around to the office door and found it was open.

"Come in, Sharon," Alison said. "Pearlene told me you wanted to talk about something?" She motioned to the high-backed chair opposite her desk, so Sharon took a seat.

Obviously uncomfortable, Sharon cleared her throat nervously before beginning. "Well, I didn't want to take too much of your time, but I really needed to talk to someone who knows about these things, and you were the first person who came to mind." She paused, trying to collect her thoughts.

Alison had learned from years of experience that the best approach to the reluctant or uncertain patient is silence. People tend to say things when they're ready, and if you don't give them a chance to speak, you'll never hear their story from their perspective. Worse, if the interviewer suggests an approach that leaves an easier avenue than meeting the problem head on, some patients will choose the path of less resistance, circumventing the real issues. In such cases, she simply sat still, wearing her most earnest and attentive face, and waited for more.

Sharon finally continued. "You see, well, it's kind of a funny thing because I just turned twenty-eight and a half which really isn't a bad thing, but I've spent all my life thinking about that day because if I don't meet someone by then, how can I get married by thirty? I mean, I need to date him for a while, right?" The last two sentences came out practically in one breath and she needed to stop for a moment. So many thoughts raced through her mind at once that it was difficult to catch the important ones. "I guess I'm really trying to say that I need to take control of my life so I can do the things I want to do. The first thing is to get in shape. I have always had a weight problem, and I know that I would feel better about myself if I could fix it. Then I could fit in better so that guys would want to date me. I...." She stopped talking and looked to Alison expectantly.

Alison responded at a measured pace, hoping it would help Sharon relax a bit. "You know, that's a lot more than you've ever told me about your personal life. Do you want to discuss this as friends or would you prefer for me to be a doctor?"

"What? I, uh, I didn't mean for either, really. I just was wondering if it would be worth me seeing someone. You know, for counseling or something?"

"Well, what do you think you could get from counseling?" Alison was probing gently, trying to determine if there was another issue at stake.

"I don't know. I guess I could tell them how I feel... I mean, what I'm feeling about myself and my weight and my age and the whole relationship issue. I could tell them about those things and they could tell me if I'm crazy, is all." She had stumbled through this last answer in another long breath while still trying to get all the words to come out with the right meaning. Hearing the tinge of desperation in her own voice only made the situation feel worse.

"Do you think you're crazy?" The doctor role was coming to the surface now, but it was really the only role Alison knew. Years of medical training had all but eradicated every other response.

"No, I don't think so. But sometimes I feel like I could do anything and other times it seems like I'm stuck right where I am."

"Have you ever had psychiatric counseling for anything before?"

"By a doctor? No. I used to talk with my mother about dieting. She helped me with almost every diet there is, but I could never manage to stick with them long enough to change. I'd lose some weight, but it would come back a few months later. It was frustrating because the old habits were so hard to break, and the frustration made me eat even more."

"What are you planning to do now, then?"

"I'm on a diet now, actually. I started it a few days ago, and it's been going pretty well, really. I haven't been as hungry during the day, and I made sure I don't have any food around me to snack on."

"What are you doing that's different than before? Sometimes it helps to change things a little."

Sharon considered telling her about Ascendiac, but she didn't want to seem like she'd turned to medications before she tried talking with her. Unconsciously, she looked down, and Alison's clinical eye caught the brief gesture, although she didn't have enough information to know exactly what it meant. "Nothing, really. I think I just decided this time I'm going to stay with it. I think I'm going to stay motivated because of this whole age thing."

"Well, Sharon, I'll tell you this. I'm a few years older than you, and I went through a similar thing around my thirtieth birthday. I never had a weight problem, but I did have other things. I don't think you're crazy, but I do think you need to talk about this some more. I can give you the name of a friend of mine who sees adult patients here on campus. He's very good and I think you will like his style. Or, if you want, I'd be happy to set aside some time each week for us to talk. It wouldn't be as formal as a real doctor-patient relationship, but I honestly don't think you have a problem that we won't be able to work through. If you need it, you can always see my friend Patrick."

"Oh, that would be great, Dr. Sonders. Thank you so much for that." Sharon was suddenly overcome with emotion and a tear escaped from her eye as she considered how generous this offer was.

"Please, call me 'Alison.' I think you'll feel better if you do."

"OK, Alison. Thank you. I'm going to go now." She stood from the high-backed patient chair, unsure whether she was about to cry or laugh. She did feel certain of one thing: Alison was one of the finest people she knew. She closed the office door behind her and headed to the garage.

Alison tapped a pen on the edge of her desk for a moment. *What an odd interaction. We never discussed anything of significance before, but now, out of the blue, she tells me more than she has in the past how many years? For all the time I've known her, she seemed so emotionally together, but today it all came undone. She's never seemed manic, but some of her answers felt so pressured that it really can't be ignored. Then again, mania doesn't fit with the constant overeating that she reported. Depression is common enough, but she doesn't have a history of anything needing treatment. In fact, the resolve to change her weight and get things together is exactly the opposite of what I'd expect if she were depressed. There were no psychotic symptoms, no obvious ulterior motives.... She didn't even ask for a day off from work! Maybe I was right the first time. She's a single woman dealing with the pressure of a job and a low self-image, and she just needs someone to talk to about life.*

Looking at the computer, she considered starting an electronic file on Sharon, but she noticed that the third year medical student lecture was only forty-five minutes away and she still had three other patients to chart. *At least I can check up on her easily.* After entering the office visit notes into the computer, Alison printed a copy of her lecture notes, grabbed her coat and bag, and headed off to the school. On the way, she quietly rehearsed the introduction to her talk entitled "The Psychology of Human Perception."

"The human brain is a remarkable device. At birth, it is not even capable of processing simple visual input, but after being exposed to light for several weeks, it not only learns to interpret this information, but it actually rewires itself to become an efficient and sensitive image processor. Yet, it accomplishes this task — one that the most advanced computers cannot begin to emulate — without a single absolute frame of reference. Seeing is much more complicated than simply detecting photons as they strike the retina. It requires *perception*, a cognitive process which necessarily involves a comparison between the visual signal being sent to the brain and the collective experience of all previous visual signals which have already been analyzed. The brain's own experiences provide the information from which the visual processing system of that brain is built."

"This functionality leads to two problems. One, which is more of a developmental topic, is how the brain is able to pick itself up by the bootstraps and learn to see. The other, which is the focus of this lecture, is how the lack of reference points can come back to haunt us in psychiatry."

"For a moment, let us stay on the subject of vision. Color blindness is a genetic defect in one of the eye's color receptors, resulting in the inability of the person to distinguish between certain pairs of color. Those with normal vision, for example, may see a red swatch next to a green swatch, whereas the color blind will not know which is which. While this makes for interesting clothing choices, the more sanguine question is, 'What do color blind people actually perceive?'"

"It seems to make sense that they would see the world in shades of grey, but this is definitely not the case, as any such person will attest. Instead, they perceive the world in full color despite the fact that they cannot distinguish the swatches. If they are then told that the colors are, for example, red, the brain will accommodate by subtly shifting the perceived hues to make them appear that color. Because the visual system also 'knows' that colors shouldn't change on their own, the alteration in perception happens with minimal fanfare. The color blind person does not feel like he is in a B-grade psychedelic movie because the brain simultaneously changes the memory of the perception so that the person feels as though the swatch had always been that color."

"Now, before you think that's too strange a concept, consider this: Look at a color in dim lighting and it will appear dark and indistinct. Perhaps a green tint will look brown or purple. When you turn on the room lights, the color is now vivid and clearly different than what you thought it was, but the change is not shocking to you. 'Sure,' you say, 'colors often look different in poor lighting,' but the real reason it seems natural is because your brain simply changed your recollection of the perception when the lighting improved."

"Of course, this not a lecture on vision, but it is a good starting point. Information comes to the brain in many ways, some of which are from external sources, such as the senses, and some from internal, such as through reasoning and emotions. We perceive happiness, pain, sound, and color, but if the brain can so easily change that perception, how can we rely on it? We can turn the room lights back down and feel certain, based on past experiences, that the color has not changed. This is our perception of the situation, but there is no way we can be sure this is true. Worse yet, what happens when the act of perceiving itself is altered, allowing a patient's perception of reality to shift uncontrollably?"

"We call such a state psychosis. In the vernacular, the word conjures up images of ranting, babbling people in white straight jackets, but for physicians it has a much more specific meaning. Patients who have lost the ability to discern the difference between reality and their own internal thoughts, are clinically diagnosed as psychotic. The term can be applied as easily to a schizophrenic who believes his hallucinations are real as to a manic patient who believes that he is invincible and perfect at everything. Because there is no internal benchmark... because we have no reference point except our own experiences... it is our perception alone that decides for each of us, every minute of the day, what is real and what is fictitious. That is why verbal psychotherapy without pharmacological adjuncts is never sufficient to cure psychosis and return to the patient the necessary function of perception."

Alison found the students assembling in the lecture hall when she arrived. Most of them were wearing or carrying their short white coats, having come directly from their clinical psychology rotation on the wards. As she strode to the lectern to arrange her notes, she felt the building excitement that always accompanied the opportunity to share her hard earned knowledge with another generation of students. She smiled to herself as the last of the students filed in.

31.

The sun was setting as Sharon walked towards the garage, and although the light grew incrementally dimmer with each step, the changes were far too subtle for her to notice. Her mind was focused on the meeting with Alison. *I thought I was going to ask her to refer me to someone, but somehow I ended up asking her to do things for me. Jesus, I can't even remember what I went in there looking for in the first place. Like she needs some neurotic, overweight office manager tying up her work time! How inconsiderate was that? Well, it is her job, at least, but then again, if it's her job then I shouldn't be using her for free. I have to thank her for the offer then ask her for her friend's name tomorrow.*

Will that seem like I don't trust her, though? I don't want her thinking that I think she's not good enough. Maybe if I tell her that I just don't want to bother her because she's my boss. That sounds so fake, though. She always asks me to call her Alison and she tries not to seem like a boss, so I'd be insulting her if I said that. I guess I could just look for someone myself and not tell her at all, but then how could I explain that I didn't need to meet with her after all? Damn it, Shar, you really screwed that up, didn't you?

She got to her car and climbed in. She was a little less winded today, but she had been walking slower, engrossed in thought. She turned the key and the engine started up immediately, but Sharon remained preoccupied. She opened the glove compartment and began rifling through the contents distractedly. After a moment, she closed it and opened the center storage bin, peering inside as the automatically dimming overhead light finally extinguished. *What are you looking for? The garage card is in the ashtray!* Shaking her head once as though to clear out the cobwebs, she grabbed the card and drove to the gate, hardly aware of what she had been doing.

Traffic was moderate tonight, and her mind wandered from Alison to the subject of what to make for dinner. *Pasta. What else do I make anymore? Bland pasta with sauce. At least it's low-fat so I can stay on the diet. What I wouldn't give for some good garlic bread and butter, though. Or pizza, or.... All right, let's not go there. I'm happy with the pasta and that's that. I'm not going to start thinking about all the things I can't have because that's what kills the diet each time. No dreaming about ice cream, chocolate, cheese, Snickers bars, or anything else. And definitely no thinking about cookies or muffins at work.*

Shut up, Shar! Thinking about what not to think about is just the same as thinking about it. What's wrong with you? Don't tell me you're going to find a way to backslide this time. Her hands were clenched tightly around the steering wheel and she could feel the disgust starting to build even though she was still technically succeeding on her diet. She got off the highway at her exit and tried to refocus. *All right, just calm down. You're just overreacting to the meeting with Alison, and you can find a way to work that out. Just go home and get back into the routine. You'll feel better once you eat something.*

Inside, she hung her coat on the rack and started rummaging through the cabinets, looking for a suitable meal. *What was I thinking in the store the other day? I didn't even buy interesting sauce for the spaghetti, and I don't have sausage to spice it up. OK, well, at least I still have some wine in the fridge.* She pulled out a pair of pots and filled the larger one with hot water then put it on the burner. The other got a portion of tomato sauce to which she added oregano, hot peppers, fennel seeds, and a touch of minced garlic. Covered, she set that up to simmer while she washed out the wine glass that was sitting next to the sink and poured herself a small glass of the Chardonnay.

Hey, a few bread sticks would go well with this. She had picked up a package of them at the store when she saw the large "low fat" label on the front, and she figured they'd go well with her "primarily pasta" approach to shopping. At the time it seemed amusing, but tonight she was in no mood for humor so she tore open the end of the package and pulled one out. It tasted bland but at least it gave her the sense that she was eating something while she waited for the water to boil. *It's not that bad after all, right? You're doing it, but there are going to be good days and bad days, just like every time.* She was mindlessly wandering around the kitchen, setting the table and measuring out the dried spaghetti. *Today was one of those bad ones but it's not the end of the world.* The first bread stick was gone and the wine glass was getting light, so she opened the refrigerator to refresh it. Before closing the door again, she picked up the butter dish for the table then sat back down. *Alison is so lucky to have her career and also stay in such good shape. She's really got it all, so….*

Sharon stopped in mid-thought, horrified by the sight of her hands coating the bread stick in butter. "What am I doing?" she nearly screamed as she dropped the food on the plate. Without even thinking, she had reverted to her old eating habits, and the realization that it was happening against her will made her even more distressed. She struggled to her feet and stood silently at the table's edge, staring blankly at the greasy mess which somehow seemed to be mocking her. *It's happening again and I can't control myself. How pathetic can you get, Shar? Even when you want to win, you find a way to fuck it all up and lose anyway. Good job, Tubby.*

The water was beginning to boil over, but Sharon didn't notice it for several minutes as she continued to stare at the plate. Finally, the hissing from the burner caught her attention and she wandered over to the stove, still fixated on the butter and now starting to feel the effects of the wine on an empty stomach. Disgusted, she turned off the burners and wandered into the bedroom, leaving the kitchen in relative disarray. It was only 7:30, but she'd had enough of today, so she undressed, leaving the clothes on the floor, and curled into a ball in bed.

The cold, dark room left everything to her imagination as she lay, numb, between the sheets. Slowly, mockingly, episodes of her life paraded through her waning consciousness to remind her of every challenge she failed and each goal that was unattained. The time she got caught lying to her parents to hide the fact she had gone to a party, the high school boyfriend who left her in the movie theater, the college formal for which she never managed to find a date, and the recurring inability to exercise an iota of control over her appetite all swam through her head in a deliberate, nauseating procession. There was no escape from it because the 'it' was her mind itself, and no amount of energy seemed to allow her to refocus its attention on anything else. It seemed only sleep could silence the derisive inner voice, but sleep would not come for more than an hour. In the interim, she suffered in silence, praying for some sort of help.

Surrounded by darkness, the only response she heard to the prayer was that she wasn't worth helping.

32.

Involuntarily, one eye opened and focused lazily on the digital clock. *3:37. Great, I'll never get back to sleep at this hour and I'm going to be tired all day.* Sharon stared at the ceiling for a while, thinking about last night's dieting crisis. *I guess that's OK, though, because what difference does it make, really? No one will care if I'm tired. It doesn't matter. They all know I'm a quitter, a failure. Who's it going to bother if I just lie here awake in bed until the alarm goes off? No one. If I stay in this apartment all day and tomorrow too, it won't change a thing. I don't matter.*

It wasn't like her to have so bleak an attitude, and part of her consciousness was troubled by this unusual nihilism. Another part was troubled by the fact that these dire thoughts weren't accompanied by an emotional response of self-pity, sadness, or even distress. Unfortunately, her inner voices of reason were relegated to the role of bit actors, almost impossible to hear above the din of her self criticisms. All the internal warnings which were meant to alert her to the fact that something was wrong with her line of thinking had become lost in the increasingly insistent sea of negativity.

I just don't matter. I don't even have friends who'd notice if I just disappeared. Of course, I don't have a place to disappear to. I could even.... No, that's not right. How would dying make anything better? It's just the quitter's way out.... But then again, that's what I am, really.

3:40. That's it, keep going. Another meaningless minute wasted in my life.

She turned over in bed but was equally uncomfortable. The image of the pot on the stove drifted through her mind. *Shit. I even screwed up cooking.* Robotically, she dropped a leg off the bed and slid her hips to the edge. Pushing her torso up deliberately, she stood momentarily, then shuffled into the kitchen where she stopped and stared at the mess she had left.

Well, what do you think of yourself now? There was no answer. Nothing came back within her. She felt numb. *I don't matter.* Part of her figured she should wash the pot, but she stood in place, not really thinking. Time passed but there was no inner monologue arguing for or against action until she noticed the kitchen knife on the counter. Her eyes locked onto it as graphic scenes played in her imagination. From behind herself and slightly above, she saw in her mind what looked like blood on her hands and she idly wondered if it was from her wrists or throat. It would be an easy way out, she knew, but her feet still remained planted. Finally, looking down at her hands, she saw the skin was unbroken and the knife remained untouched, on the counter.

Quitter.

Minutes crawled by before she finally turned around and wandered back to the bedroom, then into the bathroom. The mirror on the medicine cabinet revealed a three quarter length view of her body, and her mind distorted the image, brutally mocking her latest failure to lose weight. She studied the mirror, thinking about the warnings on the bottles of pills stored within, but even as she confronted her reflection with the mental image of a handful of white tablets, no one seemed to be looking back. Her blank eyes were looking through her, vaguely focused on some invisible scene that was yet to play out.

That's how worthless I really am. I just don't matter.

Her legs ached from standing still. She walked into the bedroom, scarcely noticing that her bare feet were now on the clothes she'd left on the floor last night. She could perceive almost nothing around her as her mind increasingly embraced the narrow, focused, bleak view of her life. Her eyes found the clock again.

4:16. Nothing matters.

Mechanically, she climbed back into bed and stared into the darkness, not even recognizing the absence of emotion after such stark contemplation of her own death. In the silence, she could feel within her chest the relentless beating of her heart. She waited for it to stop, but cruelly, it continued on its own, in spite of her.

33.

Jack was accustomed to waking up a few minutes before the alarm, but this morning he'd opened his eyes nearly an hour too early and he stared at the wall feeling far too alert. His thoughts turned to the study. *Come on, Jack. You know that depression is common, so settle down. I'm sure the California people will call you today and tell you that the guy who killed himself had a history of suicide attempts or something. Even if he didn't, how could this drug be responsible? Even drugs which are so-called depressants don't usually provoke suicide except in people who are already depressed, and there's never been any evidence that Ascendiac causes depression. In fact, most people seem to feel better when they're taking the drug! This has all got to be a coincidence.*

He turned to the right to watch his wife who was sleeping beside him. Her blonde, shoulder-length hair was spread out on the pillow slightly, and though it was a little tangled from the night's sleep, it still reminded him of a sunburst behind her head. He looked at her forehead which was smooth and peaceful at the moment. *Unexpressive, I guess, is a better word. Despite what the poets may think, all the "peacefulness" of sleep is really just an absence of animation and emotion. How strange that, as humans, we'd want to feel peaceful, but the way to achieve it is to give up emotions, the things which make us most human.*

Sandra's lips were slightly parted and Jack could just barely hear her breathing. He studied the shape of her chin and the way her cheek bones pulled the skin taught across her cheek, leaving the delicate curves which caught his attention across a crowded room so many years ago. In the ten years he'd known her, time had changed her body in countless ways, not the least of which was during her pregnancy. For all the differences, though, he was happy that the angular, self-assured chin had remained unblemished, and even in the early morning, without makeup, her face appeared as beautiful as ever.

As his eyes followed the jaw bone back to her neck, he realized that he was starting to feel aroused. He studied the graceful delicacy of her neck, thinking about how she moaned softly whenever he caressed her there, and how sometimes he'd tease her when he got home from work by greeting her with a kiss there, rather than on the lips. She'd start to melt in his arms, but before she could really enjoy it, Lisa would come bounding in to see her daddy. *God, we haven't had much time for ourselves since she came along, huh? How could we have let go of the days when we'd make passionate, spontaneous love in the kitchen while the food got cold on the table?* The sheets were pulled away slightly from Sandra's body, affording him a glimpse of the dark blue satin night slip that covered her breasts. He wasn't sure if he could make out the shape of a nipple in the dim glow from the hallway light he left on for Lisa's peace of mind, but his imagination was stimulated just the same.

He saw there was still about half and hour left before he needed to get up, and his hand started moving even before his brain had decided whether it was OK to disturb his sleeping lover. Reaching under the covers, he gently slid his finger tips across her belly, relishing the smoothness of the satin as it slid gently across her skin. As he reached the far side and moved slightly down to her hip, her eyes flickered briefly and she took a breath through her nose.

"Jack, what are you doing?" she asked, still mostly asleep. He didn't answer, but instead he moved towards her and kissed her lips. "Oh!" she uttered, now more aware of his intentions. Her right hand found its way out from under the sheets and onto the back of his neck as he pressed his lips against her face. "This is a nice way to wake up in the morning," she said in a sexy half-whisper as he moved towards her throat.

They were unconsciously careful not to make too much noise, but the attempt to be discreet made the act all the more exciting. They both achieved their pleasures simultaneously, in a way that only some longtime partners ever manage. Basking in the afterglow, wrapped in the other's arms, they laughed quietly together, acknowledging how serious those pleasures sometimes seemed.

Although they wanted the moment to last, the alarm eventually sounded, and Jack offered one final kiss before he got out of bed. He smirked, then said, "Not bad, but it needs a little work. How about we try again tomorrow?"

"Tomorrow you're going to be at your parents, remember?"

His tone suddenly got solemn. "No, I didn't, actually." They tried to divide the visits to the grandparents equally, and since they'd spent a few days with Sandra's parents in Virginia last month, they were supposed to visit Jack's in Pennsylvania this weekend. "This is really not a good time for me to be away. The Ascendiac trial is starting to get a little complicated and I'm not sure I can afford to be out of town."

"Well, they're your parents."

"Any chance you'd go with Lisa?"

"What, without you?"

"Uh, yeah, I guess. I mean, I know it doesn't sound like much fun."

"You know I love your parents, but I think they want to see you, too. You are, after all, their son."

"Oh, right, that's what I am," he said sarcastically, with a chuckle. "I know you're right. Look, let me see what we find out today, and I'll call my mom and see what she thinks. If they're going to be around next week or so, maybe we'll just change it to then. Otherwise, if you don't mind the drive, maybe you can just bite the bullet and suffer through a day of antique shopping with Lisa and her."

She wagged her finger sarcastically. "You just love the fact that you're on the cusp of finding a way out of going to the flea markets, don't you? OK, I suppose I could do that, but you'll owe me big for this one!"

"Right, like you won't spend the whole time talking about me with Mom anyway."

"Hey, if you're not there, it's your own problem!"

"You know, Sandy, you've made me a lucky man."

"Or at least a man who just got lucky," she joked.

Jack shook his head and walked into the bathroom, already thinking about the trial again. *How many more cases will we have to see before we call this thing off? Another suicide? Two hospital admissions? Five milder cases where people dropped out but basically got better after a few days of rest? Man, that's a slippery slope when we're not even sure that the symptoms are related to the drug. I guess we'll have to get a psychiatrist involved to give us a sense of how much depression we should expect to see in this population. One of the statistics guys will be able to figure out if our rate is higher than what we'd expect to see in that group.* He climbed in the shower and let the hot water pour over his back as he allowed his thoughts to drift. The lyrics to "Real World," a late 90's rock song by Matchbox 20 came to mind and he started singing as he soaped up the wash cloth.

The whole situation would be so much simpler if we just had some solid information. Everything we're trying to do is based on two cases and a number of drop-outs from the study. We need to know where everyone went.

Then maybe we can retire and the real world really will stop hassling me. Suddenly, he felt a sickening lump in his stomach. *Oh, damn it! I never called the New York site to find out if they have seen anything like this. If they're sitting on something they don't even recognize, we'll be crucified. All right, don't panic now. The enrollment numbers are still much smaller in Manhattan, so the odds are in our favor for now. I don't even know who our contact is, though. That's going to be the first order of business this morning. Maybe we can have a conference call between Joel and the New York guy in Dave's office. That way, there's no question that we're being totally open here.*

He turned off the faucet and waited a moment while the water worked its way out of the hair on his arms and legs, then he stepped onto the tile floor and began drying off in front of the mirror. With little fanfare, he shaved, combed his hair, and finished the standard morning routines before returning, naked, to the bedroom. Sandra had been energized by their morning passion and she apparently decided to get up and make some coffee in the kitchen, so Jack pulled on his boxers and started picking an outfit. He chose a conservative power tie because he knew that, if push came to shove, he'd need all the advantages he could get to keep Dave on the right side of the FDA.

He walked downstairs to find that Sandra had set the table for him and was busy getting his coffee. "Wow," he remarked, "I guess we should start every day like that."

"Yeah, you talk the talk, but let's see what you can deliver."

"Oh, a challenge, eh?" He kissed her and sat down to a bowl of his cereal. "Hey, I'm really sorry about tomorrow. This drug just has me worried, you know. I mean, it's my baby in a way, and if we can see it through the trial successfully, it'll mean a lot for all of us."

"I know, sweetie," she replied. "I'm not complaining because I know you've always made it your business to put your family first. It's not a big deal." She paused pensively. "I just hope you're not letting the money thing cloud your judgment though. I've never known you to be indecisive about anything, so the fact that this trial has you worried makes me think that you're not being totally honest with yourself about something."

"Well, it's not simple from any perspective. I mean, the company has invested a significant amount of money and manpower into this drug, too. We've got two main trial sites and they both took a lot of effort to get going. If we make a false move, all that goes out the window. Of course, if we don't act when it's appropriate, the whole company could be held responsible. What really bugs me is that we're trying to make this decision based on only fragments of information. We can't even tell if either of the people who turned up were on the drug at the time. I think it would be so much easier if there were a way to look at the whole picture at once, but that's life."

"OK, so don't worry about us for the weekend, then. Lisa and I will go to your parents' house and you try to sort this out. If you promise not to make a habit of it, I'll let you slide this time." She smiled at him, and he found himself thinking again how wonderful it was to have her in his life.

"I'll make it up to you, I promise." Standing, he put his arms around her waist and squeezed her tightly as he kissed her goodbye. "I'll see you Sunday. Drive safely."

"You too," she said, smiling warmly.

Jack climbed into the Porsche, checked that the gearshift was in neutral and cranked the starter. As the engine slowly settled into a rough idle, Jack dialed Dave's office number on his cell phone. After the announcement, he said, "Dave, Jack here. We need to meet this morning to discuss the developments in the trial with our New York people. Let me know how soon after eight-thirty we can get together." He remembered, then, that California was three hours behind which would preclude an early three-way conference call. "Well, California won't be in until later, but at least we can figure out what to do. Thanks." He hung up, then observed to himself, "...another hassle of the real world." He turned on the radio and decided the car was ready to drive, so he backed out of the garage and headed to work.

34.

It was quarter to eight, and Dave had just finished listening to his voicemail messages. The first three told him that the monthly board meeting had been moved, first to Thursday, then to Friday, then to the second floor conference room on Friday. Dave wished someone would finally get around to changing the format for these updates to e-mail so he would only have to read the most recent one to find out what he needed to know. As it was, he had to listen to two minutes of carefully articulated speech just to find out that the next message was another two minutes worth of changes. Such inefficiencies got under his skin. The next message was a wrong number, and the final one was from Jack. He eyed his schedule for the morning and saw that he had an eight-thirty meeting with the legal department to discuss the updated sexual harassment policy. The meetings were mandatory so that the company could limit their liability, and changing your scheduled time was simply not allowed. They were invariably tedious and painful, but Dave had read about enough lawsuits in the newspaper to know that the board couldn't afford to allow anyone to slip through without attending. He confirmed that it would take no more than 45 minutes, so he sent an e-mail to Jack telling him that he should be at his office by 9:25 to finalize the plan for the FDA and figure out how to get New York up to speed.

Since he was already on the computer, he clicked on the web browser icon and took a quick look through this morning's news stories before getting to work. In the Health and Medicine section he was shocked to see a story detailing Excella and their west coast trial of Ascendiac. As he waited for the story to load, he wondered how the reporters had heard about the potential problem with the high drop-out rate. *This could be a PR disaster if someone leaked sensitive information. It better not turn out to be an underhanded attempt to try to control the course of this trial.* Once he read the first few paragraphs, though, he realized that the story had nothing to do with drop-outs, but rather it was a recap of the morning TV show's report on the drug. At the bottom of the article there was a graph of the company's stock price, showing an 18% gain in value over the last three weeks.

He picked up the phone and dialed Bobby's cell. It rang three times before the call was answered, but Dave didn't hear anyone on the line.

"Hello?" he asked. "Are you there, Bobby?" He listened and thought he could hear indistinct talking in the background. A moment later, Bobby spoke.

"Yeah, it's me. I was in a meeting. What do you want?"

"Look, I need to talk with you. Where can I call you?"

"Don't. I'll call you in 10 minutes."

"I'm at the office."

"I know. The phone has caller ID." The line went dead.

"OK, goodbye then," Dave said as he put down the receiver. *Someone's going to have to teach him a little lesson about manners if he really thinks he has a future in politics.* He looked at the papers on his desk and decided that nothing was of a pressing nature, so he brought back the Lightfoot screen and checked out the new figures, which continued to show a strong recruitment effort and a significant drop-out rate. He idly moved the mouse around and clicked on one of the numbers by accident. A new window appeared next to the original one, with this one containing more details on the category he had inadvertently chosen. *Hey, I didn't know there was more to this. I wonder what else I can do.* He closed the new window, then tried clicking on the "lost to follow up" heading. Another new window appeared which contained several paragraphs of text at the top.

Reading it, Dave recognized that the text was from the New Drug Application that they had submitted to the FDA for the trial. It was a reprint of the study's "lost to follow up" definition as well as a brief overview of the approach they planned to use in order to treat the data appropriately. At the bottom was a button marked "Show Data," and Dave clicked on it.

The window's contents were replaced by a list, in alphabetical order, of all the patients who were currently classified as drop-outs. Dave clicked on one and the screen showed that patient's entire study record, including the responses to the screening questions, their initial weight, how many days they had received the drug and placebo, and any comments they made. At the bottom was a section where the investigators could enter information which was not specifically required, but which they thought may be useful. There was a considerable amount of information on the screen which Dave was trying to decipher when his phone startled him. He jumped slightly, moving the mouse to the edge of the screen as he turned to answer the call. The computer dutifully switched to the slowly morphing color screen saver which kept the monitor from damaging itself as a result of showing a static image for a long time.

"Hello, Dave Aswari," he said, once he'd regained his composure.

"So, how is your friend Jack holding up?" Bobby asked.

"What? Jack is fine. He's towing the line better than I had expected, but that's not why I called you." Bobby was already trying to get the upper hand in the conversation and Dave hated being manipulated this way. "The stock is up 18% so far, which is a decent profit no matter how you look at it. The thing is, the FDA is now getting interested in the specifics of the study and I'm not sure what they're going to find."

"Is there something you're not telling me, Dave?" Bobby asked pointedly.

"No, God damn it! Just listen for a minute. We think that the drug is fine but there are a few questions surfacing about possible side effects. It should all turn out to be nothing, but all of a sudden, the waters aren't that clear." He thought again about the scare he'd had while reading the Internet news headline. "All it takes is one news story alleging a problem and the speculative gain we've seen in the stock price will evaporate. It will eventually recover, when the drug hits the market, but I think you should protect your investments, if you know what I mean." *I don't even know why I'm beating around the bush here. I've already given him what would be considered insider information, so I should just make my point and get him off the line.*

"Shit. It won't be enough by Tuesday." Bobby suddenly sounded more like Dave's baby brother than the gangster he was trying to be when he called. It was so good to hear the old voice that Dave nearly missed his point.

"Wait, Tuesday? You really shouldn't wait the whole weekend, Bobby."

"Well, Mr. Financial Genius, our 'broker,' who funded the move, is out of town for a few days on business."

"Funded?" Dave's tone suddenly became more concerned. "What sort of investment arrangement did you make?"

"One that, if the price doesn't change by Tuesday, will show me about a 450% return on my investment. Not bad considering I only had to put up 10% of my own money, which I even got on credit."

"Are you saying you *leveraged* the deal? If anything happens this weekend, you'll never recover from it. I wish you had talked to me first!" Dave was stunned. Bobby had apparently borrowed nine times more money than he had access to, which probably came out to well over half a million dollars riding on the investment, Dave figured.

"I guess I didn't," Bobby replied in a very matter of fact tone. The gangster voice had resurfaced. "So, I suggest that you keep running a tight ship and on Tuesday, we can all forget this whole thing."

Dave didn't know what to say. He thought about the expected profit, which would be much more than Bobby had said he needed, and asked, "Why so much, Bobby?"

"What is the matter with you?" Bobby snapped. "Do you really think I'd be doing this if it were just twenty grand I owed? I knew you'd never help me if I told you the real figures. Now don't you or anyone else screw this up. I'll be watching." He hung up.

Dave stared at the phone, unsure of what to do about his brother. If their call to the New York site turned up anything even remotely suspicious, they'd have to involve the FDA or risk the entire company by keeping quiet. On the other hand, as soon as the Feds were involved, the news would spread to Wall Street immediately. Suddenly, everyone looked to Dave like a potential source of problems. Anyone involved in the study, including the research techs at each site, could bring them down with a single injudicious remark. *Too many variables. This thing is completely out of control now. The only thing I can hope for is to get a little insurance for myself.*

He stood up from his desk and walked to the door, trying to figure out where his escape route would be in case of trouble. He reflexively checked his watch and figured he had about twenty minutes before he needed to be present for the meeting. *That should be enough time.*

Although the various computer windows were hidden by the psychedelic color show, the Lightfoot data automatically updated themselves once again.

35.

By 9:20, Pearlene had started to worry a little, and when Alison came out of her office to get a cup of coffee, she called her over to the reception window. "Dr. Sonders, Miss Sharon didn't call you to say she'd be late this morning, did she?"

"No," Alison replied. "Why? She's not in yet?"

"No, Ma'am. She always calls if she's stuck in traffic, or if she's running late or has an appointment or something." She furrowed her brow. "Do you suppose I should call her at home? Maybe she slept past the alarm?"

Alison was trying to remember the specifics of her conversation last night with Sharon, but although the whole interaction had left her with a funny feeling, she still couldn't put a finger on any particular reason why that was. She wondered if she'd missed some underlying message. "Well, that certainly wouldn't hurt, I guess."

Pearlene picked up the phone and dialed Sharon's home number. After what seemed like an eternal series of rings, the answering machine picked up. Pearlene waited for the message to end, but before the beep, the office door opened and Sharon walked in, carrying a paper bag with her.

"Sharon!" Alison greeted. "We were starting to get worried and...." She stopped mid-sentence when she got a better look at her demeanor. "Sharon? Are you OK?" She was walking slowly towards the back office, hardly acknowledging Alison's question. In her right hand, she had a half-eaten donut, and the paper bag in her left bore the name of a local bakery. Her clothes were remarkably wrinkled, and Alison was pretty sure they were the same ones she'd been wearing yesterday. Her hair was unkempt and her makeup was smeared. Alison persisted. "Sharon, what happened to you? Did you not go home last night?"

"It doesn't matter," she replied almost inaudibly as she trudged past the two women and into the break room.

Alison turned to Pearlene and asked in a low voice, "Has something been going on that might make her act like this? Is she being abused or something?"

"Not that I know about, Doctor. She's been trying to lose weight recently, but that's all she's said. I don't know why she'd be eating donuts if she's on a diet, though."

"She doesn't... use drugs or anything, right?" Alison asked.

"Good Lord, no," replied Pearlene. "But now that you mentioned it, she had been in some experiment for losing weight. I think she said it was at the University Medical Center. I told her she shouldn't be letting them test things on her and she said she stopped taking the pills that very day. I think it was Wednesday. You don't believe that could be what's wrong, do you?"

"I have no idea. I'm going to go back and talk to her for a minute. I only have two patients today, right?"

"That's right. They're both in the early afternoon."

Alison nodded, trying to figure out what she was going to say. She trusted Sharon with her whole practice's business matters, but now she realized just how little she knew about the woman behind the title. She walked into the break room to find Sharon sitting at her desk with a whole bag of donuts in front of her. Her eyes were focused ahead, but it didn't seem that she was looking at anything in particular. Alison observed that Sharon's movements were calm and coordinated, making her feel a little more assured that she wasn't currently intoxicated. There were no obvious cuts or bruises, tears in her clothes, or other signs of a struggle. For all the oddity of her appearance, she just sat there quietly, eating the donut. When she finished it, she reached into the bag and took out another without even acknowledging Alison's presence.

Making sure she didn't appear confrontational and still unsure of what the underlying problem was, Alison slowly sat in a chair off to the side of the table. She decided to start with very general, open-ended questions. "How are you today, Sharon?"

Without looking at her, Sharon quietly replied, "Fine."

"You seem as though something's on your mind. What is it?"

"It doesn't matter," she replied slowly.

"What doesn't matter?" Alison probed.

"I don't matter." She finished another donut and looked down for a moment. The bag was nearly empty, and Alison figured she must have eaten about eight so far, given its size. "I'm such a failure." She started looking around the room as though she were trying to find something specific. Her eyes locked onto the knife they kept next to the coffee maker for cutting bagels.

Alison saw that she was staring at the knife, and she was relieved she had fortuitously ended up sitting between it and Sharon. "What are you thinking about now?" she asked. "Are you considering hurting yourself? Killing yourself, maybe?" It seemed pretty clear to Alison that Sharon was suffering from an acute depressive episode so the questions were routine but essential.

"It doesn't matter."

"You keep saying that, Sharon, but the truth is, it does matter. I think it's obvious that you're depressed right now, and that the depression is making it seem like nothing matters because depression changes your whole perspective on life. Now I don't know what may be causing you to be depressed and I won't promise that I can change whatever it is. Either way, though, it is important that you tell me if you're thinking of hurting yourself or someone else." Establishing a safety contract with her trusted office manager felt somewhat surreal, but Alison knew it was the right thing to do at this point.

"I'm a failure, a quitter," Sharon repeated to herself. She looked back at the donuts, ignoring Alison's attempts to redirect the conversation. "I'm worthless. I can't even stay on a diet." Another donut came out of the bag.

At this point, Alison knew that because Sharon wasn't agreeing to the contract for safety, there wasn't much choice but to have her admitted to the inpatient psychiatric ward for her own protection. Although the stress of approaching age milestones can sometimes cause depression, Alison was convinced that the onset was far too rapid and profound to be explained by that alone. Falling off a diet plan could cause a short-term change in attitude, but the depth of the depression also seemed to exceed what would be reasonable if this were the only factor. She decided that, once Sharon was safely admitted, she'd try to determine what drug trial she had enrolled in to see if there was any impetus to suspect that as a cause.

"Pearlene," Alison called gently. "Come here, please." She kept her eyes on Sharon to make sure she didn't attempt an escape or worse.

"Yes, Doctor?" Pearlene replied from the doorway.

"Call the inpatient ward and let them know I have an admission for a one-to-one observation bed. I'll also need an orderly here now, OK?"

"Yes, right away." She left the room and Alison slowly stood up and walked over to the knife. She picked it up and put it in the back of the drawer where it would be much harder to grab in a scuffle. Sharon stayed in place, staring at the wall and showing no sign that she was even conscious of her surroundings.

"Sharon, I think you should spend some time with us while we help you get this sorted out. We're going to keep you safe while we work through this together. I know it must feel awfully dark and lonely where you're at, but I promise that we'll be right here with you. Depression takes away your perspective and makes everything seem worthless, but it just isn't true."

Sharon remained seated, motionless, and only dimly aware that Alison was even speaking to her from outside the suffocatingly narrow, black tunnel that had become her world.

36.

"Dave back from his meeting yet," Jack asked Laura, "or are we alone here?" He raised his eyebrows suggestively, then chuckled.

"He should be back any minute, but that'll probably be enough time for you."

"Ouch! I was trying to be pleasantly flirtatious and that's what I get?"

"Hey, a girl has to protect her reputation. Besides, didn't you go to that sexual harassment meeting yet? That's where Dave is now."

"No, my number isn't up until next week some time."

Just then, Dave walked around the corner. He was carrying a small grey plastic box which had some wires dangling from one side. "Good," he said, looking at his watch. "Let's get on with this." They both entered the office and Jack shut the door. Dave sat as his desk and put the grey box next to the phone. It appeared to Jack to be an electronic device of some sort, and he watched as Dave started attaching the wires.

"Is that an answering machine?" Jack asked. "I would have thought the voicemail was enough of a hassle without a machine, too."

"It's a little different," Dave replied cryptically. Now tell me.... What is it, exactly, that you're trying to accomplish with this New York site phone call again?" His eyebrows were lowered slightly as he tried to take the offensive.

"Well, I think it's pretty important that they know we're dealing with the FDA to satisfy their demands regarding surveillance of the drop-outs. I also think it's in our best interest to make sure that both study sites have all the same information so that, in hindsight, we don't look like we tried to keep secrets. As it stands, we don't even know if New York has seen any cases of patients who develop depression, but if they have and we don't know about it, we're going to be hung out to dry by the FDA. Since Stanford has reported a possibly serious side effect, I think it's imperative that we involve New York in the investigation."

"OK, but let's make sure we have our terminology straight. We don't think that depression is a side effect since that should be reported in the daily checkup logs, right? I think it's important that we keep to the facts, and the fact is that we have a higher than average drop-out rate, and we're trying to establish whether these people are dropping out because they are more likely to be depressed, possibly due to frustration with dieting."

"Yes, that's a reasonable spin on the question. I don't think we're causing depression either, given the data we have so far. I am a little worried, though, when I think about what to do if we find more cases. How many before we decide it's enough?"

Dave looked up from his wiring job and admitted honestly, "I just don't know." He shook his head slightly, then continued. "I guess at some point it will be obvious that we have to sit down with the FDA and our statisticians and try to sort this out. I just don't want to screw this up before we know there's actually a problem."

"I agree. I've got the number of our New York site coordinator in my e-mail account so I'll get it and call him now." He walked around the desk to Dave's computer and moved the mouse to turn off the screen saver. The colorful display was immediately replaced by several Lightfoot windows which Dave had left opened. Jack stared at the screen for a moment, trying to make sense of what he saw. Suddenly, he realized what he was looking at. "What the hell is this?" he uttered.

Dave had his head under the desk, trying to plug in the new machine, but when he heard Jack's voice, he had the sickening realization that he'd carelessly left the Lightfoot windows visible again. He panicked and grabbed the nearest plug, yanking it out of the wall. Unfortunately, the plug was for his printer, leaving the computer screen completely untouched. In the process, he hit the back of his head on the desk, and when he finally extricated himself, his eyes were watering from the pain.

"What are you doing with this information?" Jack demanded. "This is supposed to be hidden. If *they* knew you had this, we'd never get a study in the United States again!"

"For Christ's sake, calm down, Jack. The information is secure and nobody is going to know about it. If you think it will invalidate the study then just forget you ever saw it, OK?" He started rubbing his scalp, then stopped to check his hand for blood. It was clean, so he went back to rubbing.

Jack wanted to say several things at once, but he paused for a moment to collect his thoughts. "Have you been following the study all along?" he asked.

"Yes, pretty much," Dave answered, his tone having switched from irritated to guilty.

"And you know which arm people have been in when they dropped out?"

"Do you really want to know? I mean, don't ask me questions if you're just going to say that you know too much now and we have to call off the study."

"Dave, I'm really on our side on this. I... I just didn't know we had access to this sort of information. Let me think for a minute." The silence was palpable as Jack tried to figure out how to handle this revelation. "You're probably right. Don't tell me anything more for now and we'll see what happens. But Jesus, Dave, you can't be leaving something like this in plain sight. You know we have unannounced inspections from time to time."

Relieved but just a little suspicious that Jack was willing to overlook this so easily, Dave agreed. "You're absolutely right, Jack. I won't run it again."

"Yeah, that's probably a good idea.... Well, I guess if you don't tell me specifically what's going on, though, it shouldn't matter, really. I mean, it would be pretty helpful to know we could keep an eye on things." Jack was privately desperate to know what the numbers showed and if there was an association between the drug and the drop-outs, but he was fighting the urge to ask. Eventually he shook his head. "All right, let's just get on with things now." He clicked the mouse a few times until he got to the phone number he had set out to find. He dialed Dave's phone and sat back down in the chair.

"Hello, this is Gheena with the Ascendiac weight loss study. How can I help you?"

"Hi, I was trying to reach Doctor Todd Ulster."

"May I ask who's calling?"

"This is Doctor Jack Finnegan. I'm calling from Excella Pharmaceuticals."

"OK, doctor, I think he's still in his office. Hold on a moment, please." After a pause, Jack heard the phone ring again.

"Hello, this is Todd Ulster." The voice sounded slightly pressured, as though the call had come at an inconvenient time.

"Hi, this is Jack Finnegan from Excella Pharmaceuticals. I'm the physician in charge of the Ascendiac trials."

"How did you hear about this already?" Todd was clearly surprised by the call.

"Uh, hear about what?" Jack asked nervously.

"Our second admission. Is it just a coincidence that you called now?" He was now more puzzled than surprised.

"It must be. What's happening there?"

"Probably nothing, really, but I just got a call that one of our study patients was admitted to our hospital with an acute depressive episode. We had one other who was admitted here, also for depression, last week, but we sort of wrote that off because he had a history of it. The new one is apparently the secretary or something for one of our psychiatrists, though, and she called to find out if this was a side effect of the drug. She said the patient had never been depressed before, but about two days after withdrawing from the study, she sort of crashed."

"Wait," Jack interrupted, "she left the study *before* the symptoms?"

"Yeah, apparently a few days before, but you never know if it's some sort of residual effect or something. Of course, we don't even know if she was taking the drug or placebo at the time."

"Well, is she doing OK?"

"I don't know," Todd replied. "I was on my way over to see her now, then I figured I'd call you to find out if this is something you've been seeing in the patients. Don't you have a site in California?"

"We do, at Stanford. They think they had one or two cases of depression, too, but in looking at the total number of patients enrolled, it was hard to tell if it was within the expected range for that population."

"I would figure it is, but this psychiatrist was pretty inquisitive and it got me wondering if there was a relation. Oh, she wanted to talk to someone at the company, so I found your number in the site resource package and gave it to her. She said she'd try you today. Anyhow, if you didn't call for that reason, what did you intend to talk about?"

"Well, we've been a little surprised by the high drop-out rate and we wanted to try to follow up with people to see if they left the study for reasons that need to be addressed."

"I wondered that, too, the first couple of times I studied diet drugs. I'll tell you, though, from my experience it's a real hit or miss kind of thing, not unlike dieting itself. I think the numbers are within expected limits for weight loss studies."

"Just the same, the FDA wants us to document that there aren't any underlying problems, so we're planning on contacting the drop-outs for a sort of surveillance study. The computer can provide us with the data we need in order to call them, but we thought it was best to let you know what we're doing so we're all on the same page, so to speak."

"Knock yourself out, Jack. Hey, I'll tell you, though, I think you've got a real blockbuster here. The ones who finish the study have been raving about this drug. They not only don't feel hungry all the time, but they actually seem to feel *good* while they're dieting. If this goes through, I might just have to open a weight loss clinic so I can keep up with the prescriptions!"

"So you don't think there's any problem with the drug, then?"

"What, because of the depression? It's hard to say for sure, but I don't think I know of a drug that *causes* major depressive episodes like this. Most depressants *act* like depressants first, but Ascendiac doesn't have any Valium- or alcohol- type effects. And since it's not a stimulant, it seems unlikely to be a stimulant-withdrawal type of depressive reaction, either. I don't think there's any reason to link the two at this point."

"Great. Well, let me know what you find out about this woman, OK? We'll keep you in the loop in case we find something during our surveillance."

"Good talking with you, Jack." They hung up.

Jack rubbed his temples. "I didn't think it could get more frustrating, but it did. They have two patients who were admitted with depression during the study, and they're practically bookends for the ones in Stanford. One had a history of depression, the other apparently didn't. This guy, Todd, has apparently studied several weight loss drugs and he thinks that the numbers are about what could be expected for this patient population."

"You don't want to stop the study, do you?" Dave asked nervously.

"I don't *want* to," Jack replied. "The woman who was admitted in New York works for a psychiatrist, and Todd said she's going to call me. I can't imagine what she'll tell me that will sway my opinion, but I'll see what comes of that. In the interim, we probably need to continue our efforts to contact the drop-out to see what that uncovers. Maybe the

Stanford people have tracked some of them down and we can go from there." Jack paused for a moment, wrestling with the next question. "*Were* they on the drug?" he asked sheepishly.

"Damn it, Jack, why do you keep asking?"

"I'm human, Dave. I want to know what's going on here. Were they?"

"No, most of them weren't. In fact, it looks like they all lost weight during their week on the drug, then they switched to the placebo for a few days, then they dropped out. That's exactly what your man, Zach, did, as well."

Jack couldn't decide if that made him feel better, but he was pretty sure it had to be a good sign. "Huh," he mumbled, scratching his cheek. "That's not what I expected you to say." He turned towards the door, less certain than ever about the next step.

"Let's just proceed cautiously here so we don't make a mountain out of a molehill," Dave said.

"I just wish I knew what 'being cautious' meant in this case," Jack replied.

37.

Getting Sharon admitted took a good part of the morning and now Alison was behind on her office paperwork. She generally set aside Friday mornings for administrative duties so that she'd have a shot at enjoying the weekend, but between the lectures, the text book chapters, and the various other activities she managed to get involved with, she often spent part of her Saturday mornings working as well. *I'm sure I'll end up driving back here tomorrow to see how Sharon's doing, so I can squeeze in a few hours of work then.*

Alison had full admitting and patient care privileges in the University Medical Center, but she decided it was more prudent to have one of her colleagues take charge of Sharon's care. It is generally agreed that, in order to ensure that the doctor remains objective, physicians should never treat family members or close acquaintances. There is no strict definition of 'close,' but when there was a grey zone, Alison always thought that the more conservative approach was the safest. So, she called Harold Regan, one of her own mentors from residency who also had privileges at the UMC, and he said he'd be happy to involve himself in Sharon's care. She discussed the scant facts of the case with him when he arrived at the ward, and he promised to spend a few hours with Sharon that afternoon to try to determine the cause of her illness. For now, he started her on a promising cocktail of antidepressants, combining a next generation selective serotonin reuptake inhibitor with an older, broader spectrum tricyclic antidepressant.

When they were first marketed, the tricyclics were a major break-through in the treatment of depression since they needed to be taken only once or twice a day, they had relatively mild side effects such as sleepiness and dry mouth, and they were capable of improving symptoms in 4-6 weeks. These drugs blocked nerve cells from scavenging free neu-rotransmitters from the brain, thus greatly increasing the amount of epi-nephrine, norepinephrine, and serotonin molecules available to stimulate nerves. They were the mainstay of treatment until the early 1990's when another drug called fluoxetine revolutionized the field again. Marketed under the trade name Prozac, it represented a new class of drug which selectively enhanced the function of the neurotransmitter serotonin. Not only were the side effects of this new class of antidepressants less severe, but the patients also showed marked improvement in just 2-3 weeks. Furthermore, while the tricyclics could be toxic in overdose (an unfortunately common problem associated with depression, both as a suicide attempt and as the result of memory disruptions from the illness itself), the selective serotonin reuptake inhibitors, or SSRI's, as they were generically known, showed much larger safety margins.

Prozac and its chemical cousins became so popular that they almost reached the stage of designer drug, being prescribed for every minor variance in mood. Their market value soared, but their true medical importance was still rooted in their ability to help relieve the crippling symptoms of severe, major depression. As physicians sought to improve the efficacy of these drugs further, several different combinations of medication were tested in an effort to magnify the speed of recovery. Many psychiatrists found favorite drug mixtures and dosing schedule which they employed heavily in their practices. Harold's preferred approach seemed as reasonable as any, and Alison was glad he decided to begin immediately with combined medical therapy given the speed of onset and severity of Sharon's symptoms.

"Pearlene," Alison said as she walked back into the office from the UMC, "I'm going to come in tomorrow to get some of this work done. Would you mind collecting the billing information from this week so I can figure out what Sharon managed to get done and what I'll need to handle. I don't know how much she was able to do for the last few days." A feeling of guilt came over her as she realized that her own office manager may have been exhibiting signs of a mental illness that she completely missed.

"Oh, of course, Doctor Sonders. I think she said she was still using the old billing program for the time being so it should be easy to tell where she left off. How is she doing now?"

"Well, depression is tricky. It can take a few weeks to recover, and sometimes even longer. We started her on the standard medications and Harold Regan is with her right now. I think she'll do well, but it may be a little while before we see any significant improvement."

"You know, Doctor, I really appreciate you taking care of her. She's such a sweet woman, I'd just hate to think anything bad happened to her."

"I would, too, Pearlene. What time is my first patient?"

"Miss Yulli is coming at 1:30. I took the liberty of ordering your lunch for you. It should be here in a few minutes."

"You're the best, Pearlene. I've got a phone call to make, then I'll come out and maybe we can sit and eat together."

"That's a nice idea, Doctor."

Alison closed her office door and sat at her desk. She found the number for Jack Finnegan and dialed his office. After a few rings, Jack answered.

"Hello, Doctor Finnegan, this is Doctor Sonders calling from the University Medical Center. I understand you're in charge of the clinical trials of a weight loss drug?"

"Yes. Are you the psychiatrist whose patient was just admitted?"

"I am. Did Doctor Ulster contact you already?"

"I spoke with him this morning, actually, and he mentioned that you might call. What can you tell me about this patient?"

"Not a lot, really. I was hoping you might be able to help me. Her name is Sharon and she's my office manager. She has apparently been dealing with a few minor personal problems lately, largely related to the fact that she's approaching thirty. Although it's been on her mind, she gave no indication that she was experiencing any significant depressive symptoms beyond what would be considered a completely normal attitude. Yesterday, though, she came to my office after hours, to ask me for some advice and support. It seemed reasonable at the time, and although she was clearly concerned about something, she lacked any definitive criteria for Axis I or II mental health diagnoses."

"I see, Doctor. Tell me, has she ever been treated in the past for depression?"

"You can call me Alison. No, she denied prior treatment or symptoms. Although I didn't suspect anything yesterday, it's still so routine for me to ask those questions that I got at least a brief history from her, all of which was negative for mental health symptoms. Anyway, this morning, she showed up to work in the midst of a full-fledged depressive episode with all the classic symptoms: Minimal physical energy, a melancholic and flat affect, paucity of speech, lack of interest in her physical appearance, and so on. I caught her eyeing a knife, and when I asked her to make a contract for safety, she simply ignored me. I had her admitted to the inpatient psych ward for one-to-one nursing, and she's starting a medication regimen now. That's when a friend of hers told me that she had been taking your weight loss medication. Apparently, she enrolled in the study at the beginning of the week, but her friend talked her into quitting the trial the other day. I was just wondering if you have seen anything like this in any of the other patients."

Jack's scientific conscience was beginning to nag him again as he continued to wrestle with the question of whether the depressions were possibly related to the study drug. He hesitated before responding. "I wish I could give you a clear answer on that, Alison, but it's actually hard to say. As you know, the population we're dealing with here has a high risk of depression to start with, given that most of them have spent their lives being overweight and dissatisfied with their appearance. There is going to be a significant fraction of patients who have underlying symptoms which become apparent around the time they are in our study. We have seen two such patients so far, which is probably a smaller number than we would expect given the size of our study groups."

"How about patients with no prior history, though?"

"So far, just your patient and possibly one other," Jack said, wincing when he reminded himself that the other was forever silenced by a rope.

Alison was beginning to think that Jack was merely a company tool, shielding the business at all costs, and her mounting frustration got the best of her. "With all due respect, Jack, I get the feeling that you're not being completely forthcoming with me. I understand that your company needs to protect its interests, but I'm talking about a human being here, not some money-making cosmetic drug. I don't mean to be blunt, but if you can't help me, would you mind letting me talk to someone who can? I am worried about this young lady, and I need to know if her suicidal depression is related to your drug, OK?"

Her directness and obvious concern for Sharon caught Jack off guard. *Have I really been that isolated from the patients that I stopped thinking like a doctor? Dave, Stephen, the study coordinators, and even that graduate student in Stanford who found Zach... none of them are really taking care of these people directly. All of these people have wives or husbands or family members who expect us to watch out for our study patients, but the only thing we're actually looking at is a list of numbers. Maybe what we need is a real, live clinician to give us perspective again. Hell, I needed to speak with an expert in depression anyway and this psychiatrist seems motivated enough that she might be willing to help us just out of professional courtesy. Of course, I'm sure anything I tell her will be probably be confidential corporate information, and there's no way Dave is going to authorize any outside involvement no matter what I say. How does that old adage go? 'It's easier to beg for forgiveness than ask for permission.'*

"Your office is in Manhattan, right?" Jack asked.

"Yes, at the University Medical Center, but I don't see what that has to do with Sharon."

"I'd like to come talk to you about her, and the sooner the better. Do you have any time that we could meet?"

"Well, I have a lot of work I need to do today but I only have a couple of patients to take care of this afternoon. Hang on." Alison checked with Pearlene, who told her that she'd have some time after four, but it would cost her tomorrow. She clicked back on the line. "Can you get here by four?"

"Absolutely. Look, I'm sorry we all sound cagey, but this whole FDA approval process is very tricky. We really do want to succeed with this drug and we'll obviously never do that if we put patients at risk, so Sharon's well being is really in our best interest. I'll tell you more this afternoon."

Alison was skeptical, but she had never seen a pharmaceutical company react in such a personal way before, sending a physician to her office to speak with her. She figured it was either a genuine act of concern or there was a very big secret they were trying to hide. Whatever the case, she decided it would be in Sharon's favor if she could get more information about this mysterious medication. "OK, Jack, but I expect you to be open and honest with your data so that we can better treat this woman. If you're not, I'll go over your head to get the information I need."

"I'll see you at four," he replied and hung up. As he thought about the specifics of the meeting, he started to get nervous again. *Breaching corporate nondisclosure agreements can lead to termination, remember. You'd lose your job, the stock options, and everything else you've been working for, so I really hope you know what you're getting into.* He punched in Stephen's extension and waited for the answer. "Yo, Homie, I need you here for a few minutes. Got some time?"

"Uh, sure thing, Blood," he replied sarcastically. "Do we have to keep up the Gen X lingo, though?"

"No, that's about all I know, really." He hung up and started typing at his computer, looking through some of the preclinical and phase I trials of Ascendiac. He stopped at one which was the first to show an association between the new serotonin receptor and the experimental compound EP-792 which was later given the slightly sexier moniker, Ascendiac. After a brief scan, he decided it might be useful so he clicked the print button and waited for it to emerge on paper.

"Jack, what's the story?" Stephen asked from the doorway.

"Come in and shut the door. I just got a call from the psychiatrist whose office worker got admitted for depression. Seems she was in our trial for a few days, then got talked into dropping out. Two days later, she got admitted to the psych floor, so the shrink calls us up to ask if there's an association between the two. Apparently, this woman has no history of mental health problems."

"We still don't know if she was on the placebo or drug, of course."

"True, but the point is this: She wants to talk to us about Ascendiac and depression, and we really need some insight into both as well. Either they're related or they're not, but I just don't know yet. Anyway, I have an appointment with her at four and I want to get a folder with a decent array of papers so I can show her the basic science behind what we're doing. You know this literature as well as I do, so I could use your help. Plus, it will take a while to print all this stuff out and collate it intelligently."

"I appreciate the backhand compliment, but why are you printing them all out? I thought I'd finally managed to make you paperless, and you go and shatter my image of you! Here, watch." He displaced Jack from the computer and started typing. A moment later, he had accessed a web page which was titled, "Excella Pharmaceuticals Medical Reference Library."

Jack raised his eyebrows. "Can anyone get access to that?"

"No, that's why it's asking for a password. You just type your name and password here, and you get a secure link to the whole reference library. There aren't any corporate secrets stored in this server, mind you. The Internet is only so good at keeping things safe, so the files only contain published data and non-confidential internal information. It will give you what you're looking for, though, and you can even access some of my data through a little Java program I inserted in my home page.

That way, you'll be able to get the virtual 3-D images we were playing with the other day, too."

"OK, Boy Wonder," he said sarcastically, "just write down the web address for me, then. I can't be expected to remember *everything!* That's why I have you." He laughed.

"What are you going to tell the shrink?"

"I'm not sure, yet. I need to feel things out a bit. If she seems genuinely cooperative, I think I'll try to get a sense of how many people she'd expect to see develop symptoms of depression given the patients we have. If not, I guess it will just be a PR gesture to keep her from running to the FDA just to stick it to us."

"For what it's worth, I'll keep my cell phone on. If you need to extricate yourself at any point, call me and I'll try to cover for you."

"That's probably smart. *Looking* guilty can be worse than *being* guilty, so I should keep a few escape routes open." The phone rang.

"Jack Finnegan."

"Jack, it's Joel Williams from Stanford. Look, I wanted to update you on our drop-out follow-up."

"Bad news?" Jack asked nervously.

"Well, it doesn't clear anything up. We contacted about 80% of the people so far, and most of them withdrew for personal reasons. I think they're just the ones who got frustrated, like we figured. Then we started going door to door to find the rest, with much lower success percentages, but with more pathology. We found two people with histories of depression who were tearful and frustrated, but functional. They were out of the study for more than five days, though, and they felt they were getting better just using their usual therapies. These two basically said that this happens to them almost every time they diet, so we pretty much felt OK about them. A third wasn't so simple, though. This person's father answered the door, and he said that his daughter was still in the hospital six days after being admitted for depression. Her husband had found her at home, lying on the sofa, surrounded by half-eaten plates of food. That morning she had seemed distracted but otherwise normal, but when he found her in the afternoon, she was almost catatonic. The father said all this was new for her, and they are justifiably concerned. We called the hospital but we can't get much information about her because of confidentiality issues. It would be easier if she were here, but the family had taken her to a local hospital closer to their home."

"So you found one with a new onset depression, but there are some people still unaccounted for. They could have a similar story or worse, I guess."

Joel agreed. "That's what worries me the most. The ones we can't find could be the worst cases, but they're either in the hospital or not answering the door and phone for one reason or another." The implication was grim.

"All right. Keep looking, Joel. I've got an appointment with a psychiatrist today and I'm going to try to figure out whether we have any reason to think this is related to the drug. Call me immediately if you find any more of the new-onset patients, OK?"

"We'll do that. I've also got our nurses screening for depression, both before and during the study. They're asking a few extra questions so that we can try to keep tabs on this. Hopefully we can pick up on mood changes before they become profound and maybe that will give us some insight here. I still don't understand how the drug could be related, though."

"Neither do I, but we can't afford to find out at the expense of our patients. Thanks, Joel." They hung up and Jack dialed Dave. "Dave, it's me. Listen, I just got a call from Stanford and they have another admission for depression. The patient went into the hospital about a week ago and apparently is still there. The problem is that they can't find a few of their drop-outs which is exactly what might happen if they had also become profoundly depressed."

"Do you think they're *all* getting this depression thing?" He asked incredulously.

"Well, most of them did drop out for other reasons, which we were able to confirm. It's just that, if the few remaining people all have the same symptoms and we didn't find out, we could be in serious trouble here."

"What are you suggesting, Jack?"

"Nothing yet, but I think we're on the verge of having to make a move. I know the implications, but if a few more cases surface, we're going to have to intervene. I've got a contact in the field of psychiatry and

I'm going to speak with her this afternoon to see what her thoughts are regarding dieting and depression."

"Remember to keep it clean. You can't be discussing the details of an ongoing study, especially one with corporate implications like this."

"Yeah, I know. OK, I just thought you needed the heads up on this. So far, everyone seems to be willing to explain it as coincidence."

"Just be sure that you don't make *any* moves before you clear it with me, got that? It's for your protection, too, Jack." He hoped this reminder would be persuasive enough to keep him on top of the information chain.

"You're the boss. I don't want that responsibility right now, trust me." They hung up.

38.

"So, Thomas, how was the didactic session today?" Harold asked, knowing full well that the Chairman of Psychiatry, Samuel Northrop, was delivering the medical student lecture that afternoon. Sam gave one lecture every month to the students rotating through the psychiatry wards, and it was always on his own favorite topic, electroconvulsive therapy, or ECT. He took them through the history of shock treatment, starting with the early, sinister days when it was employed more as a punishment than treatment. Without supporting evidence for its use, it was administered indiscriminately to thousands of patients, many of whom were women, to "treat" anxiety, depression, personality disorders, schizophrenia, and almost any other mental health ailment known. Without the aid of modern anesthetics, the treatments were painful and dangerous, with many people breaking teeth or bones during the electrically induced seizures.

As a result of the unscrupulous application of ECT, it fell out of favor, no doubt aided by the movie *The Snake Pit*, which brought its abuse into the limelight. Fortunately, it was never entirely forgotten, and as hard, scientific data eventually accumulated from carefully designed studies, it became clear that ECT was one of the most effective treatments for severe depression. In the days before the oral medications, it established a small niche in medical science. Furthermore, with the advent of short-acting muscle paralytic medications and intravenous anesthetics, the more dangerous side effects of ECT were severely curtailed, thus magnifying the therapeutic benefits. Even now, ECT is considered the first line therapy for certain types of depression, and its success in terms of speed of recovery and overall remission rate is yet unrivaled by even the newest medications and psychotherapy. One of the biggest impediments remaining for its current use is the lingering stigma attached to the treatment itself.

"It was really amazing," Thomas answered enthusiastically. "I didn't even realize that we still used ECT, much less how valuable it can be. Dr. Northrop had some fascinating case reports that he's collected over the years."

"That's great to hear. Sam has been giving that lecture since I was a medical student, and when I heard him speak, it was probably the first moment in my medical school career when I thought about being a psychiatrist. I credit him for single-handedly convincing me to join the department here. Anyway, while you were away we added a patient to our roster. She's an employee of a colleague of mine, but I want you to be with me when I examine her."

"What's she got?"

"Well, let's just say that this is a medical student diagnosis, OK? It's one of the more profound cases I've seen in a while, and I believe you'll see why we consider it such a devastating disease when you see it's true form, rather than what the popular press would have you believe is true."

"All right, well I'm ready for the challenge."

"Good. Let me tell you a few things first. She's not on any sedatives right now, but I have started her on some oral medications which won't have started to affect her just yet. She has no previous medical history of note, and specifically no known psychiatric history. Apparently, earlier this week she was asymptomatic, and her current state developed over about a 24- to 36-hour period. As an outpatient, she takes no medications, but she is reported to have been enrolled in a weight loss trial during which time she may have received a few days worth of an experimental medication, although she may have just been getting the placebo."

"Sounds like a mystery already."

"In a sense, it is. Let me ask the questions now, and we can talk about her after we leave, OK?"

"Of course."

The locked psychiatric ward of most hospitals is fundamentally very different from the other wards. Entrance to the ward itself is carefully controlled, with two sets of locking doors preventing entrance or exit without both a key and a closed-circuit TV clearance from a guard. The floors of the ward are carpeted and there are large central areas where group meetings can be held. The furniture tends to be large and comfortable, helping to invite patients out of their rooms and into a more social environment. The patients themselves look different, since most of them wear street clothes and walk around inside, untethered by intravenous drips. The individual rooms are similarly decorated, with armchairs, carpeting, and pictures in most rooms.

Other, more subtle differences are even more telling. The windows, with tough plastic rather than glass panes, only open a few inches, reducing the risk of jumping. There are no dangling curtain cords, no telephones, no electrical wires, no shower curtain rods, and no exposed pipes in the ceilings from which someone could hang. The doors to the room and lavatory do not lock from the inside, but the room door can be locked from the outside with a key, when necessary. Also, the beds, which more closely resemble household than hospital ones, have reinforced metal attachments in several places to which leather restraints can be fastened to control violently agitated patients while emergency medications are taking effect.

Sharon's room had one further addition: A full-time orderly was assigned to watch her every minute of the day. She was considered to be at high risk for a suicide attempt, and the most effective way to prevent her from succeeding was to keep a person next to her around the clock, with one-to-one attention. Sharon was sitting in the armchair, staring blankly at the wall across from her. Harold and Thomas nodded to the orderly as they entered and sat on the bed, across from Sharon, who failed to acknowledge their presence. Despite her apparently indifferent state, Harold treated her as though she were listening to him. It was an approach that had been taught to him, and he felt that this sort of conversation helped give his patients a sense of familiar ground so that they would have some reference point from which to find themselves again.

"Hello, Sharon, I'm Doctor Regan, remember? I brought a friend with me named Thomas Sullivan. He's a medical student and he's going to help me take care of you today." Sharon didn't react visibly to the introduction, but Harold proceeded, undaunted. "Now, Sharon, part of what we're going to do today is what we call a history and physical exam. I'll be telling Thomas things from time to time so he can learn how to take care of patients. Let's start with a few questions about your medical history. Have you ever been in the hospital before?"

Again, there was barely a hint of reaction to the question. It appeared as though she was completely unable to perceive Harold at all. Without missing a beat, Harold continued. "Good, so you've been healthy most of your life. Are you currently on any medications?" Still nothing. "None, fine. How about any other products such as medicinal herbs or folk medications?"

The questions continued despite the fact that Sharon seemed to be disconnected from the interview. Thomas was puzzled, but he held his questions as he was told. Finally, Harold sounded as though he'd reached the end. "Now, before we examine you, I have one more question for you, and it's a difficult one so I want you to think about it before you answer. How are you feeling today?"

For a moment, Sharon's eyes moved towards him, then they drifted back to the wall again. Thomas was so surprised by this that he couldn't decide if he had merely imagined it. Harold nodded knowingly to him. The physical examination was unremarkable, revealing normal heart and lung sounds, adequate vital signs, and intact reflexes. The entire process had lasted twenty minutes, and at the end, the two nodded to the orderly and left Sharon, who had not moved perceptibly during the time they were present.

Outside the room, Harold and Thomas walked to the office to discuss the interview out of the earshot of other patients. "So," Harold began, "what do you think?"

"Well, I thought she was a catatonic schizophrenic until that one moment when she seemed to look up at you. She didn't have the characteristic waxy posturing, either, so I don't think that's the right diagnosis. Then I started thinking about drugs that can cause a dissociated state, but she didn't seem to be looking around at hallucinated things, so I thought that wasn't likely, either. I mean, it's like she wasn't really listening to you at all, except for that one time, when I really think she was. I don't know what to make of it. Was she faking the whole thing?"

"Malingering is always a possibility, and some patients have been in and out of the hospital so many times that they learn most of the tricks. It can occasionally be very difficult to pick out the malingerer from the real patient, but in this case, without a history of that sort of behavior and without any obvious secondary gain, I don't think that's what we're dealing with here. But, that's why I wanted to show you her examination. Sharon has many of the classic symptoms of severe major depression with melancholic and some catatonic features. It's one of the most pronounced cases I've seen recently, mainly because the onset is usually over a much longer period of time, during which patients generally receive some sort of treatment. It seems that every general practitioner prescribes antidepressants these days, so we don't often see someone as far along as this."

"That's *depression?*" Thomas asked incredulously. "No wonder ECT is used to treat it! I can't imagine she's even able to eat in that state, much less take oral medications for three weeks as they slowly start to work."

"That's actually a very astute observation, Thomas. Her symptoms are pronounced enough that she's a good candidate for it. Usually, we'll wait 48 hours to see if there's any noticeable change in her affect — God knows we've been wrong once or twice about drug use — but if she stays this bad, I'd argue to start ECT sooner rather than later. OK, since you'll be following her with me, why don't you write up the history and physical we just did, then take some time in the library and read up on depression. You can present her on rounds tomorrow."

"Absolutely! Thanks, Dr. Regan. I'll see you tomorrow, then." He headed out of the office.

39.

The white Ford Taurus stopped in the parking lot while the driver pulled out a piece of paper from his shirt pocket. The numbers on the license plate and the description of the car matched the ones on the paper, which he quickly folded again and returned to his pocket. He eased the Taurus through the aisles and parked about a hundred yards away, careful to choose a spot that gave him a clear line of sight to the target. It would only be a matter of time before the owner, a Jack Finnegan, according to the paper, would be leaving work.

Sitting in the parking lot, the Taurus was about as inconspicuous as a car could be, with a body style so ordinary that it blended into the scenery as though it were camouflaged. The tinted windows and quiet V-6 motor attracted little attention, and there were no chrome pieces or flashy mag wheels to make it stand out in a crowd. It was the ideal stake-out vehicle, in short. The interior was navy blue, making it just that much harder to see inside clearly, but its large windshield afforded the occupant a broad panorama of the outside world.

The driver was a stocky man in his late 30's, with dark, thinning hair and bushy eyebrows above intense, brown eyes. He wore a blue short-sleeved shirt even though it was March, and a necktie that was years out of style, giving him the unfashionable appearance of a laborer-turned-manager, resulting in a level of anonymity unmatched except by his car. His eyes, however, told a different story, even though they were disguised behind a pair of fake glasses. They never stopped moving, searching the horizon then scanning closer, watching everything within sight. They were the eyes of a great hunter, and great hunters required patience, vigilance, and cover so that, when the unwitting quarry finally appeared in view, he would instantly be ready for action.

Today, the quarry arrived earlier than the hunter had anticipated.

...

Jack pulled out his car keys and unlocked the driver's door. He walked around the car to check the tires, then climbed in and started the engine. It was a habit he'd developed years ago, after wrecking a passenger-side wheel because a tire had gone flat while he was at work. The leak started in the morning and was slow enough that he couldn't hear it when he got out of the car, but by the end of the day, the tire was completely empty. Since he was driving alone, he never saw the passenger's side, and although he'd only driven a few hundred feet on it, a shallow pothole bent the rim before he recognized the problem. The replacement wheel set him back a cool $650, which was a costly enough lesson to convince him to check the wheels before he drove. Satisfied that the tires appeared fine, he sat back in the driver's seat and waited for the engine to settle into a regular idle.

Frowning to himself, he considered the trip ahead of him. *This would have been a real mess if I hadn't weaseled my way out of seeing Mom and Dad today. Sandy's right, I do owe her one for this. I guess it will all pay off once we get this drug trial over with.* He shook his head. *I can think about that later, though. Now, I've got to figure out how to handle my little improvised meeting. I guess the biggest problem at this point is figuring out how frequent this sort of depression is in overweight people, and from there, we can figure how many of our patients we'd expect would have these symptoms in our study regardless of whether they got the drug or placebo.*

The engine had warmed up, so Jack shifted into reverse, backed out of the space, and drove off towards Manhattan. The weather had cooperated that day, so he unconsciously pushed the speed up a little, enjoying the drive while he mulled his work issues. Meanwhile, the Taurus moved from its spot only after Jack had turned onto the public road, and it followed him from a generous distance.

Of course, no matter how we figure it, Dave says these people were all in the placebo arm of the trial, so I just don't understand what I'm looking for here, unless there were some sort of mistake or something.... He groaned out loud as he hit the rim of the steering wheel with his hand. *Yeah, or something like data tampering, maybe? Jesus, how could I have missed that? All along, we've been wondering which group these drop-outs and people with depression were in, and now it turns out miraculously that they're* all *in the placebo arm? I can't believe that didn't make me suspicious! The other day, Dave asks if it would matter what group they were in, knowing full well we'd be hard pressed to blame the drug if all the patients were getting the placebo when the depression hit. Today he shows me a screen full of data that he claims are the real results and I start believing his story that everyone has been off the drug for a few days!*

The frustration began to build as he chastised himself for even listening to Dave's alleged representation of the data. *Damn it, Jack, there's a good reason scientific studies are carried out the way they are, and this is what happens when you think you're smarter than the collective experiences of everyone before you.* It took him a few minutes to calm his emotions, but when he did, a new thought struck him which was even more troubling. *So, let's say that Dave was lying about the data. Does that make the drop-out and depression problems any easier to understand in the context of the study? After all, Dave couldn't change the specificity of the drug for its target receptors, so even if these people were getting the drug rather than placebo, it shouldn't make a difference. I guess the only real difference would be that, if these people were, in fact, getting the drug, we'd stop the study sooner to find out what was happening. Either way, with everyone in one group or the other, I don't see how it makes much sense. Of course, if this is just a coincidence, we'd expect the people to be split about evenly between the groups.*

The more intensely he thought about this, the more his speed crept up. There was something soothing to him about the way the car slithered around turns, changing direction effortlessly as he piloted it along the wooded highway. All the miniscule corrections in steering, changes in the pressure on the pedals, and the occasional gear shift occurred in a thoroughly unconscious plane, freeing his mind with every drumming of the tires over the expansion joints. Even reacting in a blind curve to the two slower cars ahead which were driving side-by-side required little thought, with the right foot gently tapping the brakes and instantly scrubbing 20 miles per hour off his speed. Jack was so focused that he completely missed the State Police car hidden on the roadside, zapping the passers by with invisible radar. Fortunately, the traffic had pushed his speed down near enough to the legal limit that he didn't even trip the radar gun's alarm, which the trooper had set to 69 miles per hour for this assignment. When the cars ahead returned to single-file, Jack eased left and drove on.

...

The Taurus' speedometer read 82, but occasional bursts into the high 90's were required to keep up with the Porsche while remaining far enough back not to attract attention. Convincing a family sedan to cruise smoothly around slower traffic required a much heavier foot, but the car was up to the task of just keeping the Porsche in sight on the straight-aways, although it disappeared each time the road curved. The driver was getting used to navigating the bends at uncomfortable speeds despite the howling of the tires around each. There was enough noise from them that the radar gun's alarm was entirely superfluous as he tripped the gun at 78 miles per hour. The car was far enough back from the shoulder that even the hunter didn't see the ambush until it was much too late.

Most people instinctively tap the brakes when they know they've been caught speeding, announcing their guilt to the constabulary. The Taurus driver knew better, and he kept his eyes on the road but immediately lifted his foot off the gas and shifted the automatic transmission out of overdrive to slow the car as much as possible. It was a game of psychology at this point, but even a brief stop for a traffic violation would mean losing the trail he'd been following. He pulled out his cell phone and prepared to place a call in the event he was sidelined. A quarter of a mile later he saw the flashing lights on the side of the road, but mercifully, the officer was already busy writing a ticket for another unlucky motorist. The radio message from the upstream partner about the speeding white Taurus was never received.

Relieved, the driver shifted back into overdrive and resumed his pursuit.

...

Jack was still contemplating the upcoming meeting. *This should be easier than I'm making it out to be. I'll give her the pharmacology data we have, which is all at the FDA anyway, so it's not secret. When she sees how the drug works and how meticulous Stephen was with his computer modeling, it should be a done deal. What more can we give her, anyway? It's not like we're hiding something here. If she has questions about the other patients, she'll have to understand that we can't divulge patient information, and anything else she wants to know about the drug itself, I can probably tell her. And, if Dave was actually lying about the data, I just wish he had spread out the patients into both groups. It's so hard to explain away findings when they're all concentrated in one arm of the study. If they were more random, it would actually look better for the drug.*

His thoughts drifted as he continued the journey across the George Washington Bridge and into New York City, and he never saw the stealthy Taurus which now kept about a block or so behind him. When he arrived at the University Medical Center, he followed the signs for the garage and parked inside, in a corner spot so that the car wouldn't be damaged by a neighboring car's door which might be carelessly opened.

He consulted the signs for directions to Alison's office, and headed towards her building.

...

The Taurus stopped on the street outside the parking garage and the driver pulled out his cell phone again, dialing with one hand as he watched for Jack through the window.

"He's in New York City now. Just parked at the University Medical Center. Should I follow him in?" He listened to the response. "OK. I'll advise when he reaches his next destination." He hung up the phone as Jack emerged from the garage, and he tracked him carefully as he walked along the street and eventually disappeared into the crowd.

40.

By 4:00 p.m., most of the office staff had left for the weekend, but Dave was busy finishing the proposal for the FDA to satisfy their concerns about the Ascendiac trial drop-outs. Two confirmatory phone calls and three faxes finally settled the last of the minor issues, freeing him up to contemplate the latest data from Lightfoot. He couldn't see any significant changes from the last time he'd looked, and the weight loss numbers continued to be promising. He shut down the program and started poring over a memo from Stephen outlining a new project he was proposing. Outside, the office had quieted down enough that the phone startled him when it rang. He pushed a button on the new box and picked up the handset.

"Hello?"

"What's he doing in Manhattan?"

"Oh, Bobby, it's you. What's who doing in the city?"

"Don't play games, Dave. Your man Jack is at the University Hospital now and I want to know what he's doing there!"

"That's one of our study sites, and I guess he's just checking in on them." The conversation already had Dave nervous. *How did he know where Jack was? I didn't tell him that, and I don't think I even said where the study was being done.*

"Don't lie to me, Dave," he snarled. "If he's going to screw this up, I can't let him. I told you, nothing can change until Tuesday, and I mean it, so tell me what he's doing there, God damn it."

"I told you," Dave said, though his voice was becoming more strained, "he's just checking on the site. We've had a few people from the study who got admitted to hospitals and he's trying to find out if there's a connection between them and the study, that's all. He told me this afternoon he needs to meet with some of the doctors there to find out what they think is happening." His palms were starting to sweat as he waited to hear Bobby's response. *Does he have someone following him? If he does, what if he figures out that the person Jack is seeing isn't someone from the drug study? But wait, he doesn't know who's performing the study anyway, so how could he know that? I'm getting paranoid here. I've still got the upper hand, so I have to calm down.*

"Just understand that nothing changes until Tuesday. It would be a shame if he didn't understand that and something happened to him, you know."

"Is that another threat? Because if...." He stopped talking. *What was that? I know I heard something. There's someone outside my office. Jesus, does he have someone following me, too? It could be a cop or one of his new goon friends from the mob.* His heart rate had leaped up to 140. *He can't come after me, I'm his brother! What the hell is he thinking?*

"Because what?" Bobby retorted.

"Uh," Dave stammered, "I mean, we're *brothers*, Bobby. What's gotten into you? You're really scaring me, man."

"Then I guess you're starting to get the picture." He hung up.

Dave was panting, and beads of sweat were starting to appear on his forehead. He put the phone down gently and pressed the button on the machine again. Then he took the tape out and searched around his desk for a suitable container. He found a small, nondescript brown envelope which was large enough to hold the tape and he quickly slid it in, closing it with the attached string.

The sudden knock at his door sent a bolt of fear through his chest. He threw the envelope into the back of his desk drawer, wiped his forehead, and desperately tried not to let the terror show through. As a last ditch effort, he picked up the phone and dialed security. As the call was going through, he called out, "Yes, who's there?"

The door handle turned slowly and the door started to swing open. "Hello, security, what do you need?" he heard on the phone.

"Yes, hi, it's Dave Aswari in the Channing building." Dave could see part of the person opening the door now. It was a middle-aged man wearing a dark shirt and pants, and he was pulling a large trash barrel behind him.

"Just h-h-here to empty t-t-the trash," the man said as he walked over to Dave's desk. His stutter was significant and Dave was sure he had never seen the man before. He was bracing himself for some sort of surprise, although he wasn't even sure what it might be.

"Sir," the security officer said, "can we help you?" There was a note of irritation in his voice. The janitor picked up Dave's garbage and dumped it into his can.

"Yes, um...." Dave stalled, hoping to keep the man on the line until the janitor left. "I was just wondering, um, when the last time the fire extinguishers in this building had been inspected." The janitor looked around the office slowly, ostensibly searching for other trash cans. "You know," Dave said to the janitor in a voice loud enough to be heard over the phone as well, "I don't think I've seen you here before."

"N-n-no? Well, I've s-s-seen you," the janitor replied. He turned and pulled his trash barrel out of the office, closing the door behind him.

"What's that?" The security officer asked, still sounding annoyed. "Seen who?"

Dave tried to cover himself. "Oh, the janitor was just here. New guy, I guess." He could barely think straight.

"Yeah, well, I don't know much about the fire extinguishers." His tone conveyed copious irritation. "If you really need to know, you can call the maintenance department on Monday, OK? We're security."

"Right, of course, maintenance. OK, well thanks." He hung up and tried to stop his hands from shaking. *What did he mean, 'He's seen me?' Was he trying to tell me something, or is he just a janitor that I've never paid attention to before?* He looked around the office, trying to decide if he was being watched somehow. Nothing appeared out of the ordinary, so he opened the desk drawer again and picked up the brown envelope. *How am I going to keep this safe in case I need it? The first place he'd look is my house. He's already got Jack in his sights, so that's out, too. Come on, think. Where could I store this so he can't find it, but I can get to it if there's a problem.* He sat still, thinking for a moment. *Ah, that'll work.*

He slipped the envelope into his pants pocket as he dialed the phone. His mother answered. "Hi, Mom, I'm glad I got you. Listen, I was wondering if I could stop by tonight and pick up some of my CD's. I'm finishing up the entertainment room and I realized I didn't have all of my music yet.... Yeah, around seven, maybe?... What are you making?... Sure, I'll have dinner there, then." *If I'm there for dinner, maybe it won't seem suspicious.* "OK, I'll talk to you later." He put the phone down and pulled the tape out of his pocket again. On the label, he wrote, "Jailhouse Rock," trying to enjoy the irony as he dropped it back into the envelope. *I don't think your political aspirations will survive the public release of this baby. Putting it in my old tape player in the basement is the way to hide it in plain sight!*

He sat back in the chair and tried to regain his composure as his eyes fell on the phone line tape recorder and its empty mechanism. *That looks a little strange, being empty like that. Doesn't Laura have a radio by her desk? I wonder if she's got any tapes so it's not so obvious I've taken this one out.* He walked to the door and peeked outside but didn't see anyone. The radio, which Laura had locked to her desk, had a tape in it with a symphony by Strauss. Dave snatched it from the player and walked back into the office, closing the door again. He put the tape in the machine and closed the cover.

Now, what am I going to do about Jack? He realized his options were pretty limited until the tape was safely stored somewhere. *Bobby didn't say he was going to do anything if he's not provoked, so Jack should have some time. It's going to be tricky to explain to him anyway because he already thinks I'm only interested in the bottom line here. All right, one thing at a time, then, and remember to stay calm.*

41.

"Hello, may I help you?" Pearlene asked in her polite, receptionist tone.

"Hi, I'm Jack Finnegan. I have an appointment with Dr. Sonders for 4:00."

"Yes, Doctor, she's expecting you. Please have a seat and I'll let her know you're here."

Jack looked around the cozy waiting room and realized that he had once envisioned a similar room for his own patients. While he was in residency, he never expected there would come a day when he would have "sold out," as the feeling was then, and gone into the business side of medicine. He noticed the personal touches such as the water cooler and the paintings on the walls. They weren't exactly fine art, but Alison had insisted that they all be originals which she bought from local, unknown artists for bargain prices. Even the furniture was comfortable, a drastic departure from the usual waiting room seats, and the whole effect was very soothing and homey.

"Hello, Jack. I'm Alison. We spoke on the phone." Alison was walking out of her office and extended her hand to him.

"I seem to recall," Jack said, chuckling and shaking her hand. "I just don't remember you looking so attractive on the phone." He was very good at benign flirting, but it was always a big risk when meeting female physicians for the first time. Patients, nurses, and ward secretaries routinely assumed women in white coats were nurses, a stereotype which was difficult to overcome. Even name tags were ignored, and when female nurses wanted to be especially catty, they would intentionally treat female doctors with a surprising lack of respect. Alison had stopped counting the number of times a nurse would turn to a male physician, in her presence, and question an order she had written, as though it wasn't good enough until it had come from a man. As a result, anything that could be interpreted as gender biasing could easily result in resentment and mistrust.

Alison, however, was flattered by the compliment when she saw Jack's wedding band. "Oh, I hadn't mentioned my looks?" she said jokingly. "Anyway, I don't want to take too much of your time so let's talk business, shall we?" She invited him into the office and he had a seat as he took in the décor. The dark wood paneling and large rug made it feel like a study, intimate enough for private conversation but yet academic in a way that kept the mind on the work at hand. He wondered if psychiatry residency had a rotation in interior design, since it seemed each nuance was carefully aimed at making the room a more effective place to dabble in the inner psyche.

"OK, so I'll give you a little background," Jack started. "The weight loss trial your patient was in is investigating a new drug we call Ascendiac. Excella Pharmaceuticals developed the drug using a model of a newly discovered serotonin receptor which was isolated as a result of the Human Genome Project. With a computer model of the receptor, we created a molecule which can bind to the new serotonin receptor sub-type and enhance the binding characteristics for its natural target."

"There's a new serotonin receptor, now?" Alison asked. "I haven't read about that yet. As I'm sure you know, serotonin is intimately related to mood, so I am surprised I haven't heard about it."

"To be honest, there isn't much written yet. We first learned about it from some colleagues at Yale who began studying its distribution in the human brain shortly after the gene was discovered. They took fresh cadavers, sectioned the brain into thin slices, and stained it for these new receptors, which showed up in a few, very reproducible places in the brain. So far, I think our company is the only one to have suggested a possible biological purpose for them, and because it's been the target of our drug design, we have been a little reluctant to make our findings too public. Unfortunately, that's how the pharmaceutical industry works, unlike academics, where there's a much freer dissemination of new information." The last admission stung since physicians are taught to value information above all else. The fact that potentially important discoveries would be kept secret for business reasons never pleased him, but secrecy was the only way a company could protect its intellectual property from being pirated by others.

Jack explained the evidence suggesting that the new receptor was related to eating and specifically to the feeling of satiety, and he took her through the experiments they had performed to prove the correlation in both mice and humans. He also told her how the company had succeeded in making a drug capable of binding to a location on the receptor which was not the place where serotonin bound, thus preserving the basic functionality of the receptor. Patients would continue to have hunger feelings, but the receptor would increase its apparent sensitivity as a result of the drug's presence, thus making the difference between hunger and satiety shorter, diminishing appetite. The drug's long half-life, he added, would stretch the dosing interval to twice a day, making the drug easier for patients to take.

Listening intently, Alison took in all the information Jack could provide. She was extremely knowledgeable about receptor physiology, so her questions were precise and succinct. When her attention turned to the information about the receptor locations, Jack asked if he could use her computer. He pulled the web address out of his pocket and typed it into her browser, bringing up the Excella page Stephen had showed him. A few minutes later, he had pulled up the Yale paper, complete with the pictures and graphs.

"I'd like to read this, if that's OK." Alison said.

"Of course, take your time," Jack replied as he re-read the abstract on the screen. "It's been a while since I've seen the original report, so I'll read it with you."

She was a quick study, Jack realized, as she'd click to the next page before he'd finished three quarters of it, and this was her first exposure to the topic. When she got to the illustration, she clicked on it, but nothing happened. "Is there a way to see the rest of their data? They included this sample photograph of the brain tissue they examined, but I'd like to see the other brains they stained as well. If you're right about them being involved in satiety, they would represent a whole new subsystem of the brain that has never been described before. It's really a stunning finding, given how little we know about the brain's physical organization." The neuroscience discussion was becoming very exciting for Alison and she had temporarily forgotten that the reason Jack was there was because her office worker was seriously ill. For all the triumphs of modern science, the human brain has managed to thwart almost all attempts to discern its architecture and function. Crude maps can be made of certain functions, such as where vision or movements are processed, but even these are extremely schematic. Emotions seem to be processed by several parts of the brain known collectively as the limbic system, but to find such a specific and basic function associated with a precise area was remarkable.

"Hmm. I don't know that I've seen those myself. This is the actual article the Yale guys published, so I guess I'd have to have them send us their original data. Let me see if I can call their lab. I think I've still got the phone number on my computer." He moved back to the keyboard, opened a new window, and logged into his home page then clicked through his phone book. "OK, here they are. Can I use your phone?"

"Of course. Just dial '9' first. Would you like me to wait outside."

"No, that's fine." He dialed the lab's number and the phone rang several times before it was answered.

"Hello, this is Chris," Jack barely heard over the background din. It sounded like they were having a raucous party, and Jack briefly wondered if he'd dialed the right number.

"Hi, I'm looking for Roger Pullman. Is this the right number?"

"Yeah, hang on a sec." The noise became slightly muffled, though he could clearly hear Chris shout Pullman's name at the crowd. There was a click, then a muffled, "I've got it." The background noise diminished significantly.

"Hello, this is Dr. Pullman."

"Roger, this is Jack Finnegan from Excella Pharmaceuticals. Am I interrupting something?"

"Jack, how's it going? No, we have a little party every other Friday here. Keeps up morale, you know. A few of us buy some cases of beer and pizzas for the graduate students and they all blow off a little steam. Also fosters some inter-lab discussions. You'd be amazed at how many new ideas pop up during these things. Anyway, how's the work coming on your new drug?"

"So far, we've been impressed. We're already in phase III trials, if you can believe it, but that's why I'm calling."

"Wow, I know we have different time frames in academics, but kudos to you for turning this finding around so fast! How can I help you?"

"As with any large scale trial, we've encountered a few strange responses in our patients. I'm working with a psychiatrist right now and we're trying to determine whether there's any neuroanatomical reason to suspect the drug." He winked at Alison to emphasize the overstated collaboration he described. "Anyway, we figured we'd act like good scientists and start from the beginning, with the hard data. Is there a way I can get the pictures of the rest of your brain sections from that mRNA study you first did?"

"You guys are really digging deep, eh? Let's see, I think that study was one of the first we did using our digital imager. Hang on here, it should still be on our server." The music was still loud enough in Roger's office that Jack couldn't hear him typing. "OK, yup, here it is. They're big files because they're at full resolution. Do you have a high speed Internet connection or are you using a modem?"

"No, I don't think it's a modem." Jack looked at Alison who shook her head.

"All right. I'll put copies of them in a public folder and you can look through them all you want. Are you at the computer now?"

"Yes."

"Type this address into your browser." He had to repeat the extended address twice before Jack got it exactly right. A long list of files appeared on the screen, each with a cryptic name consisting of a few letters and several numbers. "Each one of those files is a separate slice, OK. The first three characters identify the patient, and the next three numbers indicate the slice. The higher the number, the more rostral the slice, right to the top of the cortex." Jack had to remind himself that rostral was the opposite of caudal, and meant 'closer to the top of the head.' It was one of those annoying medical terms that seemed like it could be replaced with a more common word to make everything easier to understand.

"Great, Roger," Jack said. "Now, don't let me keep you from your hard work up there!"

"Yeah, this is really brutal. The grad students have a gentleman's agreement that they won't allow any leftover beer. I spend most of my time making sure they can still walk home, although we do have couches in the lounge that come into play occasionally." They both laughed.

"I'll call you next week to let you know how things are going, OK?"

"Thanks, Jack." They hung up.

Jack checked his watch and was amazed to see it was already after five. The discussion with Roger about pizza had made him hungry, and he figured it could be at least another hour or two before Alison was through looking at the data from Yale. "This may sound a little sacrilegious given the purpose of this drug, but I suspect we'll be here for a while, going over the slides. If you want, I'd be happy to order us some dinner."

"That's very thoughtful, Jack. We actually have a break room in the back and there's even a computer there that we can use. I've got a menu from a good Thai place around the corner, if that suits you."

"Great. Why don't you order so you can give them the right address. Do they take credit cards?"

"I think so, but I'll check."

"Order either way. I've got some cash on me, too." They picked their dishes and Alison phoned in the request.

When she hung up, she said, "You know, I really appreciate the effort you're making here. You still haven't told me whether Sharon's case is unique, but I'm guessing you've seen this before and you're trying to figure out what to do next. Even so, I feel like I'm doing everything I can do for Sharon, and that's important to me. She's been a faithful worker and even though she only came to me a few days ago to talk about her personal problems, I feel like she's one of my patients now."

Jack was suddenly a little embarrassed to have had his intentions read so clearly. *These shrinks can be pretty astute when it comes to motives, huh? I'll have to remember that.* He cleared his throat uncomfortably. "Yes, well it's a reasonable question, and the answer is that we have had two other admissions this week for depression. Both of those patients had no history of it, as far as we could tell, and both presented with pretty acute and profound symptoms." He looked down. "Also, one person seems to have committed suicide, but there was no note and no indication what the reason was."

Alison didn't react to this the way Jack had expected. "You know, people don't think of depression as a dangerous, life-threatening disease the way they think of heart disease or cancer. As it turns out, it's even worse. Severe major depression has a 15% mortality due to suicide alone. That's one in seven who dies from it, and many of them are young — in their 20's, 30's and 40's. Now, if your study is attracting people at higher than average risk of depression, then maybe it's just chance that you got four of them. Arguably, chronically overweight people may be at higher risk, although the cause and effect isn't as clear as people might think. Tell me, do you believe that people are overweight because they're sub-clinically depressed and as a result, they overeat, or do they overeat, then feel depressed because of it?"

Jack thought for a minute. Both sounded reasonable, but he couldn't decide which was more likely. "I guess I always thought it was overeating then depression, but I'm not so sure now."

"Don't feel bad, Jack, because *no one* has answered that question yet, although most people think the same way you do. Thing is, that's probably just a cultural bias. If you look at cultures where weight gain is socially desirable, people you'd call overweight are much less likely to feel depressed than people of the same weight in societies that value an athletic, low-fat stature. Notice, though, that I said, 'feel depressed.' Just feeling depressed isn't the same as having a diagnosis of major depression, although it's definitely one of the symptoms. If you compare cultures and the relation between weight and a diagnosis of major depression, the numbers are virtually identical on both sides. The *disease* major depression is very different than simply feeling blue."

"I have to admit, I wasn't thinking that clinically about things."

"Hey, that's why I have a job, right? Now here's why I'm so interested in your work. For the first time, we may have a way to tease apart the influences of hunger and satiety from depression. You see, there's a growing feeling that overeating and major depression may actually sometimes be *the same disease,* rather than a cause and effect as I suggested earlier. If it is, then having a drug capable of curing just one symptom— in this case the overeating— would have no direct effect on the other symptom of depression. On the other hand, if the two are dependent on each other, then altering one side could result in significant changes on the other. Your drug may be that magic bullet, so to speak, and it could give us some very helpful insight here."

"For what it's worth, we've gotten some subjective feedback from our patients and many of them report feeling better in one arm than the other. We wondered if it's that they were getting slightly depressed while in the active arm of the study, and when the drug was withdrawn, they were improving. However, according to the people at our study sites, it's actually an improvement in mood during the week they seem to be losing weight."

"I'm sure you see how that doesn't answer any of the questions we have, right? You could be seeing the result of effective dieting if it's a cause-effect relationship, or you could be seeing the direct suppression of depression if the two are more closely related. Of course, we're still talking about mood rather than the disease major depression."

Jack, frustrated by his failure to keep that distinction straight, shook his head. "I'm sorry I'm having trouble keeping that subtlety in mind. I think we are so hopeful that this drug will work that we've been explaining away our findings using simplistic models."

There was a knock at the outer office door, and Jack stood up. "Saved by the bell!" He walked to the front, paid the delivery man, and followed Alison to the break room where they laid out the spread.

Alison smirked as she took the opportunity to return a little of the flirtatious attitude Jack had displayed earlier. "Does your wife mind that you're spending Friday night eating take out in a New York City psychiatrist's office?"

The question caught Jack off guard and his face became much more serious. "Actually, she's at my parents' house with my daughter. I was supposed to go, too, but I'm concerned about these people and I realized that, at heart, I'm still a physician. Sometimes, you've got to make sacrifices for your patients."

"Tell me about it," she replied as they started to eat.

42.

The dashboard clock read 6:32, but the man in the Taurus had gotten out of the car about half an hour earlier. The sun was setting and it was getting harder to see faces from across the street so he was paying more attention to the cars which were exiting the garage than to the people who were constantly passing by. He wasn't sure how much longer he'd be there, but he knew that at some point, concentration lapses, especially in the dark and comfortable confines of the car. Caffeine was out of the question, too, given the fact that he couldn't afford to leave to answer nature's call. So he stood next to the car with a street map spread out on the roof, pretending to search for an address while he watched and waited.

A bodega behind him was selling fresh fruit, among other products, and he decided he'd be able to maintain a clear view of the garage if he purchased a snack there. Eating an apple was a very natural-appearing reason to be standing on the sidewalk next to a car, so he picked out a large, red one and paid with a bill. He dropped the change into a collection jar in the store and returned to the car with his food. He habitually left all change behind and he never carried more than one key in any pocket so that he could walk more quietly.

Shortly after his arrival, he had taken a quick look around the garage to ensure there were no other exits. Finding only one, he decided there was no chance he'd miss the car when it left, and he knew better than to call in to reconfirm orders despite the unexpectedly long wait. His only surprise when his cell phone began vibrating was that it took them that long to try to contact him for an update.

"Yes," he answered tersely.

"Where are you?"

"Same place. He hasn't come back yet."

"What? Not yet?"

"No," he said with a bit of attitude.

"Do you know where he went?"

"Inside." It was an intentionally meaningless answer, suggesting that he knew his job, and his ability shouldn't be questioned. The caller seemed to get the point.

"Shit. All right, well just stay there until he comes back. He's got to go home some time."

"You're the boss." The line went dead.

43.

It had taken Dave an extra forty minutes to reach his parents' house because he took several back roads and made a handful of intentional U-turns to try to be certain he wasn't being followed. When he finally reached their driveway, he figured there was nothing more he could do to ensure he was alone, although the fact that there was a car behind him at the final turn still unnerved him slightly. It was a tense drive for that reason, and he was relieved when he finally killed the ignition in the driveway. He hadn't heard himself yelp when the ringing of his phone startled him.

"Hello?" he asked nervously, after seeing that the caller ID was private.

"You're a tough one to catch up with," said the female voice. "I've been trying for half an hour now."

"Who is this?" he demanded.

"Oh, I'm sorry. It's Missy. We met for a drink last week and we were going to try to get together again tonight. Did I catch you at a bad time?"

He took a breath and remembered who she was. It was originally an arranged date through a friend. She worked for an advertising company with an office in New York, but most of her work was actually done at a graphics house in New Jersey. She had seductive eyes and a pretty smile which he now recalled he had desperately wanted to kiss at some point during the evening, but the moment never arose. He had intended to call her on Wednesday to make plans, but now, all that seemed so distant. "Missy, yes, I'm sorry. I've been getting these, uh, sales calls and I thought it was another one."

"Oh, I hate those, too. Don't worry about it."

"Yeah, well, I'd love to make plans but I can't tonight. Something came up at work and it's going to keep me pretty late, I think."

"That's too bad," she said, obviously disappointed. Normally, that would have been a big turn-on for Dave, but his mind was on other matters. "OK, well, do you want to try another day?" she offered.

"Another day... yeah. Let me call you back, OK? Maybe tomorrow or the next day. I'm sort of busy right now."

"Sure... Well, I hope it all works out for you."

"So do I. Goodbye, then." He hung up before she could respond. A moment later, when the phone rang again, he assumed she was calling back because he'd been so abrupt. "Hi, sorry about that. I'm just thinking about something else is all."

"You'd better be thinking about what your friend is doing in New York for all this time," came Bobby's response. The sound of his voice made the hairs on Dave's neck stand up. "What sort of an idiot do you think I am?"

"What's the matter now?" Dave asked, trying to level the field by coming on a little strong.

"Oh, getting tough, are you? Why has he been at the Medical Center for three hours, huh? What sort of a site check takes that long?"

"I don't know, Bobby. I'm not a physician and I've never been involved in one of these drug studies before. I told you we're having problems with this drug and it probably takes a long time to debrief these people and keep them from canceling the study themselves. Remember, they're trying to help other people and they get very nervous when serious problems crop up. Maybe compassion is a sentiment you should work on for your political campaign."

His approach seemed to be working because Bobby was momentarily speechless. "Don't screw with me, Dave...."

"Or else what?" he interrupted. "Tell me, what are you going to do? You had your chance, Bobby. I don't know what's gotten into you, but I'm not playing by your fucked up rules any more. If Jack thinks this drug needs to be pulled, then we're going to do what's right for our patients and our company. I'm still hoping that things will work out because it will be good for our business and it will get you off my back, but I've had it with you as a person. And if you really think you'll have any future outside of prison after the recordings I have of your phone calls get out, then put your money where your mouth is." He pressed the 'end' button on the phone, then he turned it off completely. His hands were shaking considerably but he felt like he'd won that battle, although he had the vague feeling that Jack may still be at risk. He tried to concentrate but he couldn't decide how to deal with that problem right now.

There was a knock at his car window and his heart was in his throat as he looked up slowly to see his mother's face in the window. He opened the door to hear her say, "Are you going to stay in there all night or what?"

"No, Mom, I just had to take that call. I'm coming."

44.

The labeled slices of brain were exactly as interesting to Jack as the file names that identified them. Alison examined slice after slice, eventually focusing her attention on roughly the middle third of each set. It contained the highest proportion of positive areas, and it was apparently a good cross-section of the bulk of the limbic system. Even with a high-speed connection and a fast computer, they were covering only one patient every fifteen minutes or so. Each file had, associated with it, a comments section which described an assortment of details about that particular experiment. The date and time the study was performed, the operator, any procedural notes, and occasionally some other descriptions were included with each image. The primary worker was a graduate student named Vincent, according to the files, and he seemed to be getting more efficient as the study progressed. In the beginning, he was imaging one brain every four days, but by the middle, he was doing two at a time, every other day.

"I bet old Vincent never figured anyone else would be reading this stuff," Alison commented after reading an especially long discourse on the benefits of a new software patch that had apparently been installed.

Jack was amused by the conversational nature of the notes as well, and added, "I kept anticipating he'd include his shopping list, too." They both had a laugh as a break from the tedium. The next image loaded, though, and Alison's laughter stopped prematurely.

"What happened here?" she asked rhetorically. The image showed a considerably larger area containing the new serotonin receptor than any of the previous slices had shown. They checked the data and realized that this was the first image they were seeing of this particular patient.

"Maybe it was a lab error. Check the next slice," Jack advised. Alison clicked on the appropriate file but it, too, showed a very large region which was positive for the receptor. Glancing at the annotation, it was clear that Vincent hadn't been pleased with the results, either.

Alison read the note out loud. "The abnormal pattern of staining in this brain is puzzling. Given the homogeneity of the previous patients, I suspect a reagent or procedural error may have led to this radical departure from our previous findings. Although my technique has remained constant, I cannot rule out the possibility that our DNA probe has become contaminated with others from the lab. Given the fact that the undergraduate lab section started yesterday, I think this is a likely cause. If the other specimen stained today shows a similar pattern to this one, I'll suspend further studies until the DNA reagent can be re-ordered."

"Did they mention this in their paper," Alison asked. "I don't remember anything about a second pattern anywhere, but I didn't read the footnotes. When a labeled piece of DNA is used to stain a sample, it's usually unbelievably precise, relying on an exactly complementary match of the DNA sequence. It would almost take a miracle for a contaminant to have just the right sequence to match sequences of mRNA in the brain slices."

"I don't recall hearing about another pattern," Jack replied uneasily.

She clicked through a few subsequent images from this patient and the abnormal pattern persisted throughout. "Look at that. It's actually mapping out the entire limbic system here," she observed. "You see, in the previous patients, the stain showed up in very focused areas of the limbic system, but in this one, it's all over the place. Let's see what the other patient that day showed." She searched for the proper date with a different identifying name code and clicked on one of the middle slice files.

"Looks pretty similar, doesn't it?" Jack asked when the new image appeared on the screen.

"Hmm... yes it does." She loaded a few other slices from this patient to confirm that it was again marking the limbic system. "That's strange, though. I mean, you'd expect that if one patient had an abnormal distribution of receptors, the next one would be normal again, right? That's Vincent's logic and it makes sense. If two in a row are totally different than what you expect, you start to think the problem is on your end."

"I'm with you so far," Jack said. "What's the problem with that?"

"Well, somehow, the proposed contaminant miraculously marked the same basic part of the brain we were looking at in the other specimens, *and* it had whatever chemical properties it needed to react in this experiment. If it really was due to an undergraduate mixing two bottles, say, what are the odds that they'd pick something so similar and that would work just right for this very delicate reaction?"

"It sounds like you don't think it's all that likely. What did Vincent say?"

She opened the appropriate file. He wrote: "Damn, I was afraid of that. Well, I guess losing two samples isn't the end of the world, but it worries me that such an expensive set of custom made DNA probes could be ruined like that. I guess I'll just take a long weekend here, and when the new reagents show up Monday, we'll be back on track. It's too bad I can't verify this by re-staining the sections with the fresh probes. Unfortunately, the half life of our radioactive probes is considerably longer than it will take even me to finish a Ph. D!"

"I'd give him half-credit for being a scientist there," Alison said dryly. He realized he should confirm that it was a reagent problem by re-examining the sections with the new probes, but he didn't pick up on the exceedingly unlikely coincidence that the contaminant happened to be a perfect substitute in the experiment."

"So, how can we find out more, then?" Jack asked. He was starting to wonder if she'd picked out something significant that the Yale team had overlooked.

"I don't know. It just doesn't make much sense that the two would have the same change unless they...." She stopped, mid-sentence. "Where do they get these brains from?"

"Donors, I think. You know, people who pledge their bodies to science in the event of their death."

"How can we find out who these people were?"

"I don't know if we can. The best person to call would be Roger again, but I'm pretty sure he's not going to be in his lab at this hour. What are you thinking?"

"It's a long shot in a way, but let's suppose that there *was* something fundamentally different about these two people than everyone else in the study, and that the findings weren't a mistake after all. How could you explain that you got two in a row that were abnormal?"

"Well, I guess if they were twins or something...." Jack was starting to see Alison's point.

"Or maybe siblings? There were only twenty or so subjects in this study. If two were variants, that could already be 10% right there. That's well within the number of people you've found who may have responded differently to your drug, right? They could have been in a car accident or something, and died on the same day. That way, they'd both end up in the lab together and we'd see back to back samples with this other pattern."

"So you think these people had a mutation and that's why they both had this pattern?"

"Not a mutation, really. That's usually very uncommon. Think about it this way. What proportion of people are left handed?"

"One in ten, or so," Jack guessed.

"Sure. Now, is that a mutation or is that just an uncommon trait?"

"I see your point. You're suggesting that this other pattern is considerably less common, but it's out there just the same. If the Yale study only looked at two dozen brains, they may have only found a few like that, and it was just bad luck that they showed up on the same day, making them think the experiment was fouled up."

"We need to find out where those brains came from. If that new receptor is as widespread as it looks like in these samples, then we may have our answer already."

"I can call Roger tomorrow morning. I know he shows up early most Saturdays to get his grant paperwork done. Give me your phone numbers and I'll call you once I've gotten hold of him. For now, I need to go back home and talk with my boss to start planning how to handle this if your theory holds."

"Well, I've got some thinking to do, too. Even if we're right, I'm not entirely sure how to explain the depression. Sharon stopped taking the medication a few days before hers manifested itself."

45.

Another hour had passed but there was still no sign of the Porsche. He was considering another stroll into the garage to make sure it hadn't somehow slipped out behind a truck when his phone rang again. The caller ID showed the same number as the last time. "Yes?" he answered curtly.

"Has he left yet?"

"No."

"I want to know what he was doing in there."

"You want me to bring him in?"

"No! Follow him home and talk to him there. Tell him you're with the S.E.C. and you're investigating stock price manipulation."

"And if he doesn't talk?"

"Persuade him to." They hung up.

He checked his watch and considered crossing the street when he spotted Jack as he passed directly under the only working streetlight on that block. "It's better to be lucky than good," he said to himself.

"You say you're looking to get lucky, honey? 'Cause Neville can show you a good time, you know." He didn't know if the woman had been watching him or if she was simply passing by, looking for a John, but he was mildly amused by the come-on.

"Lot of cops around," he said plainly. "You should be more careful." She thought about answering him, but instead she just turned and walked quickly into the darkness. He opened the car and started the Taurus' motor, waiting for the Porsche to leave the garage.

...

Jack started his car and stared at the wall ahead of him, still deep in thought about the possible implications of their findings. It occurred to him to call Dave, so he dialed his cell phone number but got the voicemail. He left a brief message telling him he needed to talk as soon as possible. Then he tried his home number but he got the machine. *Best communications network in the world and it seems I can't get anyone when I really need them.* He put the phone in the hands-free cradle, found his parking stub, and drove to the gate.

"You want a receipt, sir?" the attendant asked.

Recouping the $18 dollar charge was the last thing on his mind at the moment and the question caught him off guard. "Uh, yeah, OK. Thanks." He took his change and the paper ticket and he pulled onto the street, about 100 yards ahead of the Taurus. The traffic was surprisingly light for a Friday, and he made decent time uptown, to the George Washington Bridge.

All right, let's go over what we've got so far. This whole thing starts because we seem to have a high drop-out rate from the study. When Stanford tries to track them down, it turns out that most of them simply called it quits because they got frustrated. Dave claims they're mostly second-week placebo patients, meaning that they had good results during the first week, then they saw the old habits return the second week and they quit. Some of them— especially ones who have been treated in the past— have a mild relapse of depression, but nothing even remotely like a major depressive episode. A few others, though, fall off the deep end and plunge into a severe, incapacitating depression in a matter of days. Does that mean that prior treatment can prevent the more serious case? Or are they two distinct entities and people with mild symptoms are just at that side of the spectrum, whereas the ones with the severe depression are the serotonin receptor variant people?

The Porsche had found its rhythm on the Palisades Parkway, and Jack was letting the car's surgically precise steering carve a path towards home when his phone rang. He stayed in the right hand lane and pressed the answer button. The microphone, which was mounted in the sun visor, worked surprisingly well, but he still preferred not to divide his attention while driving. "Hello?"

"Jack, it's Dave. What's the matter?"

"It's going to be a long story. Let me call you when I get home. The brief version is that the drug may have a problem for some people, but it's the sort of thing we probably won't be able to screen for ahead of time."

"Is it bad?"

"I'll talk to you later about it, OK?"

"Yeah, OK. Uh... there's another problem, and it involves you, in a way."

"What's that," Jack asked suspiciously.

"Well, I've got to come clean with you on this. My brother owns some stock in Excella and he's been sort of pressuring me to get this drug through."

"Damn it, Dave! I'm not going to compromise my ethics or proper patient care for you! I've got as much of a stake in this as anyone, but I will *not* put people at risk so you or your family can make a few dollars."

"Jack, listen, I know. And I admit I've been making bad decisions because of this, but that's not what's important right now. You see, he's an assistant D.A. and I think he may have had you followed. I don't know who he's got involved in this whole thing, but...."

"But what?" Jack asked, starting to get scared by the unspoken implications.

"But I just want to make sure you don't get caught up in any of this."

"What should I do?"

"For one, I don't think you should go home tonight. Is your family there?"

That question sent a chill straight through Jack. "No, thank God. They're out of town for the weekend."

"Good. Look, is anyone following you?"

"I don't know. I'm on the Palisades and there are a few cars around, but I didn't notice anyone."

"OK, well, I know this sounds strange, but I'm at my parents' house and they would be happy to let you stay here while I get this sorted out."

"You really think that's necessary?" Jack was hoping he'd say it wasn't.

"Just meet me at the office in 40 minutes. Stay in your car and make sure you're not being followed. Make a few U-turns and keep an eye out for anyone acting strangely."

"Dave, I'm a research physician, not a spy. What the hell is going on?"

"Just drive carefully and I'll explain more of this later." They hung up.

Who's back there? He took a look in the mirror but all he could see was the glare of headlights, and they all looked the same to him. *Let's see if anyone wants to keep up with me.* He dropped down from fifth gear to third and blipped the gas to spin the boxer engine up to the appropriate speed. There was room in the left lane, and he mashed the gas pedal to the floor. The Porsche responded immediately, rushing past 90 in a matter of seconds. He snapped the transmission into fourth and kept his right foot planted. In the mirror, he saw a car attempt the same maneuver, although the Porsche was much quicker and was steadily pulling away. His heart was racing already, but the fact that there really did seem to be someone in pursuit flooded him with adrenaline.

...

Shit! What's he doing? He could barely see the Porsche's tail lights on the straights now, and he was using every cubic inch of the Taurus' V-6. Even when he could use both lanes through the curves he was losing ground quickly. His only hope was that traffic might help him close in.

...

Ahead, a slower car was taking up the left lane, but Jack saw an opening on the right. He lifted off the gas slightly and dove into the right lane, passing the car like it was parked. The lights of the pursuer loomed in the mirror, a little closer than they were before. *110 isn't fast enough for you, eh? Let's see if you'll do 130, then.* More traffic appeared just over the hill, though, and this time there wasn't an easy way out. He slowed to 90 and considered a very risky pass on the shoulder, but the other car was bearing down on him quickly now that he was slowing. He hesitated, estimated the closing speed of the other car, which looked like it would catch him in a matter of seconds, then moved to the extreme left side of the left lane. *Get it right, Jack.* He found third gear again, and at the last second he veered right, missing the approaching car by inches as he streaked up the exit ramp at more than double the posted speed. The Porsche's tires scratched and squealed but held on through the turn.

The other car— a BMW sedan, Jack decided as he barely missed its chrome grille— had no hope of following him. He stopped at the end of the ramp, shaking badly. *I can't stay here long. He could back up on the shoulder and catch up with me again.*

...

Although the Taurus was too far back to see exactly what transpired, the unique tail lights of the Porsche betrayed Jack's hasty exit. *Is he trying to race that guy or kill him?* He braced himself and threw his car onto the exit ramp curve at its limit. Suddenly, the Porsche came into view around the bend, and it was stopped dead directly ahead! He jumped on the brakes but even the anti-lock mechanism couldn't halt the Taurus in that short a distance. Fortunately, since the computer kept the brakes from locking, he was able to steer wide, onto the shoulder, and miss ramming the Porsche's rear bumper. He came to rest 30 feet past Jack's car.

That was too close, but now what? I can't follow him if I'm up here. Come on, get going....

...

The white car that barely scraped past him on the shoulder was the final straw for Jack. He shouted, "What the hell is wrong with people? I'm getting followed by a BMW and a Ford nearly kills me?" He considered his next move and decided to get right back on the Palisades. *If the BMW is coming back, he'll never suspect that move.* He gunned the engine and took off down the entrance ramp on the other side of the road.

...

Sneaky move, Jack. I can't follow you there without tipping my hand. You're smarter than I thought, but I know where you live....

...

Jack took a few more exit ramp detours but he didn't see any other cars that caught his attention. When he got to Excella, he saw that Dave was waiting for him, parked next to his spot. His legs wobbled when he stood, still suffering from the effects of the adrenaline that seemed to have replaced his blood.

"What happened?" Dave asked.

"I think I was being followed, but I managed to get away. Now tell me what's going on, will you?"

"OK, but get in my car first. We'll leave yours so if they come looking for you, they'll have to search the whole campus before they realize you're not here."

"Who is 'they?'"

"I don't know for sure. It could be the cops or it could be the mob." That was enough to get Jack into the car. "Don't think about that for now. What happened with the drug?" Jack told him about the Yale study anomalies, and the conclusions that he and Alison drew, given the information. As they drove, Dave tried to understand the biology involved, with some success.

"So," Jack summarized, "we have to find out if there's any way the two people were related. It's always possible that they aren't related but they still have the same pattern, although it's going to be a much stronger case if they're genetically similar."

"What's it going to mean for the drug?"

"Probably nothing good. Obviously, if it turns out that some people are going to end up with a severe case of depression, that's going to be a serious problem. Maybe there's a way to alter the course or even prevent it. Remember, some of the people only developed a mild depression, so if we can find a common thread there, it might help. That will take some time, though, and the FDA will probably want a lot more information before they approve anything."

"All right, well let me be clear on this, then. You're in charge of this project from now on, and I'm not going to question your decisions. If we can wait until Tuesday to make any of this public, my brother will no longer be a problem. If we can't wait until then, I'll handle him, but you may have to lay low and keep your family out of town for a few extra days."

...

The white Taurus was parked outside Jack's house for nearly three hours before the driver finally started the engine once more. *Looks like I underestimated you again, Doctor Finnegan. That will be the last time, though.* He pulled the transmission lever into gear and drove off into the night, a defeated hunter who'd temporarily lost the trail of his prey.

46.

The alarm in the guest room rang at 6:30 but Jack had been awake for hours. The problems with the drug alone would have been enough to keep him up, but he could barely relax knowing that he was being stalked, too. An image of Sandy and Lisa flashed through his mind, and he was embarrassed that he hadn't called last night to make sure they were OK. *Sandy's usually up by now.* He opened his cell phone and saw that the battery was getting low. *Can't charge it today unless Dave's got the same model.* He dialed his parents' and waited for an answer. His father picked up. "Hi, Dad. It's me. Listen, is Sandy there?"

"Hello, Jack. Yes, she's upstairs, asleep, I think. You want me to wake her?"

"Yes, I need to talk to her."

"How's work? I understand that drug of yours is coming along."

"Well, we've hit a bit of a snag. Long story, really." He could hear his father knocking on the door in the background, then he handed Sandy the phone.

"Jack? How are things?"

"Well, the drug may have a problem. We're working on that right now. You and Lisa OK?"

"We're fine. Why?" Her maternal instinct told her something was definitely wrong.

"Things are a little crazy here right now. I'd appreciate it if you could stay at my parents' for a few more days."

"We can't stay! Lisa has school on Monday. What's this about, Jack?"

"It's probably nothing, but it seems that some people are worried that the drug might not make it through the FDA."

"Who's worried? Dave? What is he going to do?"

"It's not Dave, honey. It's some stockholders or something. They're trying to put pressure on us by harassing us. I'm really not concerned, but I wouldn't want you to get mixed up in their nonsense."

"You're hiding something, aren't you? Have they threatened you?"

"Look, it will all be sorted out by Tuesday, so please just stay there for a few more days."

"I want you to call the police, then. If they're threatening you, it's the only thing you can do."

"That won't work, Sandy. Some of them *are* the police. I know it sounds like a movie, but I need to get some work done right now, and I don't want to have to worry about you and Lisa."

"And how am *I* not going to worry about *you*?"

"You probably will. Just try to stay calm and I'll call you later."

"Be careful, Jack. The money isn't important enough for you to get hurt."

"I know, Sandy. The problem is that I have to take care of the patients who are relying on us to keep them safe. They're the reason we have to get this done right now. I'll call you later. I love you."

"I love you too, Jack."

He could hear her voice start to crack as they hung up, and the fear he had been feeling started to turn to anger. *Whoever you are, if I can make you pay for this, I will.* A few minutes passed as he sat on the edge of the bed, running over the facts when there was a knock at his door.

"Jack, you awake?" Dave asked.

"Yeah, hang on a second." He pulled on his pants and opened the door.

"Here's some stuff for a shower. Bathroom's through there, and there's coffee downstairs. If you can't find something, let me know."

"Thanks." He headed for a much needed shower, hoping it might help to clear his head. Although he was stuck with yesterday's clothes, the shower and caffeine were a good start. Dave even had a disposable razor, so he got a quick shave in as well. Sitting at the table, it was easy to forget that Dave was his boss. The setting was so different from the office or planning rooms that he was struck by how much he looked like just an ordinary person, maybe a relative he saw a few times a year. Jack was struck, too, by the realization that Dave wasn't as driven by money as he had originally thought. Part of that, he reasoned, was self-preservation, because if the FDA found out he was trying to push a dangerous drug through the study, they'd destroy him. There was more to it, though, and the way he admitted his mistakes yesterday revealed a level of integrity that Jack had never seen in him.

"So," Dave said, "I think we need to make a plan here. If I understand you correctly, the real deciding factor now is whether the two people from the Yale study will turn out to be related."

"I think that's going to be an important fact, yes. I don't know if it will necessarily answer all the questions, but it will be a good start."

"OK, so if they *are* related, what do we do?"

"If they're related, the assumption would be that the pair of patient results that Yale thought were lab errors were, in fact, people with a different distribution of these receptors. It's not clear exactly what that would mean, but we would have to assume that they might respond to the drug differently. They could easily turn out to be the people who end up with severe depression from the study. It would be a serious blow to the study, that's for sure."

"And how would we handle people who are currently on it in the trial?" Dave asked.

"I think this Alison Sonders is the right person to ask that question of. She's an expert in the pharmacology of mood disorders, so hopefully she'll have some recommendations for us. To be honest, I'd guess we'd have to terminate the study immediately and keep a very close watch on everyone for a few days at least."

"Now, if the two people *aren't* related, what then?"

"Well," Jack replied, "it would definitely change the odds that the findings in the Yale study were real. I think the next step there would be to re-examine, if possible, the brain specimens as well as the DNA probes. Maybe they could run them through some analyzer to see if they're actually contaminated with something else. It's still possible, though, that the brains really do have that pattern of receptors and it just happened by chance that they both showed up on the same day. It's really a matter of odds, though, and we just don't know how common that sort of pattern would be, so we can't figure out what the chances are of finding two in a row like that."

"Either way," Dave summarized, "I guess we have to figure out why there have been these four cases of depression like this."

"I don't imagine the FDA will simply overlook that."

"All right, well I've got a phone call to make. Then, if you're interested, I'll buy us some breakfast on the way in to the office. There's a very good diner on the other side of town."

"What are we going to do about your brother?"

"I'm going to sort that out right now." He walked out the front door and took a seat in his car. It was the only place he'd get enough privacy to speak to his brother candidly. So far he'd managed to shield their mother from the conflict, and he was going to do his best to keep her from learning the truth. With the door shut and the engine running for a little extra noise, he opened the cell phone and dialed Bobby. The phone rang several times before he heard his brother's sleepy voice. "Wake up, Bobby. It's Dave. Just keep your mouth shut and listen. I've discussed with Jack everything that's happening with this drug trial. I told you it doesn't look good, and that's still the case. However, if there's any chance *at all* that the trial will continue, it's going to come down to whether Jack can figure out why there's a problem. That means that he can't be distracted by your goons or anything else. Period. We all want this trial to succeed, and if we can salvage it, we'll all benefit. Right now, nothing has been decided about the study, but if Jack or I get so much as a phone message from you, that tape I have will hit every news station on the East Coast before the answering machine beeps. Is that perfectly clear?"

It sounded like it took every ounce of strength for Bobby to utter, "Yes." Dave was satisfied and hung up without another word.

47.

"Good morning, Sharon," Alison said as she walked in her room and saw her in bed, with her head and legs raised. Apparently, her inability to eat or drink worried the medical team enough that they inserted an IV line and were giving her a glucose and salt water drip.

Sharon raised her eyes slightly and opened her mouth, but no sound came out. After a moment, she closed it again. It was clear she was "in there," but so terribly disconnected from the world that even her own voice couldn't escape. Alison had always thought that this kind of major depression was analogous to a black hole in many respects. Black holes are so massive that their own gravitational field ensnares everything that comes near them, even preventing light itself from escaping. If Sharon could see herself from Alison's perspective, she would immediately recognize that this is what was happening to her, emotionally. However, being on the inside of black hole made it almost impossible to perceive anything at all.

"I know all this may seem very sudden and scary for you, Sharon, and you may not even understand what's been happening. But I found the best doctor I know to help get you better. Harold has been a friend of mine for years and I have complete faith in his abilities. Just hang on because this takes time to fix." The orderly, who was sitting in a chair, reading a book, looked up and smiled at Sharon, feeling slightly touched herself to hear the kind words. "Thanks for taking care of her," she said to the woman. "She's a friend of mine."

In a thick, Jamaican accent, the woman replied, "Don't you worry, Ma'am. We'll do right by her." With that, Alison left the room. Standing in the common area, Harold was leading his team on morning rounds. He saw Alison and excused himself for a minute.

"Hi, Alison. I know she doesn't look great today, but part of that is because we've got her in a hospital gown and all. The IV doesn't help, either."

"Oh, I know, Harold. I just wanted to say 'Hello.' You're the one who taught me that simply having a conversation, even when it's one-sided, can help give them a little piece of ground to stand on. What have you got her medicated with?"

"The usual: an SSRI and a tricyclic. We'll probably add a stimulant today just for completeness, but you know how often that actually works...."

"Which one are you thinking about? Caffeine?" Alison asked suggestively. She knew that IV caffeine, a modest stimulant, was also used to increase the efficacy of electroconvulsive therapy.

"Look, you know the drill as well as I do. She's pretty sick, Alison, and I think that ECT may be the direction we're heading. She hasn't been eating since she got here, and you know that even one-to-one observation isn't perfect. I just don't want her getting hurt while we wait to see if the pharmacology works."

"I know, Harold. I guess I'm just blaming myself some for this. I mean, she works in my office for God's sake, so I should have seen at least some of the signs earlier than I did.... Well, I know she's in good hands with you. I spent yesterday with a few of the researchers from that weight loss drug trial she was in. Their drug targets a new subtype of serotonin receptors which are concentrated in the satiety center in most people, but which may be more widespread in others. If that's the case, this could have been precipitated by the drug. I don't know what implications it would have now, but at least we may have an idea why this came on so suddenly."

"New receptor? Wow, when did that come up?"

"Apparently they've know about it for a year or more, but in business, secrets make money." She shook her head disapprovingly.

"Well, there's nothing you can do about that now, and I'm sure it would not have made a difference if she came in 12 hours earlier, Alison. Remember, you aren't responsible for the patient having her disease. We'll give her another day of medications here before we decide anything about ECT."

"Thanks, Harold. I mean that." She patted his shoulder and left the ward for her office.

48

The Excella parking lot was fairly deserted at this hour on Saturday morning, so as the driver of the white Taurus headed down the main entrance road, he immediately spotted Jack's Porsche in its spot. *So this is where you were last night. Sent your family out of town and you spent Friday night at the office. Well, I'm sure we'll just have lots to talk about, Jack my boy.* He stopped the Taurus about 50 yards away from the Porsche, but closer to the exit and facing out of the spot. Every detail, including maximizing the escape, was so well planned and rehearsed that he performed each step unconsciously while his mind stayed focused on his mission.

He leaned over and opened the glove compartment, revealing a pair of black leather gloves which he put in the pockets of his jacket. After double-checking that he wasn't being watched, he withdrew a 9mm Glock semi-automatic pistol from his concealed shoulder holster, checked that it was loaded and locked, and replaced it. The driver then climbed out of the Taurus and opened the trunk, revealing a medium-sized tool box. He found the heavy duty wire cutter and a screwdriver both of which he stashed in his jacket pocket. He then rummaged through an assortment of ID badges until he found one labeled "Cerberus Security, Inc." The photograph showed him wearing a short-sleeved shirt and tie, and his title read "corporate security expert." He clipped the badge to the jacket then walked purposefully towards the Excella compound. Behind his sunglasses, his eyes never rested, scanning the horizon and taking in everything.

When he reached the 12 foot high chain link fence topped with barbed wire, he turned left and followed it along the parking lot until the lower part disappeared behind a few stray bushes. There were no obvious video cameras in sight, so he casually bent down behind the shrubs as he removed the wire cutter from his jacket. Within two minutes he'd cut enough of the fence to allow himself easy access to the inside of the plant. At this point he could only hope he hadn't been seen, so he slipped through the hole and inside the plant. Without any idea where Jack's office was, his direction was arbitrary, but it was important to put some distance between himself and the fence, so he walked purposefully towards the center of the compound.

A loading dock at the back of a building caught his eye, and he moved closer for a better view. The large, retractable door was opened about four feet, and despite the limited view he had, it didn't appear that there was anyone inside. Re-checking his badge to be sure he knew his alias, he pushed his way through the opening, removing his sunglasses to improve his vision in the darkness. He scanned the room until he found, on the wall behind him, a telephone and an Excella phone directory.

Let's see where you hide out, then, Dr. Finnegan. The listing provided Jack's office extension and room number in the Channing building. He flipped through the pages until he found the site map on the inside of the back cover. After studying it briefly, he determined that he was two buildings away. The trail, which had gone cold overnight, suddenly heated up again, and the hunter was back at his game.

The Channing building was one of the newer additions to the campus and it housed a significant amount of high-tech research equipment. Consequently, the security was particularly modern, with card readers required for building access. Nevertheless, the driver knew that security was only as good as the last person to use it, so no matter how secure a door appeared, there was little harm in trying it in case it had not been closed completely. This time, however, it was locked tight, and he was about to turn around when the door burst open with a loud bang as though it had been hit from within. The sound startled him, and he instinctively took a step backwards, out of the way of a large green trash barrel that was being wheeled out.

"Oh, s-s-sorry," said the janitor when he realized he'd nearly hit the man. He was about to continue pushing the barrel when his gaze met the driver's, and he paused momentarily.

"No problem," the driver replied quickly, recognizing the break he'd just gotten. "Looks like you've got your hands full." He entered the building without addressing the puzzled look on the face of the janitor. *OK, so I'll have to settle for the second-easiest way into a locked building, then.* The stairs were predictably located in the corner, and he climbed them, checking the door at each floor to be certain he had options on the way out. At the fourth floor, he cracked the door open slightly and listened for signs of life. Hearing none, he opened the door further and peeked through to see a long hallway but no people or cameras.

Jack's lab was easy enough to locate among the numbered doors, but the walls of windows left no doubt that Jack was nowhere inside. His hands clenched slightly, then relaxed. *Patience, now. He wasn't at home last night and his car is here, so there's reason to believe we're on the right track. Let's just find a safe place to wait.* Several doors were locked, but a few rooms in the middle of the floor were open, so he began setting up a blind in which to hide and observe.

49.

Compared to yesterday's commute from New York City, the drive to Excella was pleasantly uneventful. Excella's campus housed both research and production facilities, so there was a skeleton crew on site, even on weekends. The executive amenities, though, were largely empty off-hours, so Dave and Jack commandeered a large meeting room located roughly between their offices for the morning work. This one's large, wooden table was equipped with several flat-screen computer terminals and a complement of phone extensions for the occasional international teleconferences.

On one of the computers, Jack pulled up his electronic address book and tried Roger's lab again. After a few rings, he got a machine. "Roger, it's Jack. I need to speak with you as soon as possible." He heard a click on the line.

"Jack, I'm here. Sorry, I was working under the radioactive exhaust hood when the phone rang. What's up?"

Jack took a breath. "Have you looked at the data from the serotonin study?"

"What do you mean? Of course. I think the grad student on that project was Vincent. He showed me the whole thing. It's what got him his Ph. D."

"What did you think about the two patients with the variant staining patterns, then?"

There was silence on the line for a moment. "Someone had a different pattern?" he asked weakly.

"Roger, we've got a real problem here. Vincent's notes indicate that, when he found these two people, he thought his DNA probe has been contaminated, and that was the reason the slices stained differently. It probably sounded like a reasonable enough explanation, but we're beginning to think that the results were real, and that, in some people, there's another distribution pattern for these receptors."

"Jesus Christ, Jack. I had no idea." He sounded like he'd just been kicked in the stomach. "Where did you find this out?"

"Your electronic data collection program has a whole annotation section to it. Vincent was meticulous in explaining his steps and findings for each sample. He may have made an error in judgment regarding this other pattern, but he definitely tried to keep good notes. I don't think it was an intentional cover-up, but we need to know some more information about these two people."

"Sure, I'll do whatever you need. There have been so many reports of scientific fraud and misconduct lately that we've all been scared it would happen to us. I just thought we had a solid group of people working together."

"Look, Roger, I don't think it was misconduct, but that will be for you to decide later. Right now, I need to know the names of the two patients and whether they were related genetically." He gave him the computer ID numbers from the two patients' files.

"OK, sure, Jack. I think the Medical Examiner should have that information. They don't tell us names for confidentiality reasons, but I know someone in the office over there and he might be able to help."

"Good. Call him now and get back to me immediately. This may have implications for patients who've already started taking our drug in the trial, and we need to know how to handle them."

"Of course. I'll call you in a few minutes. Give me your number." He wrote down Jack's extension and hung up the phone. For a moment, all Roger could do was shake his head slowly and wonder how his lab could have been tainted by questionable scientific information. It was overwhelming, but he managed to regain his focus and call the ME's office. The automated switchboard explained that there were no normal business hours on the weekend, but for emergencies, pressing zero would transfer him to the police desk, and from there, he could describe his problem.

"New Haven Police, Sergeant Broderick speaking. Your call is being recorded. Is this an emergency or business issue?"

"Business," Roger replied, although he felt more like he was in the middle of an emergency.

"What can I do for you, sir?"

"I'm Doctor Pullman from Yale. I'm trying to get in touch with the Medical Examiner on call."

"OK, Doctor. Hold on a minute. I think he's got a pager." The line cut out while he was on hold, then the sergeant came back on and gave him the pager number. "Anything else we can do for you Doc?"

"No, that's great. Thanks, Sergeant." He hung up and dialed the pager number and typed in his lab's phone number. While he waited, he wondered how he had managed to let his own scientific guard down to the point that he didn't personally review all the raw data from his experiments. He had been rudely reminded how easy it was to become complacent, trusting bright and energetic but inexperienced graduate students to be able to make what often amounted to very difficult decisions. Something as simple as doubting your hypotheses first, rather than the results, was a hard-learned lesson, and Roger had forgotten that it takes years to develop that keen, self-critical sense. The only one to blame was himself for not having taught his own people how to approach these issues. He'd have to have a meeting Monday to address this problem so it wouldn't recur.

The phone finally rang. "Roger Pullman," he said.

"Oh, Roger. How are you? It's Lou Lombardi. What's up?"

"Lou, I need a favor. We may have had a problem with one of our experiments and I need to know the names of two of the cadavers. Are you at work?"

"Yeah, I'm at work. But Roger... you know I can't give you that information. People trust us to keep their identities safe when they donate their bodies to science."

"I know. The problem is, a drug company based a new medication on our results, and now they've got a bunch of people taking this drug. If we had an error, then they could be at risk right now."

"You're really putting me in a bad position here. Isn't there anything else you can do?" Lou really sounded uncomfortable.

"I don't think so. Although...." He paused as a new thought struck him. "You know, I think they said that what they really need is just to know if the two subjects were genetically related. Maybe you could find that out for me?"

"Let me see. There's some basic information like 'age' and 'cause of death' that's kept in one electronic file, so I can start there. If I access the other database, it logs my name and everything, and they check that one like it's got national security secrets hidden in it." Roger gave him the ID numbers, and Lou typed them into the aging county computer system, which took its time pulling up the information. "Let's see. The first was a Caucasian female, 67 years old, 5 feet 3 inches tall, 182 pounds, who died July 14th from smoke inhalation. Sounds like a house fire," he said parenthetically. "The other was.... Looks like your lucky day, Roger. The second was also a Caucasian female, age 71, 5 feet 1 inch tall, 178 pounds, who died July 14th from smoke inhalation. Probably two elderly sisters who got caught inside. I can't guarantee they're sisters, but we rarely get more than one house fire here in a given month, so I think the odds are extremely good given their ages and similar body habitus, that they're related. You know, I've got the fire chief's number, and if you want, you can call him to see if he remembers anything." Roger jotted the number down on a scrap of paper.

"Thanks a lot for your help, Lou. This has been a real stress for me, and I want to make sure we don't cause any trouble as a result of a grad student's error."

"If you need anything else, call me, Roger. I'll do what I can." They hung up and Roger dialed the fire chief's number. When he answered, Roger could tell he was on a cellular phone, but the connection was good enough for him to ask about the July 14th event.

"Oh, right, I remember that call," the chief eventually replied. "That was a real shame. Seems one sister had recently broken her hip and the other was trying to help her down the stairs, best we could tell. They both perished before our boys could get them to safety."

"They were definitely sisters, then?" Roger confirmed.

"Yes, from a big family, too. The next of kin sent us a beautiful thank you card and a donation for the station. Felt kind of strange accepting it because we couldn't save them, but I think they knew how hard we tried."

Roger thanked the chief for his time, hung up, and dialed Jack again. When he answered, Roger said, "Here's what I've got, Jack. Both patients were elderly white women, both were overweight, and both died on the same day from smoke inhalation. I can't get their names because of confidentiality issues, but I spoke to the fire chief and he clearly remembered a house fire that day which killed two elderly sisters."

Jack thought for a minute. "Yeah, that's a pretty convincing story, huh? OK, Roger, we'll go from there. In some ways, this development is as interesting as the original concept that the receptors were specific for everyone. I mean, it might help to explain why some people depend on eating to stave off depression."

"Maybe you're right," Roger said unconvincingly. He was still wrestling with his own emotions over this finding. "Let me know how it turns out, OK?"

"I will," he assured as he put down the receiver. He told Dave the news.

"Well, that's unfortunate," he said flatly. "I guess we should get Dr. Sonders on the payroll immediately so we can show we responded to this finding, then we can figure out with her how to stop this thing."

"I'll talk to her about coming up here today. Can I offer her the standard level five consultant's fee plus 30% for the emergent nature of the problem?"

"Go as high as 50% if you need to," Dave said. "It's still going to be a drop in the bucket compared to what this is will cost if we don't get our response just right in the FDA's eyes."

"But not nearly as costly as the mistake you're about to make." The new voice startled Dave and Jack, whose nerves were already frayed from the events of last night. They snapped their head around to see the Taurus driver standing in the doorway. Dave grabbed the phone, but hung it up again as the driver leveled the loaded Glock at his head. "Please put that down. I don't like welcoming parties. Let's keep my visit here between us for now."

"Who are you?" Dave demanded.

"I am just a man with a job. My boss, however, has an important business interest in your company and this new drug you've got. That's why he's asked me to make sure you don't do anything stupid."

"Now look," Dave started, "if anything happens to me or Jack, you can let Bobby know that the tape will be public within twenty-four hours. Got that?" He hoped he wasn't shaking as much as it felt like he was.

"Oh, that's a lovely thought," the driver mocked. "Of course, I don't know who Bobby is, but if I meet him, I'll pass along the message. Now, both of you get over there, away from the phones. And, as they say on TV, don't try anything funny."

"What do you want from us, then?" Jack asked belligerently. "We're still trying to salvage the drug trial despite the problems we've had so far. We have no intention of asking the FDA to halt the investigation yet."

"Look, doc, I don't know shit about your medical mumbo-jumbo. All I know is that my boss wants this thing to work out, and he wants a little insurance to make sure you do your very best."

"Well of course we will. That's why we're here today!" Jack replied.

"Aw, now that's the spirit I need to hear. That will be perfect with the boss, too. I'll just go back and tell him you promised to do your best and I'm sure he'll be satisfied." He was shaking his head sarcastically. "That story, plus your daughter, is all I'll need."

"My *daughter?*" Jack said hoarsely. "What are you going to do with her?"

"God damn it!" Dave interjected, beginning to stand. "This has gone far enough. Get Bobby on the phone right now before he gets himself done in for good."

"Touching," the driver continued dryly as he pulled out a black silencer and methodically began screwing it onto the barrel of the gun. "Sit down, and *stay* down." The look in his eyes left no doubt in Dave's mind about the seriousness of the threat. "Now, doc, do us all a favor and tell me where your daughter's hiding out. It's the only way you'll be able to get out of this without anyone getting hurt."

Jack could barely focus his thoughts at the moment as he tried to find an alternative to giving up his precious daughter. He stared at the ground and began stammering as he struggled to utter words despite the fear and nausea he felt. "She's… I mean, you can't have her. I… Oh, God, I can't do that to my baby girl!"

Suddenly, there was a loud bang, startling in its abruptness, and Jack reflexively sat bolt upright in the chair from sheer terror. Some disconnected, irrational part of his brain was certain the driver had just shot at him, and his mind wondered helplessly if his body had been hit.

"What the…?" The driver quickly hid the gun inside his jacket. "Oh, it's *you* again."

The sound, Jack eventually realized, was from the janitor's garbage bucket banging into the door as he pushed it into the room. Dave recognized the janitor from the day before, but this time he was considerably happier to see him.

"S-s-sorry," the janitor said routinely. With the man facing the janitor, Dave and Jack tried to motion to him that they were in trouble, but the driver turned around, towards them, before any signals could be effectively communicated.

With his gaze fixed and his back to the janitor, the driver said, "Forget about it. Just take out the trash."

"OK, then, Franklin — or as your friends call you — Frankie Continenti," the janitor replied in a strikingly different voice. "You're the biggest piece of trash here, so I guess it's time for you to go." The driver turned, stunned to have been addressed by his name, to find himself at the business end of someone else's 9mm semiautomatic. "Drop your weapon and get your hands in the air *now*. I'm officer Parker from the organized crime unit." Two other, uniformed policemen entered the room and quickly handcuffed the driver. "Take our boy Frankie downstairs, would you?" he said to the officers. "He's had enough fun for today, and with his extensive record, probably enough fun for life without parole."

Dave managed to regain his composure slightly. "You're a... cop... then?" he asked.

"That, or a janitor with a keen interest in notorious crime figures," Parker replied lightheartedly. Dave and Jack were still frozen in their seats. "OK, this is the first bust you've been to, and you guys are still a little rattled right now, so I'll let that slide. Yeah, I'm a cop. The DA's office — your brother, I suspect — put me on your case, under cover. I thought it was supposed to be for surveillance, though I don't know, really, what he was looking for. Then I ran into your friend Frankie downstairs and I recognized his face from a briefing we had at the station a few weeks ago. I didn't figure he was here for a social visit, so I decided my assignment must have been intended as more of a protection beat than a surveillance one. I called in some backup and dropped by your little party here."

"B-Bobby sent you here?" Dave asked, shaken and still trying to understand what just happened.

"My orders come from the chief, but he got asked to do a favor by the DA's office. Like I said, it sounded more like surveillance when I was told, but that's what happens sometimes when the buck gets passed along. My cover's blown, but I'll have to stick around here until I get replaced or until the chief decides it's enough." As an afterthought, he added, "By the way, your phone's been bugged, and your car has a little radio transceiver on it. Sorry about that, but those were the orders I got.

We'll take those electronics back today, of course. For now, you might as well go back to what you were doing."

"OK," Dave said as he finally began to regain his composure. "Jack, you've got to call Alison and get her here." He realized that Jack hadn't yet recovered from the experience, so he added, "Everything's fine, and your daughter's still safe, OK?"

Jack looked blankly at him for a moment before blinking his eyes tightly as if to wake up from a terrible dream. "Yeah, OK, Dave. Give me five minutes. I'll call her in five minutes from my office." He shook his head to clear it, took a deep breath, and stood on his slightly wobbly legs. With a weak thumbs up to Dave and the policeman, he headed out the door.

50.

Alison announced herself at the Excella guard station and waited there for her escort inside the locked compound. Her mind was still reeling from Jack's phone call, and she kept replaying it in her head. First, she was proud of herself when he told her that her theory about the two anomalous staining patters being from relatives was right on the mark. Basic research was never her strongest suit, but she could handle the science when she needed to. Then, the request to join them as a professional consultant was an honor. They were acknowledging her intellect and asking for her expertise to help them solve their own problems. It was a feather in her cap, for sure. Then, Jack started talking about money....

"Of course, we'd give you the standard consultant's fee for your time today," he had said on the phone.

"Oh, no. I'm doing this for Sharon. It isn't about money, Jack. You people can worry about that. I'm just trying to take care of people who need help."

Jack was impressed by her altruism, but he gently persisted. "I know that, Alison, and that's part of the reason I'm so keen on getting you involved. But since you're already going to work with us, you might as well take the $40,000."

That's precisely when Alison's brain boggled. *Forty* thousand *dollars? That's more than I make in three months! No wonder people get sucked into working with these companies.* "Uh, could you repeat that number?" she stammered.

"I know it's a ridiculous amount of money, Alison, but that's just how business works. Most of the people we bring in as consultants aren't worth the bagels we feed them, yet they get paid just the same. You, on the other hand, will make a real difference for us. Take my advice and take the money. It's not going to corrupt you, and it'll give you some freedom in your own life, maybe just to cover the cost of a few more service patients." People without money or insurance were known in the business as 'service cases.' Even private practice physicians usually saw several people a month who were too sick to turn away, but too poor to pay. It was simply an expense that the office absorbed as a good will gesture.

Alison had accepted the offer, but she still couldn't grasp the number. She even managed to jot down the directions to Excella without really hearing them. Jack said he'd see her in an hour, and she agreed she'd be there as she hung up. All of a sudden, she missed Sharon more than ever because she would certainly have known what to do in the practice with that sort of payment.

Even now, as she waited to be brought into the Excella plant, she still felt in shock, as though everything were just a little surreal. The door next to the guard finally opened, and Jack walked through.

"Good to see you again, Alison" he greeted. "Come with me." They walked through the campus making small talk and eventually arrived at the Channing building. "Now, the other guy here is Dave Aswari. He's my boss, but he's not a physician. His background is finance, so I may have to explain things to him from time to time. He's a decent guy, though, and he's on our side here, so don't hesitate to give your opinion even if it seems like he's disagreeing, OK? Most of the time, it's just his way of trying to understand the details."

They got to the conference room and found Dave plugging in a coffee pot in the corner. "Thought we might need this," he said.

"Dave, this is Doctor Alison Sonders. Alison, Dave Aswari." When the two shook hands, Alison recognized a look in Dave's eyes that she'd seen many times before. It was fear, borne of intimidation by the fact that an attractive woman might turn out to be smarter than him. It was just the sort of stereotypical male response that made certain men say painfully immature things in an imagined battle for dominance. She hoped he wasn't one of them, because if he was, even forty thousand wasn't enough.

"It's a pleasure to meet you," Alison said.

"Thanks, but I think we're the ones who were lucky to have met you. Jack told me about your conference yesterday, and we really do appreciate your help." Dave realized he suddenly felt nervous, but he couldn't quite figure out what was happening. "Please, have a seat." The three sat around the corner of the table, with two computers in front of them. "Jack told you what he found this morning?"

"About the two women? Yes, he told me."

"So," Jack said, "what do you think our next move should be? I'm assuming you'd favor stopping the drug trial for now, right?"

"Well," Alison replied, "I'm sort of new at this, so I'd like to see your data first, if I can."

"Dave, you might as well show her what you've got." Jack suddenly remembered that he was still uncertain whether the data Dave had the other day was even real. "Those numbers were accurate, right? There wasn't anything misleading in them?"

"They should be accurate," he responded, oblivious to Jack's implication. "The guy who wrote the database also wrote that program as well. He said it's just a back door into the electronic file." Dave brought up the Lightfoot program and pointed out the salient features as he saw them. Alison studied the screen for several minutes.

"Is there a way to print this stuff out," she asked. "I'd like to see several of these charts at one time." Dave clicked the appropriate buttons and a hitherto unseen laser printer in the corner of the room came to life. "Nice network you guys have here," she commented.

"I keep learning new things it can do almost every day," Jack admitted sheepishly. While they waited for the printer to finish, the door opened and Stephen entered. "Good, I was hoping you'd get my message to come here. Stephen, this is Doctor Alison Sonders. Alison, Stephen Shin. He's a Ph. D. and our main computer modeling guy." The two exchanged greetings.

Alison picked up the stack of paper and returned to the table. "Let's see, now. Which people were the ones with the severe depression here?" Jack checked his notes and picked out the proper pages. "OK, now which others were the ones with mild depression?" Again, he pulled out the appropriate sheets. She looked over the data, shuffling back and forth between the patients several times. "You know," she finally said, "it's really strange that everyone was on the placebo when this happened."

"Everyone but Sharon," Jack pointed out. "She wasn't on anything at the time, right?"

"Right, but...." Alison paused. "Oh, this is interesting. How long did you say the dosing interval for the drug was?"

Stephen answered that. "We set it at 12 hours because of the relatively long half-life."

"OK, and it looks like the people who got sick showed symptoms between 48 and 60 hours into the placebo arm. That's 4-5 half lives, or just enough time for the blood levels of the drug to drop basically to zero." Alison was still trying to convince herself that her line of reasoning was correct when Stephen picked up the lead.

"I see where you're going! This could be a *withdrawal* problem rather than a drug *effect* problem. You know, it never occurred to me, but this drug may be so good at potentiating the effect of serotonin that there could even be receptor down-regulation."

Dave interrupted. "Wait, what are you talking about?"

Alison replied, ignoring the risk of intimidating Dave by taking charge of the discussion. "To answer that, let's take a step back first. This drug was designed to increase the effect of the small amounts of the neurotransmitter serotonin in specific parts of the brain. When that happens in the average patient, they feel full more quickly than normal, so they eat less food. When it happens in these other patients— the ones with the alternative receptor distribution— they also feel satiated more quickly. But, it also increases the effect of the neurotransmitter in all the *other* places they have these receptors. Basically, their whole emotional system gets revved up by the drug, making them feel good. Not 'high,' mind you, but good in the way that they'd feel if they took a quick-acting anti-depressant medication. In fact, they may be even more sensitive than other people to the interrelated effects of hunger and depression since their brains seem to be overly cross-wired in those areas."

She stopped for a moment to let the concepts sink in. "Anyway, I'm getting ahead of myself a little. In nature, almost every system has a built in adjusting mechanism so that organisms can regulate themselves, adapting to unpredictable changes in the environment. One of the things that cells do when the supply of a neurotransmitter is increased is they cut back on the number of receptors available, thus helping to bring the increased signal back to a normal level. It's like turning down the radio when a loud song starts playing. Your ears want a certain sound level, and you adjust the gain to keep the output signal the same when the input signal changes."

The analogy was a good one, and Dave nodded to Alison to continue. "That's called receptor down-regulation, and it happens at varying rates for different receptor types. What I think you're seeing here is the combined effect of relatively quick down-regulation followed by a rapid drop-off in input signal. From a biological standpoint, it actually makes good sense. In the wild, if you suddenly suppress the appetite, animals run the risk of starving. Over the course of evolution, food was relatively hard to come by, so you'd want to make that system respond quickly, thus keeping the appetite relatively intact. But, for the people who have that receptor in their limbic system, the effect on mood would be profound. First you give them a potent anti-depressant, then, once they've adjusted to it, you take it away, just like that." She snapped her fingers for emphasis. "Instant depression."

"And the difference between the mild and severe cases?" Jack asked.

Alison shrugged. "Who knows? Maybe they got treated with an SSRI before and it changed their receptor population subtly. Maybe they have a mix of receptor types and so they're more resistant to the effects of the drug. Maybe they just get depressed when they stop losing weight and it's nothing more than a coincidence."

Stephen said, "This has some real implications for our study, then. We can't let *anyone* stop taking this drug without some sort of tapering dose or they'll be at risk for developing depression."

"You're probably right," Alison conceded. "Do you think two weeks would be long enough? Jack, what's your feeling on this?"

"Don't SSRI's work by changing receptor densities?" Jack asked rhetorically. "I thought that's the theory behind them taking three weeks to work. If so, I'd vote for three weeks, just so we have that precedent to refer to in case we're wrong."

Alison nodded. "Good point. Three weeks, then. Of course, we don't have any evidence to support that plan, but that's an experiment you guys will have to organize. You know, that's probably the right approach for Sharon and the others, too. If this is an acute withdrawal, then they should respond quickly if we restart the drug."

"You know," Jack observed, "that might work, and it would go a long way to confirming this whole theory. Stephen, can you walk over to manufacturing and get a bottle of Ascendiac for us? If they give you any problems, have them call me immediately." Stephen gave Jack a thumbs up and headed out.

"Well," Dave said, "I guess I should call Andy Rheinberg at the FDA and run this by him. I'd appreciate it if you two would stay here in case he needs to know more than I can tell him." They agreed to wait, so he dialed the phone. "Andy, it's Dave Aswari from Excella Pharmaceuticals. I'm sorry to bother you at home, but we think we need to change our

Ascendiac protocol." Dave explained, to the best of his ability, the new data they had uncovered this week.

"You don't have any proof that a taper will work, though?" Andy asked incisively.

"No," Dave reluctantly admitted. "But, if the patients who manifest symptoms of depression are cured when they're put back on the drug, we think that will at least be a good reason to believe the basic premise."

"OK, well, it sounds like you're staying on top of this. I'll authorize you to administer a three week taper to the patients with the depression and anyone else who's currently on the drug."

"Or," Dave added, "anyone who has stopped the drug within the last 60 hours, right?"

"Yes," Andy agreed. "I guess they'd have to be included, too. Make sure you get that to me, in writing, by Monday morning, though. We need the paperwork to keep this legal. When do you want to send the rest of this to me?"

"Send what?" Dave asked.

"You're not going to cancel the trial, are you?" Andy asked.

Dave didn't know how to respond. He was so certain the FDA would stop the study that he wasn't prepared for the question. "You want us to continue with this?" He could hardly contain his disbelief.

"Look, if the taper works, the drug will still be useful," Andy explained. "Obesity is a serious medical problem in America, as I'm sure you've seen on the news and with your own eyes, and it's more than just an aesthetic issue. It increases the rate of hypertension, heart attacks, strokes, diabetes, and cancer, just to name a few side effects. On top of that, one of the currently approved treatments, gastric bypass surgery, has its own litany of risks including anesthesia, infection, bowel obstruction, and more. Honestly, we think this drug has tremendous preventative value in the long run. If you can find a way to make it safe to use, we all think you'd be making a tremendous contribution to public health. You may see money in the cosmetic side of the drug, but the rest of us hope to see people actually get healthier from it."

"I'm glad you see it that way," Dave said. "We'll put together a new proposal immediately, and we'll keep you up to date on the progress the other patients make."

"You folks showed a lot of initiative here, and I personally appreciate that. It sounds like you've been working hard to make sure you tracked down the problem, so it gives me more confidence to allow you to press on. Keep working with us like this, and you'll find that the United States' drug approval process is an example for the rest of the world."

The last bit sounded a little overstated, but Dave wisely bit his tongue and thanked Andy for his ongoing help. When he hung up, Jack still hadn't figured out exactly what had been said, so Dave summarized the conversation. "He wants us to get this drug through. His feeling is that being overweight has health risks, too, and Ascendiac's benefits may outweigh its own side effects. We're still in business!"

51.

Two hours later, Dave, Alison, and Jack were finally putting the finishing touches on an Ascendiac tapering protocol which they hoped would eliminate the risk of the withdrawal depressions that they had seen. Alison's expertise in mood evaluation provided them with a significantly improved tapering protocol based on daily assessments of the patient's progress. She reasoned that, since the majority of patients never developed withdrawal symptoms, their taper could proceed at a much more rapid pace, keeping the cost down and minimizing the inconvenience to the patient. Based on approximately ten questions, if one of the test subjects were felt to be developing symptoms of depression, the dose would be maintained or possibly even increased temporarily.

Jack tapped the computer screen at which he was typing. "You know, Alison, this is really very clever. I was thinking of just tapering everyone, but with your system, not only is it going to be easier for most of these people, but we'll also learn some information like how long it seems to take to taper the drug and also how many people are going to need long versus short tapers. We'll probably have at least a rough idea from this how much needs to be changed in the next study design."

Dave agreed, then said, "We've got most of what we need, now, and the rest of the work is just procedural stuff. I think at this point it would be much better if you got the Ascendiac down to Sharon and started her back on it."

"You're probably right," she agreed, "but I think I've been trying to put that off as long as possible. What if it doesn't work?"

"It won't be for lack of trying," Dave suggested. "Look, you really have some excellent insight in this area, and your concept of what this drug is actually doing fits all the facts to a 'T.' Honestly, I'd be stunned if it wasn't exactly the way you predicted." The flood of compliments embarrassed her slightly.

"That's very kind of you to say."

Jack chimed in, "It pains me to admit, but for once, I agree with Dave. Oh! I can't believe I just said that!" He laughed, taking some of the pressure off her.

Dave said, "Jack, why don't you print a few copies of the protocol so our clinical study coordinators can follow them. I need to see you in my

office, Alison, to get your billing information for our accounting office."
As they walked through the hallway, Dave explained, "The corporation
keeps track of expenses and it needs to provide the IRS with an itemized
list each year for tax purposes. Come on in." He opened his office door
and they sat at his desk. "Now, what's your office address?" he asked as
he typed the information into the Excella financial organizer program on
his computer. Alison gave him the requisite information, and when he
was finished, he loaded a blank check into the printer and it produced a
special, tamper-resistant payment for the agreed amount.

"That's a lot of zeros," Alison said when he handed her the slip."

"I don't know if it shows, but this project means a lot to me personally, and when we thought we'd have no choice but to abort the study, I
really felt like I was losing something significant. Excella and I both owe
you a deep debt of gratitude."

"I'm just glad I could help you and the patients," Alison said.

"You know, you're a very talented person, Alison. Jack and I spent
months planning this study, and you came along and saw right through
weak spots we never even noticed. That was very humbling. If you
don't mind my saying, you're quite attractive, too, and that can be very
intimidating to some men. I know I was a little nervous when I first
met you, but you've really got a great way about you." He could feel his
pulse pick up as he tried to get the next sentence just right. "In a week or
so— you know, when this business settles down and Sharon is hopefully
getting better— do you think you'd consider having dinner with me
some time?"

Alison definitely didn't expect that question. When she looked directly in his eyes, though, she saw that the fear of intimidation had been
replaced by a fear of rejection, and she found it very touching. Work kept
her extremely busy and she realized that it had actually been a while since
someone outside of the hospital had asked her on a date. She'd almost
forgotten how good it felt to know that someone wanted so sincerely to
spend time with her that the possibility she'd say 'No,' made them worried. "You know, I think I'd enjoy that. Call me and we'll make plans."
She touched his hand for a moment and they both felt certain that it
wouldn't be the last time they would meet.

Dave walked her back to the conference room where Jack was waiting with the protocol and the Ascendiac supply. He handed the papers

and bottle to Alison and said, "You're planning on starting Sharon on this tonight, right?"

"Yes, I think that's the best thing," Alison confirmed.

"Good. If you don't mind, I'd really like you to keep me informed about how she's doing. I've already sent the study site coordinators e-mails explaining the changes and the fact that they'll need to complete the documentation personally on any patient identified by your mood assessment as a potential withdrawal victim. Nevertheless, since it's all technically speculation, we need to be extremely vigilant until we show it's working."

"I'll be happy to keep you up to date on her progress, Jack."

"OK," Jack said, "I'll walk you back to the guard house, then."

Dave, hoping to keep his romantic intentions private for the moment, smiled at her and said simply, "Thanks again, Alison," as she walked past him and out the door.

52.

Alison had spent several hours with Harold late Saturday afternoon, bringing him up to speed on the proposed Ascendiac treatment for Sharon. He agreed that it was worth trying, since the next move would likely be to begin a series of ECT treatments. By Sunday, Alison still hadn't addressed any more of her growing stack of office paperwork, so she made another trip into Manhattan to try to catch up. Her first stop after arriving, however, was at Sharon's hospital room. When she entered, she was shocked to see that the orderly wasn't anywhere to be found. She pressed the nurse call button on the wall, trying not to wake Sharon, who was sleeping in bed, just under it.

A moment later, a nurse came bounding through the door and asked anxiously, "Yes, is there a problem?" Sharon began to stir from the noise.

"Where's the orderly? This patient is supposed to be on one-to-one," Alison said.

"Oh, she was, but last night she contracted for safety. The night nurse reported to me that Doctor Regan himself came back to re-evaluate her, and after about an hour, he was convinced, so he took her off."

"Doctor Sonders, is that you?" Sharon was sleepy but definitely awake.

"Yes... yes, it's me, Sharon. How are you feeling?"

"Well, I was pretty surprised to wake up here last night. I still don't really understand what happened. There was a doctor who said he knew you, and he told me some things, but it all seemed surreal at the time."

"What do you recall about the last few days?" Alison asked.

"That's what he wanted to know. I definitely remember talking to you in your office. I think I was a little upset about something, though. I went home and I started cooking dinner, and the next thing I can clearly remember, I was in bed, here, with some woman watching me sleep."

"Do you know what happened in between those times?"

"I have the feeling I got sick or something. I don't know if I was dreaming or what, but I almost have the sense that people were talking to me but I couldn't answer them. Even when I wanted to, it's like I was just paralyzed. I asked the doctor last night if maybe it was food poisoning, and he said a strange thing. He told me it was 'diet poisoning,' but he didn't explain what that was. Whatever was wrong, it seems to be getting better, I guess." Sharon shrugged.

"Give yourself a day or two more, and when you're up to it, I'll tell you the whole story. We were worried about you for a while there, but you've definitely gotten past the worst of it."

"I hope I haven't caused you too much trouble, Dr. Sonders."

Alison shook her head slowly as she thought about Dave, Jack, the check, and the slick medical detective work she had been involved in over the past three days. Smiling, she answered her. "Of course not, Sharon. And it's Alison. Just call me Alison," she said as she patted her shoulder gently.

53.

Monday morning brought the full work crew back to the Excella campus, so Dave and Jack were relegated to their respective offices until 10:15. That was the time they had arranged to meet to place their call to the FDA regarding Ascendiac's new taper protocol. After hearing their plan, Andy Rheinberg approved it on the spot, adding that he thought it was a remarkably innovative approach given the short time frame they had to devise it.

Once that was taken care of, Dave pointed at Jack and said, "You know, I was thinking about this last night. Hadn't you originally suggested that we watch these patients for a few days after the study to make sure they didn't have a rebound effect or anything?"

"Yeah, I remember mentioning that to you in one of our meetings, but I never imagined that the rebound would have anything to do with mood disorders. I was just thinking about someone scarfing down a box of Twinkies," Jack admitted.

"I thought you were totally paranoid then, going off the deep end with your cautious approach. Even before my brother got involved in this, I was trying to figure out how to limit the amount of damage you could do to the study."

"That's not exactly reassuring, Dave. I was just trying to keep our interests in line with our patients'."

"I know that now, Jack. I'm just constantly surprised by how tricky this biology and medical stuff can be. My financial training never touched on such intricate and unpredictable forces." His phone rang on the direct line, and he waited until the second ring to answer. "Hello, Dave Aswari."

"Dave, it's me." Bobby sounded considerably less aggressive than he had recently.

"Speaking of unpredictable, it's my brother," Dave said sarcastically. He considered pressing the 'record' button on the box, but then he remembered he had put Laura's Strauss tape in there on Friday. "What do you want?"

"Well, I just called to say that it looks like the whole... you know... deal will work out. I wanted to tell you I'm sorry for the way I've been acting, and I appreciate all the help you gave me despite my behavior."

"You know, I'd love to believe that, but it's just too easy, seeing that you got what you wanted in the end. I've lost confidence in you and in the quality person you actually are inside. Now, I'm not saying I won't give you another chance some day, but you're going to have to earn it based on your actions. I definitely hope you do, mostly for Mom and Dad's sake, because they tried to raise you right. But let me tell you one thing, and make no mistake about it. That tape is my insurance policy and it's locked away in a very safe place. I hope you clean up your act because it's the right thing to do, but I'm not taking any chances here. If something happens to me and there's even the chance it wasn't an accident, the tape will surface. You know I'm not a vindictive guy, Bobby, but you brought this on yourself."

Jack felt like he was seeing a bully brought to justice as Dave dressed his brother down over the phone. On the one hand, he hoped that the threat wouldn't provoke Bobby into action, but on a much more visceral level, it felt good to watch him get beaten at his own game.

Bobby proceeded carefully. "I don't blame you for feeling that way, Dave. You're right about actions speaking louder than words, so I'll just say you can be sure you'll never need to use that against me. I'll let you go now."

"Goodbye, Bobby." He hung up. Turning to Jack again, he said, "Boy, you think you know someone and then money or power changes them, just like that." He snapped his fingers for emphasis. "I just can't believe he got himself involved with organized crime."

"I can't say it makes me feel any more secure, knowing that I was being chased by a mobster. And when he wanted Lisa, I don't think I was more scared in my life. Do you really expect they'll just leave us alone?"

"Like I said to Bobby, I know he got what he wanted from us. He doesn't have a grudge against you, Jack. He just needed Excella's stock to stay up until Tuesday." He paused for a minute. "Come to think of it, I wonder how he settled his debt already. Maybe they cut him a deal?"

"It's already more than I wanted to know," Jack said.

54.

"You know what we need?" Jack asked Sandy one morning during breakfast. "A vacation. Now that we've gotten just about everyone off Ascendiac, things are going to slow down for a little while, until our new phase III study is approved. It's our window of opportunity."

"That's a great idea, but I'll believe it when I see you spend some time away from work. Remember, you still owe me for that weekend at your parents', too."

"I can't catch a break with you, huh?" he asked jokingly as he leaned over and kissed her cheek. "No, really. I was looking online yesterday, and Club Med has this package somewhere warm where they've got a beach, lots of water sports, and even horseback riding. It sounded like a great trip, and I think you guys deserve a break."

"Sounds wonderful, but Lisa doesn't have school vacation for a couple more months."

"Oh, come on. How much of her life will be changed if she misses a few days of the second grade? I mean, it may keep her from becoming a Supreme Court Justice, but that's a price she'll have to pay!"

"You really are a whacko, Jack-o. OK, I'll think about it, but if I say 'yes,' you'd better be ready to close the deal."

"Yes, Ma'am," he said as he stood up and saluted her mockingly. Then, his eye caught a headline in the middle of the front page of the paper. His body tensed as he read the report. "Assistant DA Reported Missing. New York— A New York City Assistant District Attorney was reported missing yesterday after he failed to show up for work for three consecutive days. Robert Aswari, credited recently with the break up of an organized crime drug ring, was last seen by colleagues as he left the city courthouse after preliminary hearings involving the bust. Special Agent Terrance McAlister with the FBI would not rule out foul play. 'We're following several leads right now, but I can't say more than that. We're not prepared to rule anything out just yet.' Unnamed sources reported that Mr. Aswari is believed to have converted a considerable quantity of stock holdings into cash, possibly as recently as two days before his disappearance. The company, Excella Pharmaceuticals, employs Mr. Aswari's brother, David Aswari, and the SEC is now determining whether they will launch an investigation as well. David Aswari was not immediately available for comment."

"What is it, Jack?" Sandy asked when she noticed how focused he was on the paper.

"It's this article," Jack started. *What about this article, Jack? You're not involved in this, and you had nothing to do with Dave and his brother, really. What's the worst that can happen? Excella's stock drops until the papers get tired of the story? So what? It's just money, remember? If Dave didn't do anything wrong— and with his financial training, he ought to know the laws— then he'll be fine, too. There's no reason to worry Sandy again.* "It's a scary world out there, that's all. I'm just glad I've got you and Lisa."

-- The End --